ELEVEN LIARS

ROBERT GOLD

SPHERE

SPHERE

First published in Great Britain in 2023 by Sphere
This paperback edition published by Sphere in 2023

1 3 5 7 9 10 8 6 4 2

Copyright © Robert Gold Ltd

A CIP catalogue record for this book is available from the British Library.

ISBN 978-0-7515-8281-9

Printed and bound in Great Britain by
Clays Ltd, Elcograf S.p.A.

Papers used by Sphere are from well-managed forests
and other responsible sources.

Sphere
An imprint of
Little, Brown Book Group
Carmelite House
50 Victoria Embankment
London EC4Y 0DZ

An Hachette UK Company
www.hachette.co.uk

www.littlebrown.co.uk

Robert Gold is the *Sunday Times* bestselling author of *Twelve Secrets* and *Eleven Liars*. Originally from Harrogate in North Yorkshire, Robert Gold began his career as an intern at the American broadcaster CNN, based in Washington DC. He returned to Yorkshire to work for the retailer ASDA, becoming the chain's nationwide book buyer. He now works in sales for a UK publishing company.

Robert now lives in Putney and his new hometown served as the inspiration for the fictional town of Haddley in his thrillers.

Also by Robert Gold
Twelve Secrets

In memory of my brother, James.
And for my mum.

ELEVEN LIARS

One

*'I've been around long enough
to know when my time is up.'*

THURSDAY

CHAPTER 1

My Uber driver gives me a dejected look in his rear-view mirror. For the past ten minutes we've barely moved. He points to the solid red line of congestion displayed on his map, covering the next two miles. The traffic along the river road is gridlocked. At this rate, it will take me over an hour to get from Richmond, through the village of St Marnham and on to my home in the London Borough of Haddley.

I look out at the late October evening where darkness has descended. 'Probably quicker if I jump out here,' I say. 'I can walk the rest of the way along the river.' My driver raises the palms of his hands and shrugs. 'Hopefully you can pick up a fare going in the other direction,' is my half-hearted apology, before I open the passenger-side door and climb out.

'We will see,' he calls wearily. I stand on the pathway and watch him turn his car in the road before he accelerates away from the west London traffic.

The evening is cold and my warm breath lingers in the crisp air. I zip up my jacket and push my hands deep inside my pockets. Stepping down onto the embankment path, I feel the crunch of fallen leaves beneath my feet. The towpath leads into St Marnham, before I have to cut across the playing fields on the north side of the village and on towards Haddley Common.

My phone buzzes. Flicking open the screen, its light brings a brightness to the darkened pathway. The message is from Madeline Wilson, my boss at the nation's number one online news site. I've spent the last six hours with her at her home overlooking Richmond Park, finalising the script for a true-crime podcast I'm due to begin recording in a week's time. Madeline is now messaging me with even more suggestions. That's Madeline all over – she's relentless, always ready with a stream of new ideas. Journalism is in her blood; her passion inherited from her father, Sam, an old-school newspaperman. She'd never want to admit it, but I know her unwavering determination to be the first to uncover the best possible story comes from her dad. I guess I got the same from her.

In the weeks approaching the podcast's recording, Madeline's support of me has been unflinching. Six months ago, with the help of a local police officer, PC Dani Cash, I unearthed the truth behind my mother's death and the brutal killing of my brother, Nick. Murdered when he was only fourteen, his death has held a morbid fascination for much of the country for almost a quarter of a century. It's Nick's story the podcast will tell.

I was eight when my brother was killed and the loss will stay with me until the day I die. For many years it was simply impossible for me to comprehend. The horrifying nature of his murder meant my name, Ben Harper, became known both nationally and internationally and for much of my life, I lived in shadow of his death and my family's grief. After my mother died, from an apparent suicide, I knew my only way forward was by not looking back. But then, earlier this year, that changed when new information came to light about my family's story. Once I finally discovered the truth, I wanted everyone else to know it too. I published the story for our news site and it attracted global attention as well as, much to Madeline's delight, record reader numbers. I know the release of the podcast will bring further painful attention to my family's story, but my overriding determination is for the truth to be known. Nick was my hero, and this is the only way I know to deliver justice for the life so brutally stolen from him. I still miss him and my mum every single day.

St Marnham is brightly lit by street lamps, but as soon as I reach the playing fields on the far side of the village, I find myself in darkness again. Picking my way along the path, I feel the chill rise into the soles of my feet. Through the darkness, I see flashing lights appear in the distance and moments later I step aside as two cyclists race past me on their journey home at the end of the office week. I pass a floodlit running track, where a lone sprinter braves the artic breeze, her rapid stride powering her down the long home straight. From outside the newly built brick sports pavilion, I can hear a frighteningly energetic fitness class taking place inside.

To make the shortcut through to my home on Haddley Common, saving me a mile-long walk along the road, I enter the small copse of trees at the far end of the playing fields. From there I scramble down the bank that leads through to the back of St Stephen's churchyard. At the bottom of the bank, I reach the set of iron railings I've clambered over a thousand times in the past thirty years, like so many residents of Haddley Common and St Marnham, taking this unorthodox short cut through to the Lower Haddley Road. I loop my bag across my shoulders and grip the shallow railings. They glisten with frost, and as the cold seeps into my bare hands, I hear my mum's voice asking me why I don't invest in a pair of gloves. I pull myself up and over but, as I do, my hand slips. I reach backwards to try and steady myself but, unable to grab the railing's pointed tip, I fall towards the crumbling graveyard.

I brace myself for the impact, but it doesn't come. The strap of my bag has hooked itself across the top of the railings. Cursing, I reach behind my head to try and dislodge it but it holds fast. I realise the only way to free myself is to snap the strap. I launch myself forward, the strap breaks and I hit the ground hard, my ankle twisting with a pain that makes me cry out, and I roll down the bank into the darkest corner of St Stephen's cemetery.

Lying prone, my jacket caked in mud, my ankle throbbing, I'm momentarily dazed. When I get my bearings, I see my laptop has spilt from my bag. Tentatively I push myself up, kneeling on my right leg before testing my weight on my left foot. I suck in cold air and hold my breath. I lean against a moss-covered headstone before reaching for my bag and shoving my laptop back inside. Suddenly, my attention is caught by a bright orange glow, smouldering in the trees on the far side of the churchyard.

I clamber to my feet and hobble forward. I move from one gravestone to the next before making my way down the gravel path that runs across the back of the cemetery. With each step I take, the fire appears to intensify. St Stephen's sixteenth-century church comes into view, but its only light is the lantern that hangs above its heavy oak door. I hurry around the side of the church, ignoring the pain in my ankle. I see the orange light again, now impossibly bright. The derelict community centre behind St Stephen's is on fire.

Smoke pours through its grimy red-tiled roof. Flames lick at the ivy-clad walls. I drop my bag and fumble in my muddied pocket in search of my phone. As I do, a window at the front of the community centre shatters, sending sparks crackling across the path. Burning light illuminates the churchyard and the heat is so intense that, even from this distance, I'm forced to take a step back. Finding my phone, I'm about to call for help, when a fleeting movement inside the building catches my eye.

I flinch.

I stare into the smoke and see another movement; a streak of black amid the bright orange flames.

Then, through the smashed front window, I see a figure.

Adrenaline pumps through my veins and without thinking, I run towards the building's graffiti-covered door. The door is locked. I yell at whoever is trapped inside to find a way out. They hesitate before scrambling backwards, deeper into the flames.

I ram my shoulder against the door. It doesn't move. I step back then launch myself forward, crashing my foot against the door.

It flies open and I fall forward into the furnace.

The smoke is so thick that I can only just make out the slim figure, now crouched on the floor. From the frantic way they are fumbling, they appear to be searching for something.

'What are you doing?' I scream, trying to cover my mouth as smoke fills my lungs. 'You need to get out, now!'

But pulling their hood across their face, they clamber further across the floor, ignoring my escape route.

'Stop, or you'll get yourself killed!' I shout.

Suddenly they are on their feet, spinning round to face me. For a moment they are still, as though trapped by indecision. Then they charge forward, leap over me and race away from the building. Fire flashes around me, the heat ferocious. I scramble to my feet and lurch backwards out into the churchyard.

Gasping for air, I collapse onto the path. I peer through the darkness and look towards the Lower Haddley Road. The escaping figure never breaks their stride. A passing car is forced to skid to a stop, its blaring horn filling the still night air. The figure's hand slams onto the car's bonnet, and in the glare of the car's headlights, I catch a momentary glimpse of their angular frame. Still desperately trying to fill my lungs with the cold night air, I lie on the ground and watch the distinctive bright orange trainers of the fleeing figure disappear into the dark woods at the back of Haddley Common.

CHAPTER 2

PC Dani Cash felt her breath catch in her throat as she entered the CID offices at the rear of Haddley Police Station. She glanced at the clock on the far wall. She was still ten minutes early for her eight o'clock meeting with Chief Inspector Bridget Freeman. Time had seemed to crawl since she'd received the meeting request earlier in the afternoon. Originally the appointment had been for seven, but then, as seven approached, Bridget Freeman had pushed the meeting back.

At this time on a Thursday evening, the offices were largely deserted, the pub at the top of the high street calling most detectives out of the building before six. Only two detectives remained, both eating dinner. The smell of their spicy Mexican tacos lingered in the airless room. Briefly they looked up at Dani, before one passed his phone to the other and laughed. Something in his expression told her this was a joke she would not enjoy.

Haddley was one of the last remaining Victorian police stations still in operation across the capital. For years, one badly planned extension had followed another. The building had been constantly adapted, the need for extra space met by knocking down walls, replacing offices with open-plan rooms or simply squeezing desks into the alcoves that once housed cupboards. But the detective branch remained where it had always been, right at the back of the old building, hidden away from the day-to-day community buzz. In the summer, the room became intolerably hot; in winter the radiators generated more noise than heat. The windows reached almost to the ceiling but gave little light, offering only a view of a neighbouring brick wall.

But there was nowhere in the world Dani felt more at home.

Crossing to the desk at the back of the room, Dani ran her hands along the scratched wood, feeling the notches and flaws built up through years of toil. She pulled out the battered office chair, its faux leather seat worn thin, its back stained with sweat. Sitting at the desk, she traced her fingers across the fading computer keyboard. As a child, she would type her name with one finger; her dad standing behind her, unable to type much faster himself. She closed her eyes and remembered him spinning her in the chair, her legs, not yet able to reach the floor, flying out in front of her. As she threw her head back, her blonde hair falling across her face, he would spin her until she was dizzy and tears of laughter streamed down her cheeks.

She looked out across the room, and suddenly her father's face was as clear to her now as it was twenty years before. She could see him, with his greying hair, briefing a team of junior officers, each one paying strict attention as they took in every word that Jack Cash said. She'd felt so proud.

And then a call would come in, or a shout from across the room, and he'd be gone. She'd sit in the desk chair and watch her father charge from the office, calling instructions to others as he left. How she'd loved the excitement, always wishing she could go with him. Waiting for his return, however long that might be, was all she'd ever known. If she was lucky, a friendly officer might bring her some paper and perhaps some colouring pens. She remembered ending up with colours striped across her face from licking the pens' dried-up ends. A kindly woman came to clean her up. It was her dad's boss, Chief Inspector Anders, who then took her out onto the high street. Walking beside the commanding officer, she had held her hand. Inside the shop the inspector had told Dani to choose two different packets of crayons – one to take home and one to keep in the office. Dani chose a pack of chunky colouring pens and another of brightly coloured wax crayons.

'Thank you, Chief Inspector,' she'd said, as they'd walked back towards the station.

'Don't tell anyone but my name isn't actually Chief Inspector. You can call me Christine but make sure you keep it our secret.'

Dani had felt sad when, a year later, Christine told her she was retiring. But she couldn't have felt prouder than when her dad had told her he was taking over the running of the station. She threw her arms around him and squeezed him so tight she felt she might burst.

A scrunched-up wrapper from a Mexican takeaway hit the rim of the bin and bounced onto the floor, snapping

Dani's attention back into the room. She glanced across at the detective who'd made the shot. He made no move to pick up the rubbish, simply turning back to his screen. Dani checked the time. It was approaching eight o'clock. She walked across the room, picked up the failed shot and dropped it in the bin.

Her dad had always expected his detectives to keep a tidy office.

CHAPTER 3

Dani stood alone in the dimly lit corridor outside the chief inspector's office, the last remaining private office in the station. She hesitated, her hand hovering above the door.

For over fifteen years, the office had belonged to Jack Cash. Next spring, it would be three years since Dani had last turned the rattling doorknob and entered the room to find her dad sitting behind his coffee-stained desk. Still now, each time she passed the office door, she thought of that day.

'You wouldn't know it was supposed to be spring,' she'd said, entering her father's office for the last time. Her dad had looked up from a stack of unread reports and smiled at her as she'd crossed the room to warm her hands against the cast-iron radiator. It was the week of the University Boat Race and Dani had been out on the Thames in support of the Marine Policing Unit. A northerly wind had cut through her as she'd travelled in a small boat, tasked with security-checking the bridges.

'Everything go okay?' he'd asked.

'Fine,' she'd replied, pulling a chair close to the radiator.

'Nothing out of the ordinary; probably need to watch the numbers on Hammersmith Bridge.'

'We'll bring in a few extra officers to hold the crowds back on the banks. I don't think it'll be a problem. Coffee?'

'That'd be lovely,' she'd replied, as he clicked on the kettle that lived on top of his filing cabinet. When the water boiled, he scooped some instant coffee granules and splashed some milk into two mugs.

'Biscuit?' he'd asked, reaching across for the packet of bourbons always open on his desk.

'Just one. And you should do the same,' she'd said, as her dad pulled out two biscuits for himself. He'd dip them one at a time in his coffee, the same way he'd done for as many years as she could remember.

'So?' she'd said, crossing to collect her coffee and taking a seat opposite him. She always knew when her father had something to tell her.

Jack Cash reached across for his mug. He paused and then after a moment put the mug back down on his desk without taking a sip. 'I wanted to hear how things are going, that's all.'

'Don't give me that,' she'd replied. At the end of the year, it would have been just her and her dad for two decades. Like any father and daughter, at times they'd clashed but most of the time they'd been there for each other. Dani instinctively knew when something was on her dad's mind. 'Spill it.'

She'd watched her father stand, his breath quickening, and pull his chair around his desk to sit alongside her.

'Dad, you're worrying me, what's going on?'

Jack faced his daughter before suddenly blurting out the words. 'It's time for me to step down.'

It took Dani a moment to register what he'd said. 'What do you mean?' she'd replied. 'Step down how? Do you mean you want to go back to working in the unit?' Dani knew her dad's heart had always remained in actively investigating crimes, not running the station.

'No,' he'd replied, his frustration showing. 'I mean it's time for me to finish. I'm going to step away.'

To Dani the idea was so ridiculous, she'd laughed out loud.

Visibly annoyed, Jack had got to his feet and pushed his chair back behind his desk. 'I'm serious, Dani. I'm stepping down. It's time for me to move aside, to let somebody younger take things forward. We need to modernise.'

'Are you trying to tell me you're retiring? *Modernise, take things forward.* Those aren't your words. I don't even know what they mean.'

'I can't cut it any more, not in the way I could.' Jack bowed his head.

Then it dawned on Dani. 'This is about Betty Baxter.'

'The station's lost faith in me; officers don't trust me any more.'

'That's not true. You made one mistake.'

Jack shook his head. 'No, I made a mistake twenty years ago and now I've done the same again. How many officers have I told not to be a fool and to learn from their mistakes? Turns out I'm the biggest fool of them all. I'm an embarrassment to the force.'

'Who said that?'

'I know it's what they're thinking. I spent a fortune and couldn't even bring the case to trial.'

'Dad, it happens.' Dani knew months of expensive surveillance had failed to result in any charges against a supposed drug-trafficking operation.

'The team have lost confidence in me and, if I'm honest, I've lost confidence in myself. I'd have given anything to finally nail her; perhaps my problem was I wanted it too much. I gave it my best shot, but I need to recognise that's no longer enough.'

'I can't believe after one bad case you're walking away.'

'It's time for me to do other things, enjoy the time I've earned.'

'Bullshit,' she'd replied, looking directly at her father. 'It is, Dad, it's fucking bullshit. This place is your life. For your whole career, you've said they'd have to either drag you out of here or carry you out in a box.' Much as Dani loved her father, she'd known that since he'd joined up as a nineteen-year-old and served for over forty years, only on a very good day could she hope to rank as equal first in his life's priorities. *Enjoy your time, do other things.* You can't even bring yourself to say the word. *Retire.* You could work another five years, at least.'

'No, I couldn't,' he'd replied, sharply. 'I'll get a very nice pension.' His voice softened. 'Perhaps I'll do a bit of travelling.'

Dani said nothing. She'd spent nearly all her school holidays in and around Haddley Police Station. For one week at the start of each summer, she and her dad would drive north to the Yorkshire seaside town of Filey. At the end of every week, all she could remember was her dad being desperate to get back to work. Travelling had never been high on his list of life's priorities.

'I might take up golf.'

'Now you really are being stupid.' She looked at her father's face, more ruddied than she'd remembered. When he reached for a third biscuit, she caught hold of his hand. 'Tell me the truth,' she'd said, her bright blue eyes fixed on his.

Jack's smile was a rueful one. 'It might not be completely my own choice,' he said, 'but the fact is I've run out of road. I've been around long enough to know when my time is up. Forty years is a good stint.'

'Surely you can fight on?'

Jack shook his head. 'It's time, Dani. Somebody else needs to take Haddley forward. I'm finishing next Friday. Freeman will step up.'

Dani wanted to scream at her father, but she could see his mind was made up. She leaned back in her chair and folded her arms. And despite the sadness in his eyes, Jack laughed.

'Your mum used to sit like that whenever she didn't get her own way.'

Dani said nothing. She had only a few hazy memories of her mother. For as long as she could remember, her dad had been her inspiration. She admired the passion and dedication with which he'd led the Haddley force into battle against drug crime across the borough. Had that dedication become an obsession? Perhaps. But looking at him on that day, she had to accept his fight was gone.

The following Friday, Dani had watched her father leave the station for the last time. When she'd stood beside him on the steps at the front of the building, she'd held his hand and desperately fought back the tears that pricked at her eyes. Surrounded by his fellow officers, Jack had walked up to the pub at the top of the high street and stayed there long into the night. The next night he was in the pub again, this time with a smaller crowd. And then the following night with an even smaller one. And then, finally, alone.

A year later, he was dead.

CHAPTER 4

The Monday after Jack Cash's retirement had seen Bridget Freeman elevated to lead the Haddley police force. Dani had scrutinised her closely, watching for all the ways she'd fail to live up to Jack's standards. But she'd had to admit that Freeman led with efficiency, while consistently managing conviction rates. At the same time, the police presence on the streets of Haddley, so visible under her predecessor, had gradually waned. Now, two and a half years after Bridget Freeman had taken on her role, Dani knocked on the chief inspector's office door and waited.

'Come,' called Freeman, after a moment. 'Take a seat, Constable Cash,' she continued, indicating a chair as Dani crossed the room. 'Apologies for the lateness of the hour. My liaison meeting with the Fulham and Hammersmith force ran considerably over.'

'Not a problem, ma'am,' Dani replied, stealing a glance around the room. The office was barely recognisable from the one occupied by her father. Gone was his wooden desk and dusty filing cabinets, replaced by a sleek white vinyl table, a wide-screen monitor and Freeman's own MacBook flipped open in front of her.

'You have an exceptionally strong advocate in Detective Sergeant Barnsdale,' began Freeman. 'Her recommendation of you is fulsome.' Dani dropped her head but couldn't help smiling. She'd worked closely with Barnsdale earlier in the year, investigating the deaths of Claire and Nick Harper. After the successful conclusion of a difficult case, she'd hoped Barnsdale would support her request for a transfer into CID.

'I respect the honesty she shows in her appraisal of your performance. You are still learning, Cash, and made some errors of judgement in the Nick Harper case but DS Barnsdale believes you have the instincts and potential to become a highly successful investigative officer. I am broadly in agreement.'

Dani looked at her senior officer. Coming from Freeman, these words meant a lot. She struggled to remember an occasion when Freeman wasn't fully in command of a situation. Always fully briefed on every aspect of a case, always impeccably turned out. Even now, after such a long day, her jacket was buttoned, her epaulettes polished and her hair neatly styled. Women were still judged on such things in the force and Dani guessed that Freeman wasn't going to give anyone an opportunity to find her wanting. Much as she missed her father, Dani had grown to respect Freeman.

'After taking some time to consider, you will be pleased to know I'm inclined to approve your transfer to CID.'

'Thank you, ma'am.'

'You've shown excellent initiative in the past, Cash. You

have a genuine ability to work with members of the public and have demonstrated a talent for forensic interrogation. Those are the skills that will bring you continued success and the further development of your career.'

Dani nodded. 'Yes, ma'am.'

'Results are key but so is how we achieve those results. It is important to remember that. I want to see you become a successful modern officer.'

Dani wondered if that was a veiled reference to her father. Jack Cash would have done anything to achieve a result. But Dani was her own person, and she wanted Freeman to judge her on *her* performance, not her father's. She said nothing.

'With continued development and loyalty to your team here at Haddley, I don't expect it to be long before you are being considered for a sergeant's position,' said Freeman.

'I'd like that very much, ma'am,' Dani replied. Freeman smiled and gave a nod to indicate that Dani was dismissed. Dani got to her feet, but as she did there was a knock on the office door.

'Come,' called Freeman.

'Excuse me, ma'am,' said DS Lesley Barnsdale, stepping into the room. Dani looked towards her, and both officers smiled briefly.

'I'm just sharing good news with soon to be *Detective* Constable Cash,' said Freeman, noting the exchange.

'Much deserved,' replied Barnsdale. 'If I may ma'am, we have a fire at St Stephen's church on the Lower Haddley Road. One officer is in attendance, but I'd like to send PC Cash in support to interview any witnesses.'

CHAPTER 5

I sit on a wooden bench at the side of St Stephen's church and sip from a bottle of water. I can still taste the smoke trapped in the back of my throat. The churchyard is illuminated by the fire service emergency lighting and a heavy smell of burnt wood lingers in the air. I look across at the smouldering community centre: much of its roof has burnt through, although its outside walls remain standing.

After escaping the flames and collapsing onto the gravel pathway, I quickly found my phone and called the fire brigade. Almost in an instant I heard the blare of sirens racing down the Lower Haddley Road. Their quick response stopped the fire spreading to St Stephen's ancient church, protecting its centuries-old stained-glass window and imposing bell tower.

A young police officer crosses from the burnt-out building.

'Mr Harper?' she asks, taking a seat beside me. 'I'm PC Karen Cooke. The paramedics tell me you've refused any medical assessment or treatment.'

'I'm fine, honestly, thank you,' I reply, waving away her concern.

'Sometimes in these situations it's still worth getting checked out. A small amount of smoke inhalation—'

'Really, I'm fine.' I take another sip of water. 'I probably just need to go home and get showered.'

'I can drop you home if you like?'

'No need. Five minutes' walk, no more than that. Over the Lower Haddley Road and across the common, and I'm home.'

'If you're sure. Before you go, there are a couple of questions I'd like to ask you, if you feel up to it?' I nod and wait for her to continue. 'Mr Harper, am I right in thinking it was you who reported the fire?'

I tell her everything: my short cut through the back of the cemetery, seeing the bright orange glow across the graveyard, the figure escaping from the community centre before running through the church gates. Cooke makes copious notes.

'The figure you saw – you've described a slim, angular frame. Male or female?'

'I never really had a clear view and they kept their hood pulled over their face. My only thought was how to get them out.' Cooke raises her eyes from her notebook and waits for me to continue. 'If I had to guess, I'd say probably male, possibly late teens but it really is a best guess.' My eyes still sting from the smoke, and I rub them vigorously.

'I'm sure the paramedics have eye drops, you know.'

I smile but shake my head. 'The best look I got of them was when they were caught in the car's headlights. Five nine, five ten in height, maybe? Tracksuit bottoms, hooded top and bright orange trainers. I'm afraid I didn't see any more. The driver of the car would've had a better view.'

'And you didn't see the make of the car?' asks Cooke.

'It all happened so quickly,' I reply. 'I was pretty much wiped out.'

'We'll try and trace the driver,' she says. 'Once the figure was over the road they disappeared into the trees?'

I point towards an opening at the side of Haddley Woods. 'Straight through that gap,' I say. As I speak, a second police vehicle pulls up at the entrance gates to St Stephen's. I watch as Dani Cash, the officer I worked closely with earlier in the year, steps out of her car. In the last six months, we've met only once to share a brief cup of coffee, but I wish it could have been more. My overriding urge is to run and greet her. Instead, illuminated by the fire service floodlights, I watch her swiftly make her way down a narrow path that runs along the side of the cemetery towards the vicarage garden.

'Mr Harper?' says PC Cooke, recapturing my attention.

'Sorry,' I reply. 'Really there's nothing more I can tell you. The figure disappeared into the woods and I called the fire brigade immediately afterwards.'

She keeps talking, asking me to call her if I remember any further details, but my attention wanders back to Dani Cash. She is walking slowly back through the cemetery, now in the direction of the community centre, accompanied by a man whom I recognise as Adrian Withers, the vicar of St Stephen's.

Working with her closely earlier in the year, I quickly learned Dani has a sharp investigative mind, easy intuition and an ability to get answers to difficult questions. And every time I saw her, I couldn't help but smile.

CHAPTER 6

At the end of the gravel path that wound through the back of the cemetery, a small wooden gate led into the vicarage garden. With the bright lights of the fire service fading behind her, Dani could only dimly make out the house beyond. Surrounded by graves and shadowy trees, she shivered. Finding herself on edge, when her hand reached for the gate at the same moment as the Reverend Adrian Withers emerged from the vicarage garden, she jumped back.

'Constable, my apologies,' he said, before introducing himself. 'What a terrible night.' He looked skywards. 'Please tell me nobody's been hurt. I struggle to imagine a horror comparable with being trapped in a fire.'

Dani shuddered. 'Nobody was hurt, thankfully,' she said. She'd spoken briefly with PC Cooke during the short drive from the station.

'That is a relief,' replied the vicar. 'With it occurring on church land, one can't help but feel almost culpable. I did see an ambulance pulling into the car park, though, didn't I?'

'We believe somebody was trapped in the fire, but a passer-by was able to free them.' Dani glanced over her shoulder in the direction of Ben Harper. She was relieved to see he was now standing beside Karen Cooke. 'The ambulance was purely precautionary, I'm pleased to say.'

'Good. Were you looking for me?'

'I just have a few questions.'

Adrian Withers gestured to the gate. 'Of course. Shall we?' They began their slow walk down the path towards the community centre. 'I was terrified the fire may spread towards St Stephen's. Having stood for five centuries, I would have hated to see it succumb under my relatively brief tenure.'

Dani could imagine Withers, with his precisely trimmed moustache and neatly parted hair, regarding himself as something of a charmer.

'Can I ask when you first became aware of the fire?'

'I conduct three services on a Sunday, and I like to use Thursday evening to begin to gather my thoughts and reflections. I was in the vestry at the rear of the church. It's a small space with thick walls, and no discernible light from the window. I was unaware of events until the arrival of the fire brigade.'

'And at that point?'

Withers paused. 'I came out of the front of the church – we keep the rear gate permanently locked – and was thankful to see the fire was already in hand. Once I was assured it was fully extinguished, I returned briefly to the vicarage to check on my wife. I was just coming back to the church when I met you at the gate.'

Walking beside the vicar, Dani could smell the dense smoke hanging in the air. Biting her lip, she covered her mouth with her hand. The path split and they turned away from the burnt-out building and towards the front of St Stephen's. 'It's a beautiful church,' Dani said, as they passed the sweeping arch of the stained-glass window before stopping by the steps at the main entrance.

'Thank you,' he replied.

'When you walked from the church to your home, you didn't see anybody in the graveyard?'

'Nobody living, I'm afraid.'

Dani smiled. 'And your wife?'

'My wife?' replied Withers.

'She was okay?'

'Oh, I see what you mean. Just returned from supper with an elderly parishioner.' A fire engine was manoeuvring out of the small church car park, reversing out onto the Lower Haddley Road. 'I will make a point of personally thanking the station commander for his team's efforts,' said Withers, his eyes following the vehicle. 'I know him well from a number of shared charitable endeavours. If you've nothing further, constable, I must head inside the church to ensure everything is safely extinguished for the night. I would hate to have left anything alight in my hasty exit.'

Dani watched Withers stride up the three steps at the front of St Stephen's and enter the church through its heavy oak door. Standing in front of the building, she briefly imagined herself soaking in a hot bath and scrubbing the stench of smoke from her skin. Lost in her thoughts, she was unaware of the figure, swathed in darkness, watching her from the upstairs window of the vicarage.

CHAPTER 7

Seeing Dani and the vicar part ways, I take two strides in her direction before the pain in my ankle makes me audibly wince.

'Mr Harper, are you sure I can't run you home?' asks PC Cooke, catching up with me and placing a hand gently on my elbow.

'No, I'm fine, honestly,' I say, turning back towards the community centre. Two members of the fire service are beginning to dismantle the last of the floodlights. 'All I need is a few steps to walk it off. My ankle's not even sprained.' Karen Cooke smiles at me and I laugh. 'No, really,' I continue, biting my cheek as I move along the gravel path. Breathing deeply, I turn to her. 'See? Absolutely fine.' I look across at the sprawling Victorian vicarage, a rabbit warren of rooms, which stands beyond the graveyard. A single light dimly illuminates an upstairs window.

'We'll speak to any further witnesses in the morning,' says PC Cooke, following the direction of my gaze. 'But you're quite sure for now that you didn't see anybody else in the churchyard when the fire first broke out?'

'Not a soul.'

'Nobody hanging around the church or leaving through the front gates?'

I shake my head. 'Sorry. In the darkness it was impossible to see much.'

We stand in front of the community centre's blackened entrance. What was the figure doing in the fire? Why didn't they try to get out sooner, and why hadn't they fled when I called to them? The charred remains of the door hang loose from its hinges. Burnt ivy still clings to the door's surround, a dense smell hanging heavy in the air. I reach for my phone and flick on the torch light. Inhaling sharply, I move quickly forward and before PC Cooke can react, I'm standing back inside.

'Mr Harper, what are you doing?' she calls after me, but I'm already stepping through into the room where I'd seen the figure. Wooden tables, folded and pushed to the middle of the room, are scorched black. A stack of wooden chairs is burnt through.

'Why were they here?' I say aloud to myself, shining my light around the room.

'Mr Harper, I need you to step back outside.' PC Cooke has followed me into the room. 'It isn't safe in here.'

'They were here for a reason,' I reply. 'At the height of the fire, they were still scrambling about on the floor, as if they were looking for something.'

'The fire investigator will fully examine the scene

tomorrow.' She's trying to placate me, but I've learned it's always best to ask my own questions when I can. I move further forward. Against one wall are the remains of what might have been a climbing frame. Scorched ropes hang from the roof. 'What was this place? Some kind of gym?'

'Possibly, yes,' Cooke replies. 'The building's been empty for years but in the past it was used for all kinds of community activities.'

I climb over a wooden rowing machine before tracing my fingers through the wet soot that covers an ancient bench press.

'Mr Harper, I'm going to step back outside now. I'd ask you to do the same.'

I lift my torch and scan it around the room. 'This is where I first saw them,' I say, and with my shoulder I try to push a blackened bench press to one side. Bolted to the floor, the equipment is impossible to move. The beam of my torch reflects off something metallic. I bend and see the light reflect off a knife blade.

A crash echoes through the room. The bench press collapses through the floor, coming to rest in the foundations below. I jump backwards, yelling as I land heavily on my twisted foot.

'Mr Harper!' calls PC Cooke. 'It's really not safe in here.'

Readily agreeing, I hurry out of the room. With much of the rear wall destroyed by fire, we are able to step out of the back of the building relatively easily.

'There was a knife,' I say, 'jammed beneath the bench press.'

'Can you be certain?'

'Positive. My light reflected off the blade.'

'If there is a knife, the fire investigation team will find it tomorrow.' Cooke lights her torch to guide her way through overgrown scrub, and I follow.

'Any idea yet as to how the fire began?' I ask.

'At this stage, it would only be speculation.'

'Could it have been started deliberately?'

'I hope not.'

'Because if it was, whoever was inside might've been the target?'

Cooke doesn't respond immediately. As we turn and walk down the side of the building, the devastation of the fire on the community centre is on full display. Then, quietly, she says, 'I think whoever was inside was very lucky you came along when you did.'

I stop and survey the burnt-out building. A metal drain-pipe still clings to the wall. I point my torch down towards a cracked glass bottle lying in the blackened drain-hole cover. I pick up the empty bottle and put my nose to the rim. The lingering pine-wood smell is unmistakable.

'Turpentine,' I say. 'Highly flammable.' I look up at Cooke. 'We need to find whoever was in the fire.'

Two

*'Their lives were separate and nothing
she did seemed to change that.'*

FRIDAY

CHAPTER 8

Pamela Cuthbert hated mornings. She struggled to remember the last time she'd woken up feeling refreshed. The whole night she'd been restless. Her feet tingled with pins and needles. Her legs were swollen. Her hands were stiff. Reaching towards her bedside table, she looked at her phone. The neighbourhood app was full of chatter about the fire at St Stephen's church. She had no interest in reading about it and turned on her radio for the eight o'clock news. It was all bad. One endless stream of disasters: floods, murders, corrupt politicians, innocent soldiers killed in somebody else's war. Nothing to cheer her. She switched to her favourite music station, Absolute 80s. They had a habit of playing the same songs over and over but Pamela didn't mind. They reminded her of when she was happy.

The DJ told his audience, *Here's something to get you in the mood for the weekend.* Pushing off her duvet, she wondered when people did any work. She knew by lunchtime all of Haddley's riverside bars would be packed. In her day people worked a five-day week. The song's chorus came on and she started humming. Her next big birthday was seventy-five and here she was still listening to Adam and the Ants. She smiled to herself. Who was she fooling?

She sat on the edge of her bed and gently rubbed the lumps in the palms of her hands. Every morning they ached. Some days she would wake with her hands almost rigid. When she'd shown the lumps to her doctor, she'd seen him look them up on his computer. In the end all he'd said was that it was probably down to old age, and she should take two paracetamol each morning. Was that the best he could do? She had wondered if he was even fully qualified. He didn't look much older than twenty, although surely he would have had to be. Everyone looked so young to Pamela these days. He was only a locum and she suspected it was his first real job. At least he'd made an effort and dressed very smartly. She'd ended up feeling sorry for him. On the way out she'd thanked him and hoped she would see him again. Why on earth she'd said that she didn't know. Walking out of his room, she couldn't stop herself giggling. The woman on reception must have thought she was bonkers. She'd make another appointment for when her regular doctor, Dr Jha, was back from India. She was away for a month, teaching in the city of Meerut. Pamela had never heard of Meerut and had asked Dr Jha if it was in Delhi. It wasn't, although Dr Jha had said it wasn't that far away. Pamela secretly thought Dr Jha would have been better off in Delhi. She was brilliant, and Pamela worried she would be wasted in Meerut.

Feeling a tickle in her nose, she looked in the drawer of her bedside table for a tissue. Two empty miniature bottles of gin rattled together when she opened the drawer. Dr Jha wouldn't be impressed with that. She wiped her nose and had a sip of water from the glass beside her bed. Then she pushed herself up onto her feet, stretching until her back felt relatively straight. At least she could still do that. As she stepped into her slippers, Olivia Newton John's 'Physical' came on the radio. She turned up the volume, not too loud or she'd have the neighbours banging on the paper-thin walls, and did a quick shimmy away from the bed. She followed that with a twirl across her bedroom. What would people say if they could see her? She didn't care and slowly bopped her way into the bathroom.

The small terraced house on Haddley Hill Road had been Pamela's home for nearly fifty years. Each time a lorry drove past, the windows rattled. The traffic these days seemed never ending. Walking into the kitchen she felt the morning chill coming through the back door. She'd love to have the windows and doors replaced but there was no way she would ever be able to afford that. A widow's pension wouldn't pay for new sash windows. She pulled her dressing gown tight and edged the heating up just a notch. The kitchen clock told her it was a quarter past eight. She'd have to hurry; she didn't want to be late. She put the grill on to warm and took her favourite walnut bread from the bread bin. There was just about enough for two slices. Opening the fridge, she realised she was low on butter as well. She'd have to walk down to the mini market later in the morning. She smiled as that meant she could spread her thick-cut marmalade a little more generously. Dr Jha wouldn't like that. Too much sugar, she'd say. But she was in Meerut, so she would never know. Pamela always bought her marmalade from a stall at St Marnham's farmer's market, where she went most Saturdays. It was quite a walk, but it got her out of the house, and it did do her good. When it wasn't wet, she always walked along the river path. It was a little bit further, but she enjoyed seeing people out on the water.

The farmer's market was held in the car park of the doctor's surgery, right in the middle of the village. One Saturday she was buying her marmalade and who should pop up to serve her but Dr Jha. Pamela had been taken aback. It turned out Dr Jha's husband had a business making all kinds of preserves and chutneys, and mustards as well. English mustard, which surprised Pamela. Dr Jha's husband was nothing like she had imagined. He was called Edward. They didn't have any children, which probably explained why they had time to be at the market every weekend. She thought she should be seen to support them, Dr Jha always being so kind to her, so she said she'd take two jars of the marmalade. That was when Dr Jha told her it had a lot of sugar in it, so to only spread it thinly. If it wasn't so tasty she would have stopped buying from Dr Jha's husband and bought her marmalade from Tesco instead. In Tesco they don't tell you how thick to spread it. She'd smiled at Dr Jha and said she was always careful with her sugar, only for Dr Jha to spot her five minutes later buying half a dozen cherry buns at the cake stall. Good job Dr Jha couldn't see the two bottles of red wine she had in her backpack, she'd thought, as she waved goodbye.

She retrieved her walnut bread from the grill, quickly

buttered it and slathered on a thick layer of marmalade. Then she poured tea into her favourite blue and white china cup, popped everything onto her breakfast tray and walked through into her living room. She set the tray down on the small glass table by her front window, which looked directly out onto the pavement that ran along Haddley Hill Road. She glanced at the clock on her mantelpiece; it still wasn't quite eight thirty. Just in time, she thought, as she dropped into her armchair, which faced towards the window. Biting into her toast, she looked up the road and could see the secondary school children making their way down the hill. She sipped on her tea as a few of the older ones started to come past her window. Most of them ignored the old woman in the window but there were always one or two who shouted something spiteful. But Pamela took no notice of them. We were all young once, she reminded herself.

The younger children appeared around ten minutes later. She guessed their lessons must start a little bit after the older ones. They were nearly always with their mothers, although these days quite a few came with their fathers. She'd even seen some with two dads. That didn't bother her. As long as they were happy, and the children looked after. She was on to her second slice of toast by the time Jeannie came into view.

Pamela had noticed Jeannie straight away from her red hair, tied back in pigtails, the freckles covering her face and the bright, happy smile she wore. She guessed Jeannie must be eight or perhaps nine. A few months back Pamela had started waving at Jeannie. Not a big wave, just a little movement of her fingers. After a couple of weeks, Jeannie started waving back. Soon after, Pamela started mouthing hello and then Jeannie started saying hello back. Jeannie's mother nearly always had her head down, absorbed by whatever was so interesting on her phone, so she never noticed.

Today though, there was something wrong. Jeannie was hunched over, her head bowed. Pamela leaned forward to get a better look, and her plate tumbled from her knee, spreading crumbs across the carpet. She'd have to hoover them up later but never mind about that now. She peered more closely at the girl. It was definitely Jeannie, there was no doubt about it, but she was on her own. Pamela called out and waved frantically, but Jeannie kept her eyes down and walked on alone.

CHAPTER 9

Sipping on my first coffee of the day, I stand outside the front of my terraced house.

The morning school run begins. For the residents of Haddley Common, that means a walk down to the river and then along the towpath towards the bridge and St Catherine's Primary School. Or, alternatively, a cut-through to the high street and a walk halfway up the hill to Haddley Grammar School. Seeing the children and their parents fills me with a sense of sadness. Mum, Nick and I always walked the first stretch together. Waving enthusiastically when Nick veered off towards the grammar school, I remember longing for the day when we would make that turn together. That day never came.

The air is cold, frost glistens on the common but rays of autumn sun are beginning to glint through the dense woods beyond. Reddening leaves hang from the trees while, above the Thames, the early-morning river haze slowly burns away. I have lived beside Haddley Common for almost all of my life. Despite everything my family has suffered here, this is my home.

Stepping out onto the pathway that runs beside the common, I feel a twinge in my ankle and lean against my garden wall. An impromptu five-a-side football match kicks off, with school bags piled up for goal posts. It's not long before Archie Grace and his younger brother, Ted, come racing down the steps at the front of their house in the far corner of the common. Together, they sprint across the grass and join the game. Archie neatly flicks the ball away from one of his friends before kicking it up to volley across the open space. Watching the boys knock the ball about between them, I can't stop myself thinking of the hours I spent chasing a ball around the open space with Nick. I try to imagine him today, in his late thirties and perhaps with a family of his own. More than two decades after his death, he still lives on in my thoughts almost every day.

'Ben!' cries Alice Richardson, and I turn to see my five-year-old goddaughter running down the pathway towards me.

'Alice!' I call back, as she charges down from her house, only three doors away from mine. I bend to greet her and when she reaches me, she jumps up into my arms.

'There was a fire in the church last night,' she tells me, as she hugs me tightly. 'And there were *eleven* fire engines.'

'Guess what? I saw the fire on my way home.'

'Did anybody get burned?' she asks, sitting upright in my arms. 'You have to keep away from fire. Getting burned is very painful. When I was three I got burned by an iron and you can still see the mark now.' She holds up her little finger in front of my face.

'Luckily nobody was burnt in this fire,' I tell her. 'Are you on your way to school?'

'I am, but after today it's the weekend and that means two days at home with Mummy. *And* you coming round to play in the garden in the afternoon?' she says, opening her bright eyes wide.

'We'll see,' I reply, laughing.

'I'm on reading level five and Max is only on level four!' she continues, scarcely waiting for my answer. 'I've got a new book to read about Winnie and she's a witch. On Fridays we do reading in the morning, and I will be able to show Max that I'm ahead of him. This afternoon we're doing times tables and Max likes that better because he can already do them up to seven, but I can't. Max can do sixty add sixty. I don't know what that is.' I laugh when she pulls a face.

'I'm sure you will be able to soon,' I reply.

'I'm better at reading than Max, though.'

'You're a brilliant reader.'

'When I'm older, I'm going to write news stories, just like you. And I'm the fastest girl in the class,' she rapidly continues, her thoughts racing on. 'Max is still faster than me, though. Boo!' She pulls her face again.

'He is a boy, though,' I point out.

'So?' she replies, almost spitting with outrage. I'm not sure how to reply but I am suddenly proud of Alice. Then she smiles and laughs when she tells me, 'Two of the other boys are faster than Max, so I always cheer for them.'

'Morning,' says Holly, coming down the footpath after her daughter. 'Tell me you're okay,' she says, wrapping her arm around me. Since the age of four, Holly and I have been best friends, with each the only constant in the other's life.

'Nothing worse than a twisted ankle,' I say.

'All very dramatic.'

'Somebody was determined to destroy the old community centre, that's for sure.'

'It was deliberate?'

'Looks that way. Either they wanted rid of the community centre or whoever it was that was trapped inside.'

'Madness,' replies Holly, shaking her head. 'Can I ask you a favour? Any chance you can pick up Alice from school next Wednesday? I've got a training course at work and then I said I'd meet Sarah for a quick pizza.'

'I could have my tea at your house, Ben,' adds Alice, listening carefully to our conversation.

'We'll cook it together,' I reply.

'I won't be late,' Holly assures me.

'Can Max come for tea as well?' asks Alice.

'I think Max will be at his daddy's house,' says Holly.

Alice's face momentarily drops until she spies Max leaving the front of his home. Holding his mum's hand, he carefully makes his way down the steep steps that lead up to their imposing Victorian villa. Once on the common, he races across the grass towards Ted Grace and the older boys playing football. Alice is quick to jump down after him.

'You can have two minutes' chat, Mummy. Then we need to leave for school,' she calls over her shoulder.

Sarah Wright follows the path along the side of the

common, watching her son hurl himself after a football Ted Grace has sent flying down the makeshift pitch.

'He's Max's new hero,' she says, as she comes to stand beside us. 'He'll be devastated when Ted heads off to the grammar school in a couple of years.' Max thumps a football towards us and races after Alice. I stop the ball and knock it back to Ted.

'Thanks, Ben,' he calls, picking up his football and carrying it under his arm.

'You can walk with us to school if you like,' says Holly, but Ted looks back towards his older brother.

'I should probably wait for Archie.'

'A choice between walking with us and two five-year-olds, or a gang of fifteen-year-old boys,' says Sarah. 'I can understand that choice.'

After Holly and Sarah head to school with their children, I walk back to the front of my house. I grab my coffee cup, one made by my mum in honour of my favourite football team, and head back into my garden. As I turn I notice the older boys gathering their bags from the grass, leaving it as long as possible before departing for school. Ted is some distance in front, walking alone. As he passes, I wave and he raises his hand in reply.

I make my way back inside my house and through into the kitchen. As I rinse my mug, I hear my phone buzz. I dry my hands on my jeans and then pull my phone from my pocket.

I look at the message. It's from an unknown number and is a single word.

Help.

CHAPTER 10

Pamela leaned back in her chair. Jeannie had never walked to school on her own before. Surely, she wasn't old enough. Pamela felt certain she was only eight, and if she was nine she was small for her age. Had she had any breakfast? She hated to think of Jeannie being hungry in school. Did she have money for her lunch? Perhaps they didn't need it at that age. She couldn't really remember. And her hair wasn't in its usual pigtails. Pamela reached for her cup of tea only to be startled by a sudden rap on her window. She heard a scream of laughter and when she turned in her chair she saw two older boys, late for school she presumed, disappearing up the road. She sighed, drained the last of her tea and got to her feet. Half a slice of toast was lying on the carpet. She bent to pick it up and gave the carpet a quick rub with her slipper. Then, she pulled the blinds halfway down the window to stop any passers-by looking in during the day.

Walking back across her living room, her thoughts returning to Jeannie, Pamela stopped to talk to Thomas. She knew what he'd say – that she was best to keep her nose out of it and leave well alone. She straightened his picture, pulling it forward slightly on the shelf. He was still so handsome, with his neatly combed jet-black hair parted to one side and his dress uniform with its polished buttons and red stripe down the side of the trousers. The night before he'd left they'd danced together in the living room, first to 'It Must Be Love' and then to 'Golden Brown'. Both songs still made her tear up. A week later, in the spring sunshine, among the cheering and waving crowds, they'd shared a crowded farewell on the Portsmouth docks. That autumn, she attended a victory parade, a new life growing inside her. She'd been invited to sit in a stand and watch the soldiers march past. After fifteen minutes, unable to bear it any longer, she'd made her excuses and hurried home. That night, as she'd played 'Golden Brown' over and over on her Walkman, she'd sobbed.

For the shopping list she had, the mini market would've been fine, but once she was outside, Pamela decided to walk down the hill into Haddley. By the time she reached the high street, her legs were already aching. She paused outside a café, where a chalkboard advertising artisan coffee stood. Pamela had never understood the modern fashion for coffee shops. These days there seemed to be one on every corner and a simple cup of coffee cost over three pounds. How did people ever afford it? Still, there must be some appeal because she'd walked past this café hundreds of times and it did always seem busy. She peered through the window and noticed an empty table. It was an extravagance, but it wouldn't hurt this once.

Her chair wasn't overly comfy. In fact, it wasn't a chair at all, but a stool. Pamela looked about her expectantly, trying to catch the waitress's eye, but nobody came to serve her. Just as Pamela was thinking how disappointing the service was, a younger woman, probably only in her fifties, got up to leave a neighbouring table.

'You have to order at the counter,' she whispered.

'Oh, thank you,' Pamela replied, feeling her age.

'And take my table. There's a proper chair with a cushion.'

Pamela was quick to her feet and put her bag down on the neighbouring table to claim her spot. She took her purse from her bag and went across to the counter to order. She was right – three pounds for coffee. Looking at the lemon cake on display, she thought it did look moist. She knew what Dr Jha would say but she needed to think about Jeannie, and the lemon cake would help.

Sitting back down at her table, she noticed the woman had left behind a copy of the *Richmond Times*. The same newspaper was shoved through her letterbox most Wednesdays, and Pamela had already read this edition cover to cover. She pushed the paper to one side and switched on her phone. As a rule she enjoyed the neighbourhood app, even if it was mostly made up of wealthy people moaning about how badly off they were. Somebody'd posted pictures of the community centre at the height of the fire. Somehow people managed to get photographs of everything these days. Looking at the burnt-out building only depressed her. She and Thomas had married at St Stephen's and, on that day, it'd seemed such a happy place.

This morning, on her walk down the hill, she'd stopped

to talk to Mr Nowak, the owner of the mini market. He was standing outside the front of his shop smoking a butterscotch vape. She'd thought it was an unusual choice for a grown man but had said nothing. According to Mr Nowak, a teenage boy had been seen running from the community centre. How he knew that, she didn't know. Mr Nowak was already convinced it was the boy who'd started the fire. He'd told Pamela the boy was sure to have been smoking something illegal, and in his view he'd got what he deserved. She liked Mr Nowak but felt he was always very quick to judge. She was simply relieved that whoever had been trapped in the fire was safe.

Drinking her coffee, she had to admit it did have a lovely flavour. It was very different to the instant she made herself at home but at this price it needed to be. She broke off a corner of cake and was pleased to discover it tasted as good as it looked. Now, she thought, what should she do about Jeannie? She knew what Thomas thought but she also knew Jeannie never walked to school on her own. It was too far for an eight-year-old – she'd decided that she must only be eight – to be walking on her own. And with so much traffic.

She'd only ever seen Jeannie with her mum. What if it was just the two of them, and her mum was ill? Or something even worse? She knew Jeannie's school was St Catherine's by the bridge and as it was almost lunchtime, if she walked down to the bridge now, she might be able to see her in the playground. She'd happened to be crossing the bridge a few weeks back and, if you stood at the very edge of the bridge, it was possible to look directly down into St Catherine's playground. She'd noticed Jeannie three or four times since then. Perhaps she should go there now. Then she could stop at the supermarket in the town centre before walking back up the hill. Finishing her cake, she decided that was her plan.

Approaching Haddley Bridge, she slowed before stopping to peer over the edge. Almost immediately, she spotted Jeannie. She was standing at the side of a larger group but remained too far away for Pamela to call. After watching for a couple of minutes, she decided to get moving before anyone noticed her. Not that she was doing anything wrong.

The supermarket was quiet. She quickly picked up all she needed and at the last minute added a box of miniature chocolate brownies to her basket. Back home, she realised she was late for her own lunch, but she wasn't overly hungry. She made herself a tongue sandwich, just one round, with a touch of Dr Jha's English mustard.

In the afternoon, it was always the younger children who made their way home first. Sitting back in her chair she felt a slight chill, so she lit the gas fire for some extra warmth. She was glad when she did as the glow gave the room a welcoming feel. She smiled at one little boy who was dragging his bag along the ground behind him. That bag won't last long at that rate, she thought. More children followed, quite a rush, and for a moment Pamela worried she might miss her. But then there she was, Jeannie, walking back up the hill, all alone. Butterflies fluttered in Pamela's stomach.

Jeannie was looking straight ahead, not towards her

window, so as she approached, Pamela leaned forward and knocked on the glass. Jeannie looked up, startled. Pamela waved.

'Hello!' called Pamela through the window. 'Can you wait a second and come to my door?'

Pamela got to her feet and hurried as fast as she could out into her narrow hallway, cursing her stiff and heavy legs. She scrabbled at the latch on the door, her haste making her clumsy. But when she finally got the door open, there was Jeannie, standing on her doorstep.

'Hello,' Pamela said again.

'Hello,' was the little girl's nervous reply.

'I only wanted to check you were okay. You haven't got your mummy with you today?' Pamela saw the girl's face drop.

'No,' she replied.

Pamela thought the girl was going to burst into tears. So she had been right, something was wrong.

'Why don't you come inside, just for a minute?'

The girl hesitated. 'I'm not meant to go inside with strangers.'

'I'm not a stranger, am I?' said Pamela. 'You see me every day.' She could see the little girl thinking. 'Come on, I'll make you a glass of Ribena and I've got a box of miniature chocolate brownies.'

Jeannie's face brightened. 'Can I have one?' she said, stepping inside.

'You can have two if you like,' replied Pamela. 'Now, come in here and sit down. I've got the fire on so it's lovely and cosy. Take your coat off and I'll get your drink and the chocolate brownies.'

Pamela hurried into the kitchen and put four chocolate brownie squares onto a plate. That would be a treat for Jeannie. She ran the cold tap and mixed a glass of Ribena. Then, she decided she'd have a glass as well. She put the drinks and the brownies onto her breakfast tray and carried them out of the kitchen. But when she came back into the hallway, there was Jeannie, reaching up for the latch to open the front door.

'No, don't go!' called Pamela, setting the tray down on the hall table.

The little girl turned. 'I have to go,' she said. 'I have to go home.'

'Not yet,' said Pamela, dashing forward. 'You can't go yet.' She suddenly found herself raising her voice as she slammed her hand hard against the door.

CHAPTER 11

Ted Grace sat down at the broad wooden table that filled much of his family's kitchen. He started to untie the laces on his school shoes.

'There are still two more bags in the car that need to come in,' said his mother, Amy.

Ted looked up at her, staggering under the weight of multiple bulging shopping bags on both arms. 'Can't Archie get them?'

'It's your turn and, anyway, he's not home yet.'

Ted got to his feet. 'It's always my turn,' he grumbled as he walked out of the kitchen.

'Don't trip over your laces,' he heard his mum call behind him.

He ran down the steps at the front of his house and around to the side, where his mum always parked her beat-up old Fiat. He was glad the car was kept out of sight. He grabbed the two bags from the boot and raced back inside, dropping the shopping on the kitchen table. Amy was crouching in front of an open cupboard, stacking packets of rice and pasta, and didn't turn as she said, 'Careful, please.'

'Did you get any popcorn?'

'No.'

'Crisps?'

'I've bought proper food, not rubbish,' said Amy. Ted sat down, took off his school shoes and pulled on his trainers. 'Change out of your uniform if you're going outside,' she continued.

'Can I have a sausage roll?'

'I'll be making dinner soon.'

'What are we having?'

'Pasta.'

'Again,' replied Ted, with a groan.

'I thought it was your favourite?'

Ted shrugged, but when he saw his mum's face he said, 'Carbonara?'

'Of course.'

'That's okay, then,' he replied, before smiling at his mum. 'Where's Dad?'

'Upstairs, in his office.' Ted quickly made for the door. 'Don't disturb him,' called his mum. 'He's on an important call with investors.'

'He said he'd get me a new football.' Ted stopped in the doorway.

'I don't think he's been out today, Teddy.'

Ted felt his stomach sink. He knew it wasn't worth arguing. Two nights ago, he'd heard his parents talking about making their mortgage payment. He didn't really understand what a mortgage was, but he did know not paying it wasn't good. He stood and watched his mum split open a bag of onions and reach for a knife.

'Mum,' Ted said, hesitantly. 'This is our house, isn't it?'

Amy stopped what she was doing, wiped her hands and crossed towards him. 'Of course it is,' she replied. 'What makes you say that?'

'Nothing,' he said, wishing he hadn't asked his stupid question, 'just something Archie said about the bank.'

'Don't listen to him,' she replied, picking up her knife again. 'Archie thinks he knows everything.'

'What time will he be home?'

'I don't know. I think he's working at the boathouse this evening.'

Ted waited for a moment before asking, 'Can I go and see him?'

'No,' replied Amy, without turning. 'It'll be getting dark soon. I don't want you leaving the garden.'

Ted sighed before running down the hall.

'Where's your football kit?' called his mum.

'In my bag.'

'It won't get washed in there. Put it on top of the washing machine.'

Ted pulled his muddy kit out of his bag and took it round to the garage, dumping his kit on top of the washing machine. Then, he found an old football squashed beneath his bike and started firing it against the side of the house. Slamming the ball against the wall, he found himself wishing Archie spent more time at home. He and his brother used to spend hours playing football on the common, but now Archie was hardly ever home. If only Ted could find a way to make Archie love football again.

Fifteen minutes later, his mum appeared in the garden, dressed in a tracksuit and a baggy hoody.

'Where are you going?' asked Ted, surprised.

'For a jog down to St Marnham and back. I need some fresh air. I won't be long.'

'Isn't that Archie's sweatshirt?'

'It's too cold to run in just a T-shirt,' she replied. 'It could do with washing, anyway. I don't know how many times I've told him he can't wear the same thing again and again without changing it. I'll put it in the machine when I get back, although –' she pinched the fabric between her fingers and brought it to her nose '– for Archie it doesn't smell too bad. Don't you go telling him I've borrowed it,' she continued, running over to her youngest son and giving him a hug.

For a moment Ted closed his eyes and let his mum hold him close. Then, he stood and watched as she disappeared toward the woods.

CHAPTER 12

'I've bought the chocolate brownies especially for you,' said Pamela, keeping her hand firmly pressed against the door. She clicked down the latch. The little girl's startled eyes stared up at her. 'Come on, Jeannie, they're your favourites.' Pamela put her arm around the girl and steered her back towards the living room. 'That's it. We can sit by the fire.' Pamela pressed more firmly on the girl's back and guided her into the room. Once she was sitting on the sofa, Pamela picked up the tray and followed her in.

'Now,' said Pamela, setting the tray down on her small coffee table. 'Let's get your coat off because you'll be too warm in here with it on. I've put the fire on especially for you.'

The girl stared at Pamela and slowly unzipped her anorak.

'That's it,' said Pamela, 'you can pop it on that other chair.'

The girl did as she was told and then perched back down in the far corner of the sofa. Pamela turned her favourite armchair from the window and sat looking at the girl.

'As a special treat, would you like two brownies?' she asked, already putting the chocolate squares onto a blue willow pattern plate. 'There you go.' She handed the plate to the girl. 'And that glass is yours,' she added, reaching for her own Ribena, and resting it on the small table beside her. Then, she put two brownies onto her own plate, leaned back in her chair and bit into her first cake. 'Well, this is nice,' she said, as the girl sat motionless in front of her. 'You can try your brownie now.' She nodded towards the girl's plate.

Tentatively, the girl picked up the cake and took a bite.

'How's that?' said Pamela, and the girl's mouth twitched. 'They've always been your favourite, haven't they?'

The girl nodded.

'You had to make your way to school on your own this morning, didn't you?'

The girl nodded again.

'And all the way home. That could be quite dangerous. You never know who might be waiting for you.'

The girl stared at Pamela and took another bite from her brownie.

'You seem hungry. Did you have enough money for your lunch?'

The girl shook her head. 'I don't have to pay.'

Pamela wondered what that meant. Free school meals she assumed, but she wasn't here to judge.

The girl reached for her drink.

'That's it. Ribena. You like that, don't you?'

'We don't have it at my house,' said the girl.

No, Pamela thought, I'm sure you don't. She wondered what else Jeannie was missing out on.

'Well, you can come here for Ribena whenever you like.

And if you let me know when you're coming, I'll always make sure I've got chocolate brownies or any other kind of cake. You'll have to tell me what else you like.'

The girl nodded again, and Pamela leaned forward in her chair. 'Is everything all right at home?' she said, reaching for the girl's hand.

Instantly, the girl jumped to her feet, sending her plate and the glass of Ribena flying. The girl grabbed hold of her school bag and, before Pamela could react, was racing out through the living-room door. Pamela heard the click of the latch and then the sound of the front door being thrown open.

She got to her feet and looked out of the front window. She could see Jeannie running up Haddley Hill Road. She sighed, turned and surveyed her living room. Ribena was sprayed across the carpet, right in front of the fireplace.

She'd never get that stain out, she thought to herself.

CHAPTER 13

Dani Cash exited through the front of the police station, stepped through the traffic and crossed to the flower stall on the opposite side of the high street. Picking out a spray of blue irises, her father's favourite, she held them close and inhaled their delicate scent. Despite her best efforts when she got home the night before, the smell of smoke still pursued her. Somehow even now it clung to her clothes, her hair. All day she'd struggled to keep the fire from her mind.

Spending two hours staring at CCTV footage hadn't helped. Her search had proved fruitless. Outside the church there were no cameras, while images captured from beside the pedestrian crossing, halfway up the Lower Haddley Road, caught only distant images of the slim figure running into the trees. All were too hazy to offer any hope of identification. She had successfully identified a VW Golf slamming on its brakes but with no licence plate visible, she knew it was virtually impossible to trace.

Frustrated at her failure to achieve a breakthrough, she tried to relax as she made her way back through the park towards her Haddley Hill home. When she reached her neat, modern terraced house, she paused and took a deep breath before slipping the key in the latch and stepping inside.

'You brought me flowers,' said Mat Moore, when his wife walked through the front door. It was as if he'd been waiting for her. 'How sweet.'

Without saying anything, Dani moved past her husband and into the small kitchen at the back of their new-build home. 'Thanks for clearing up,' she muttered, seeing the sink piled high with dirty plates. She opened the dishwasher and began loading the machine.

'I've been working,' replied Mat, following her into the kitchen. 'You're the one who encouraged me to get more involved with the station again. And anyway, you're so much faster than me,' he continued, as Dani emptied the sink. 'It's just easier if you do it.'

'Everyone's looking forward to seeing you back next week,' she said, attempting to inject a lightness into her tone.

'Not as much as I'm looking forward to seeing them. I cannot wait to get out of this miserable prison.'

'Barnsdale said next Wednesday was probably best. Everything should be set up by then.'

'They've only had a year to get things sorted.'

Dani wiped down the sink before filling a vase with cold water. She carried the flowers across to the kitchen table. 'Anything you fancy for dinner?'

'I've ordered up a Deliveroo.'

'What are we having?' she asked.

'I didn't know what time you'd be home.'

Dani stacked the last plate into the dishwasher, then turned to look at her husband. 'Not a problem,' she said. 'I'm not really that hungry. Think I'll pop upstairs for a soak in the bath.' She opened the fridge and reached for a bottle of Sauvignon blanc.

'I'll have a beer if we're drinking,' said Mat.

Dani took out a bottle of Peroni. The bottle opener was already on the table.

Mat manoeuvred himself across the room. 'Any crisps?'

She knelt to open the cupboard by the cooker and threw a bag of Frazzles onto the table. Then she crossed the kitchen, reached for a wine glass and poured herself a generous serving. Screwing the cap back on the bottle, she stood and watched her husband drain his bottle of beer. She'd barely taken a sip from her own glass before he held up his empty bottle.

'I'll have another.'

'My guess is you've had two or three already.'

'You're not my mother,' he replied. 'I said I'll have another.'

Dani didn't move. Mat stared at her, and for one terrible moment she thought he was going to drop the bottle on the floor. Instead, he slowly rolled it across the kitchen table. They both watched, transfixed, as the bottle trundled forward. Behind her back, Dani gripped hold of the edge of the sink. She held her breath. The bottle teetered on the table's edge. Only when it stopped did she exhale.

'I said I'll have another.' Mat looked at his wife. Still, she didn't move. He grabbed the edge of the table and aggressively pushed his wheelchair backwards. The bottle smashed to the floor; the vase of flowers tipped over, splashing water across the kitchen. Dani closed her eyes.

'I'll get my own,' he said, rolling himself around the table and taking two more bottles from the fridge.

Eighteen months earlier, not long after the death of her father, DS Mat Moore had dazzled Dani. She'd caught the attention of the high-flying sergeant when they jointly attended a body pump class at their local gym. He'd waited for her outside the changing rooms, and she'd found herself instantly attracted to his soft blue eyes, shock of cropped blonde hair and five o'clock shadow. At the pub that evening they had giggled and laughed before Dani had spent the night at Mat's rented flat at the top of Haddley Hill. In the weeks that followed, they were together whenever they were both off duty. They eagerly viewed the new-build house where they now lived and one day had planned to marry.

Then, last Hallowe'en, when Dani stopped at Haddley's riverfront gourmet supermarket to pick up dinner and a bottle of wine, everything changed. Dani's mind had been on the dinner she'd planned to cook for Mat and she'd scarcely noticed the gang as they charged past her, wearing masks of monsters and ghouls. Entering the store, she'd seen the figure with a Scream face mask pull a knife. Perhaps she was only thinking of the end of her shift, but she'd been slow to react to the danger.

She'd assumed they were kids, and that the knife was fake. Except they weren't, and it wasn't.

Her guard down, she was thrown back against the shelves at the side of the store. Alarms had sounded and within minutes police first responders broke through the rear of the store. Dani freed herself and pushed customers to safety. Bottles crashed to the floor as the masked raiders tried to flee. A struggle had led to a stabbing. A first responder was down. Hours later, when she'd sat beside Mat's hospital bed, Dani cried with relief when she heard he would live. She felt numb when she heard he would never walk again.

At the beginning of December, on the day Mat left hospital, he and Dani were married. Since then, she'd wondered every single day what she might have done differently that day at the supermarket. Perhaps Mat was right, and she had made a mistake. She didn't know. But what she did increasingly know was that in marrying Mat, she had definitely made a dreadful mistake.

Every single day, Dani desperately sought to find ways to try to make her marriage work. Together, she and Mat had bought a house on the new housing estate at the top of Haddley Hill. She'd dreamt of building a home where they could both be happy. Ten months later, they were still struggling to make the adaptations to the house Mat needed. Compensation money either never arrived or was painfully inadequate. Mat lived downstairs, she lived upstairs. Their lives were separate and nothing she did seemed to change that.

She took a large swig of her wine and opened the cupboard beneath the sink. Pushing aside bottles of cleaning spray and a large box of laundry pods, she fumbled for the dustpan and brush, somehow always thrown haphazardly to the back. Crouching beside the kitchen table, she began to sweep up the broken glass.

'When were you going to tell me?' said Mat, rolling his chair towards her. She didn't look up. There was a bitterness in his tone. 'The new queen of CID.'

Dani got to her feet and grabbed a free newspaper from the pile stacked beside the back door. She spread the paper out by the sink and tipped in the broken glass. 'I was going to tell you,' she said, turning to face her husband, 'but I only learned it myself last night.' She tossed the wrapped glass into the bin before reaching for the mop from behind the kitchen door. 'Barnsdale suggested I apply for the transfer,' she continued, before adding, 'And I wanted to.'

'You'll be my boss before you know it.'

She knew Mat would be sensitive to her appointment, but she wasn't going to apologise for it. Her dad would be proud of what she'd achieved, and so was she.

'Is that what this is all about?' she said, setting the vase of flowers upright on the table. 'Who told you, anyway? Was it Barnsdale?'

Mat sniffed. 'As if,' he replied. 'I've still got my sources.' He moved directly in front of Dani. 'I could've run that station.'

'No one is saying you can't still. When you've passed the exams, they'll make you inspector in no time.'

'How could they not? I'll be the poster boy for disability.'

There was a knock at the front door.

'I'll go,' said Dani, instantly.

'I can still answer the door,' replied Mat, looking up at his wife. And as he wheeled himself away, she was left with the image of the anger burning in his eyes.

CHAPTER 14

Ted picked up his football and walked to the end of his drive. He looked towards the woods, but there was no sign of his mum. Upstairs, the light remained on in his dad's window. He knew his father must still be working. Across the common, there was no sign of Archie returning home. He was alone.

This was his opportunity to explore the churchyard. Stepping out of his garden, he stood at the edge of the pavement. He dropped his football and volleyed it across the lane. He watched it trundle down the side of the woods before he crossed onto the common and chased after it. The cold breeze blowing in his face made his eyes water but when he reached his football he kicked it again. He stood and watched it roll all the way to the Lower Haddley Road.

Keeping close to the trees, where he knew it would be harder for him to be seen, he hurried after the ball. One last gentle kick and the ball was directly across from St Stephen's church. The Lower Haddley Road was busy with traffic. Looking across at the church, he felt his stomach tense. He gripped hold of the football but when the road cleared, he sprinted across.

Standing inside the churchyard gates, he could clearly see the burnt-out community centre. Temporary lights lit up the inside of the building. He could see people, dressed in plastic suits, still working and wondered what they were looking for.

As he crept forward into the church car park, he caught sight of a figure in a hooded sweatshirt running down the roadside from St Marnham. He moved backwards and hid behind a stone gatepost, waiting until the road was clear of traffic. As soon as it was, he ran back across and tucked himself into the trees at the side of the common. Peering forward, he watched his mum stop outside the front of the church. For a moment she lingered, looking around, before she jogged through the car park and down the side of the church.

Ted edged forward. His mother was out of sight. Where was she going? He stood beside the trees but as he did he looked back across the common and saw Ben Harper leaving his house. Wanting to avoid Ben asking him any questions, Ted quickly ducked back into the woods. He hurried through the trees and didn't stop running until he was safely back inside his own garden.

CHAPTER 15

Early in the evening I step out of my front door and cross the common towards St Stephen's. I spent much of the day working on my podcast script before a seemingly endless video conference call with the audio producers. When the conversation became long and technical, my mind returned to the plea for help I received this morning. I replied instantly when the message arrived.

Who is this?

Then, when there was no response:

Are you okay? Where are you?

And finally:

Please call me.

Since then, I've heard nothing. All I can do is wait to see if whoever it was contacts me again.

Before the last of the daylight fades, I want to revisit the community centre. Less than twenty-four hours since the fire, I struggle to understand why anyone would want to destroy the old building, unless the figure trapped inside was a direct target. But if so, who were they? I stand and wait for the number 29 bus to pass before crossing and following the narrow path towards St Stephen's. At the entrance to the churchyard, I stop to read the parish notices. Three religious services will take place this Sunday; at the end of next week there is a bake sale raising funds in memory of a parishioner who recently died from motor neurone disease; while the scouts are welcoming new members. A larger poster proclaims the Lord's love is steadfast and endures for ever. Tucked beneath the poster, I can see the edge of a council planning application. The poster conceals its details.

I enter the churchyard and see a slim figure hurrying along the gravel path, which runs down the side of the church.

'Ben,' says Amy Grace, hastily greeting me. 'I know I shouldn't have but I couldn't stop myself taking a quick look. It's so close to home.' As we stand together in front of the church, she continues: 'Why on earth burn down the old community centre? On the neighbourhood app, people are saying it was deliberate.'

'Looks that way, I'm afraid.'

She shakes her head. 'They're still working now.' She glances towards the building. 'I wonder what they're looking for. Do you think it might be something to do with the church?'

'Right now, it's impossible to know.'

'Well, the main thing is you're safe.' She briefly reaches out and touches my arm.

'I'm fine,' I reply.

'Thank God for that. Kicking in the door and charging into a fire is such an incredibly brave thing to do.'

I smile. 'I was in the right place at the right time.'

Amy looks as if she is about to say something more, but just then there comes the sound of the old bolt on the church door being lifted from the inside.

'Look at the time, I must get going. Dinner won't cook itself,' she calls, already jogging away. 'A mother's work is never done!'

Pulling up her hood, she starts to run out of the car park and by the time the church door is fully open, she is already crossing the Lower Haddley Road.

'Can I help you?' a voice calls from behind me. I turn to see Adrian Withers leaving the church. He takes three steps down and only then does he recognise me. 'Ben, I'm so sorry, I didn't realise it was you. All day, I've been meaning to visit. It really is a dereliction on my part. You were quite the hero last night. How are you?'

'I'm fine,' I reply, already tiring of this question.

'Your bravery in the face of such danger. Please tell me you suffered no ill-harm.'

'Bit of a sore ankle and a few scratches but nothing worse than that.'

'As long as you're sure?' he replies, overly earnest. 'I dread to think what might have happened if you hadn't arrived when you did.' I slowly nod before he continues. 'I understand you said last night you thought you saw a teen-age boy but were unable to say anything more?'

'I don't think I even said that,' I reply, as he moves closer to me. I take a small step back.

He pauses. 'So it wasn't a boy you saw?'

'I couldn't see who it was. It was dark and they had a hood pulled over their face.'

'I see. Well hopefully the police will get to the bottom of this terrible business. I hate to think of it happening so close to the church.'

'We can only thank God the fire didn't spread.' I smile but Withers doesn't share my humour. Together, we walk slowly down the side of the church until the burnt-out community centre comes into sight.

'Left derelict for so many years,' he says. 'I feel almost culpable in that regard, but who could have known something like this would happen?'

'The building looks a fairly simple construction?'

'It was,' he replies. 'Just the two rooms, built by a couple of local Haddley lads. Cold water and electricity but anyone needing the loo had to use the one at the back of the church. We had a few in need of a quick dash on a winter's night. If I was feeling charitable, I left a light on.' Withers smirks. 'For the past five years, I hate to say it, but the building's been left to rot.'

We approach the building where a single strip of red and white fire-investigation tape blows vainly in the wind. The front door is gone, and we are able to stand exactly where I entered the building last night. The investigating team has cleared the wall dividing the two rooms, a wide-open space remaining. All the seared gym equipment, which I saw with PC Cooke, is now piled at the back of the building.

I drop my voice so as not to attract the attention of the investigating officers. 'And since then? No plans to use the land for some other purpose? It's such a lovely spot, right by the river.'

The reverend exhales slowly. 'From time to time we've looked at how best the land might be used – for the good of the church, you understand.' I turn to Withers and wait. He touches his moustache. 'As you'll no doubt be aware, Ben, we have submitted a planning application to the council.' I raise my eyebrows. After a moment he continues. 'Three small cottages. From the outset, I've been insistent their style must be very much in keeping with the character of the church. If we were able to proceed with such a development, it would help secure the financial future of St Stephen's long after I have departed.'

'A valuable piece of land.'

'As I said, purely to secure the financial future of the church.'

'No danger of this investigation delaying permissions?' I ask, turning back towards the building.

Suddenly, a voice calls from inside the remains of the community centre. 'Please step back. This is an ongoing fire investigation site with restricted access.'

I move forward and can see the floor of the building has been removed. The two investigating officers are crouching in the building's shallow foundations. Before I can reply to the investigator, she calls again.

'I asked you both to step back.' A bright light is pointed directly towards us. Withers lifts his hand to shield his eyes.

The second officer rounds on us, his voice sharp. 'Get out, now!'

Neither of us moves. Looking into the foundations of the building, we can see the two officers are kneeling beside a battered human skull.

Three

'She briefly closed her eyes and let the relief wash over her, safe in the knowledge the police had asked her nothing more.'

WEDNESDAY

CHAPTER 16

The Reverend Adrian Withers edged back his sitting-room curtains and looked outside. Squinting through his side window, he could see the police forensic team removing what he desperately hoped were the last of the filled plastic sacks from the old community centre. This was the fifth morning he had watched them, quarantined in their protective white suits, trekking across the grounds of his church. On each morning, his heart had sunk a little further.

He decided he'd seen enough and yanked the curtains closed. What else could the police be looking for, he wondered. From what he understood, the remains of one body – a badly beaten female – were the totality of the discovery. But for five days the police had kept searching, sifting through every last grain of dust and ash in the burnt-out building. Watching the police tramp across the church grounds, he'd felt hopeless.

On the morning following the discovery of the woman's body, two police officers had arrived at the vicarage. Detective Sergeant Lesley Barnsdale and, once again,

Constable Daniella Cash. They had a few questions, they'd said. It was early, before nine, and he wasn't prepared for their visit. He'd attempted levity, telling the officers he'd buried plenty of bodies in his time, but almost always with headstones. Barnsdale remained stony faced. They had some questions, she'd repeated, and could they come in? He'd explained his wife was feeling slightly under the weather and perhaps they could arrange a time later in the day.

'We'll try not to disturb her, reverend,' Barnsdale had assured him, as she'd moved forward into the porch. She had left him with no alternative. He'd stepped back and allowed them both inside, but felt uncomfortable with the way they encroached upon his home. They would receive no hospitality from him.

From the hallway, a short corridor led to an unloved study he barely used, preferring to work in the vestry at the back of the church. 'Do come through to my study,' he'd said, and opening the door the room had smelt damp. When he'd invited them to take a seat, he'd chosen not to light the fire. And he didn't offer them tea.

Deliberately walking around his desk, he'd sat opposite the two officers. 'How may I be of assistance?' he'd asked.

'Reverend Withers,' the sergeant had begun, 'at this time, we have been able to determine the body discovered beneath the community centre is that of a woman, her age yet to be confirmed.'

Withers leaned forward, folded his arms and rested them on the desk in front of him. His lips tight, he slowly nodded. 'A shocking discovery,' he'd replied.

The sergeant continued. 'From an initial examination, it appears the skull is severely fractured, with the injuries occurring pre-mortem, probably immediately before the woman's death.'

Withers could see the two police officers studying him, so he dropped his head forward. 'We will say prayers for the victim at each of our services tomorrow,' he'd replied.

'It might be advisable to postpone tomorrow's services,' said Barnsdale.

Withers stared at her. 'We have never postponed our services on the sabbath. In such trying circumstances, the community will be looking for guidance.'

'I'll leave the decision with you,' Barnsdale had replied, 'but you should be aware we will have forensic teams working right across the weekend.' Withers had drawn in his cheeks but said nothing. 'Can I ask how long you've been vicar here at St Stephen's?'

'I celebrated my quarter of a century last year. The archbishop sent me an antique silver fountain pen, most generous of him.' Withers gestured to the slim leather case on his desk. Neither Barnsdale nor Dani Cash dropped their gaze from him to look at it. 'Prior to St Stephen's I spent many happy years in a small parish in East Haddley. The community here is a close one, and through births, marriages and eventually deaths, most do pass my way. Even now, when other professions may consider me to be approaching retirement age, I'm able to remain vital in my work.'

Barnsdale made no comment. 'Was the community centre built during your time at St Stephen's?'

'I believe construction was three or four years after my arrival.'

'The building was wholly owned by the church?'

'It was built on church land, and we led the fundraising efforts to support its construction, but it genuinely was a community facility.'

He'd told the two officers that for at least fifteen years the building was used on an almost daily basis. Not just by the church but by the scouts, guides and other community groups. He believed it had been the scouts who'd made most use of the gym equipment. A number of years ago, the church received a bequest, which allowed them to share in the construction costs of the new sports pavilion beside St Marnham playing fields.

'A much better space with wonderful facilities for all of our community groups. I hate to say it but since then we rather let the old building fall into disrepair.'

'You never thought of renovating it, using it for other church business?'

'No, we have all the space we need in our rooms at the sports pavilion and those come with hot water and central heating.'

'Was there anything on the land prior to the community centre?' PC Cash had asked.

'A smaller building, not more than a shed. It was flattened.'

DS Barnsdale gave him a long look, and Withers found himself shifting uncomfortably under her gaze. 'The investigation of the site to this point, suggests the body was most likely disposed of during the original construction of the building. The reason we believe this,' she went on, before Withers could respond, 'is the skeleton's discovery was within the foundations of the building. Hiding the body in such a way would have been virtually impossible once the community centre was complete and in active use.'

There was a long silence while Withers took in what she had said. To his dismay, he realised his brow was beginning to sweat. 'I see,' he said, eventually.

'Who built the community centre?' asked Dani Cash, quietly.

Withers frowned, trying to look ponderous. 'It was so long ago I don't recollect the details. As you can see, my study is small, I tend not to keep records for very long. But if you give me a couple of days, I might be able to dig something out.'

Barnsdale smiled. 'If you could find the time, we'd be most grateful.'

Withers couldn't stop himself reacting to her tone. 'You may consider the role of a parish vicar to be a limited one,' he began, coldly.

'Not at all—'

'But the hours can be considerable, and the commitment must be absolute.' Withers had leant forward, clasping his hands tightly together. 'But of course, I will do my very best.'

Following a further moment of silence, the officers had stood, and he'd been happy to lead them back down the narrow corridor into the hallway. Before stepping outside, Barnsdale had turned to him.

'On the night of the fire,' she'd begun, 'after speaking with Constable Cash, you went back inside St Stephen's?'

Withers nodded, waiting for the detective to make her point. 'And after that?'

'I returned to the vicarage. My wife had recently arrived home from her supper engagement. We had tea together and then retired for the evening.'

'Thank you.'

'Why do you ask?'

Barnsdale had given him that smile again, the one that didn't reach her eyes. 'In a case like this, we like to be certain of people's movements.'

'Of course, but the poor woman was killed many years ago, not on Thursday night. You can't believe there is a link between the two?' he'd ventured.

'At this stage it appears unlikely,' Barnsdale had conceded, 'but if the fire was started deliberately it could easily have resulted in the death of the person trapped inside.'

Withers nodded but said nothing. Barnsdale had stepped out onto the porch, then turned back to look at him. 'If you could find details on the community centre construction, we would be most grateful.'

A rattle on the vicarage front door disturbed his thoughts. Stepping into the glass porch, he felt a biting chill blow through the door. He knelt on the stone floor, scooped up the newly delivered stack of letters before retreating backwards and swiftly drawing the curtain closed behind him.

Even in the days of email, the church postbag still brought several letters to his home most mornings and, as he walked through to the parlour, he scanned over the mid-week delivery. There was little to interest him. Entering the small room, he closed the door behind him and stooped to light the small gas fire in the hearth.

He laid the post on the dining table.

'Anything?' asked his wife Emily, already seated at the table.

'No,' he replied, before moving through into the kitchen. The kettle had just boiled, so he quickly sluiced hot water around the teapot. He heaped in four teaspoons of tea and added hot water. He loaded the tray with their morning cups before pausing in the kitchen doorway. He looked at his wife sitting upright on a hard, wooden chair, with her outdated mobile phone clutched in her hands, her eyes closed. He realised she was silently praying. Withers sniffed, and she turned.

'Have you heard any more from the police?' she asked.

'No,' he replied.

'And they haven't asked about Luke?'

'Not yet.'

'So, what happens when the police return?' she said. 'Because you know they will.'

CHAPTER 17

Dani stood behind her husband as he hit the blue and silver access button at the rear of the police station. The newly installed doors swung open, and she watched as Mat rolled his chair forward. Inside the small entrance lobby, a second set of doors required security access. Mat felt for his pass card, which hung around his neck.

'Let me get that for you,' said Dani, jumping forward with her own pass. Instantly, she felt Mat grab hold of her wrist.

'Don't ever help me when we are inside this building,' he said.

Biting her lip, Dani didn't reply.

Mat pulled the security card out from inside his jacket, and with it still fastened around his neck leaned across towards the scanner. 'Fucking thing,' he said, still unable to reach. There was a snap as Mat ripped the cord from around his neck, reached across and slapped the pass against the scanner. The doors opened and he rolled himself inside.

A new ramp had been installed that led directly into the CID unit at the back of the station. Mat pushed himself up the ramp, a further set of double doors opening as he approached. When he entered the room, his colleagues launched into a loud round of applause. At the far end of the room, a huge banner welcomed DS Moore *home*. Cheers rang out as he crossed to his desk, untouched for the past year. Dani stood and watched as Mat's colleagues surrounded him, slapping him on the back, laughing with their returning hero.

Alone, Dani walked across to her new desk.

'Jack Cash's son-in-law,' she heard one of the older male officers say. 'He would have been bloody proud to have you as part of his family.'

Sitting at her desk, Dani hoped he would.

Logging on, she was expecting to see an update from the forensic team. Five days since the discovery of the human remains, their report had been promised by now. Glancing through her inbox, she saw there was still nothing. They were making slow progress on every aspect of the case. Uniform were yet to discover the identity of the figure from the fire, and they were no further forward in understanding what they were doing in the community centre, or why someone might have wanted to do them harm.

'So good to see Mat back,' said PC Karen Cooke, suddenly at Dani's side. 'We've all missed him so much.'

'He's glad to be back,' replied Dani. 'It's been a long year.'

'Exciting times for you. Your dad would be pleased to see you moving into CID.'

Dani couldn't stop herself wondering if it was Cooke who had told Mat about her move. Cooke was the kind of person who made it her business to pick up on every piece of station gossip.

'I should get to work,' replied Dani, refusing to engage.

'Seeing his daughter become an investigating officer, that would have made him proud.'

Dani pushed her chair away from her desk and faced Cooke directly. Following Mat's stabbing, Dani had taken five months off work, returning earlier in the year. On her first day back, she and Cooke had come to blows in the women's locker room. They hadn't spoken since. 'Don't tell me how my dad would have felt. You called him a bottler to my face. God knows what you've said behind my back.'

'That was stupid of me,' replied Cooke. 'I was parroting the rubbish I'd heard around the station. I should never have said it. I'm sorry.'

Dani didn't trust Cooke. She hated the way she flirted with the male officers, sharing in their daily banter. She turned back to her screen.

'We needed your dad here at Haddley,' Cooke continued, and the note of contrition in her voice seemed genuine. 'And then almost overnight he was gone. When you're on the streets facing up to drunks and dealers on a nightly basis, you want a boss who backs you. Your dad did that. I wanted him to stay in the fight. That's all.'

'Thanks,' said Dani, quietly. Cooke gave her a brief nod, then crossed the room to greet Mat with an all-embracing hug. Hearing them laugh together irritated Dani. She couldn't remember the last time she and Mat had laughed at the same time.

The room was still buzzing around Mat when the door at the far end of the office opened. DS Barnsdale crossed towards Mat and brief words were exchanged between the two detective sergeants. Dani knew Mat held little respect for his peer. Her failure to make any arrests following the attack last Hallowe'en had been, in his opinion, unforgivable. It was why he'd taken on the case himself. For the past eight weeks, working from home, Mat had led a small team reinvestigating the raid on the supermarket. With the anniversary approaching, the team planned a reconstruction of events leading up to Mat's stabbing. A breakthrough, Mat was convinced, was imminent.

'DC Cash,' said Barnsdale, who'd left Mat and approached Dani's desk.

'Good morning, ma'am.'

'The chief inspector would like to see you in her office. Now.'

CHAPTER 18

For the past five days, forensic investigators have occupied St Stephen's churchyard. I stand in front of the community centre, now completely boarded over. Briefly, I close my eyes and the fear I felt, as I desperately tried to smash my way into the burning building, returns. I can see the flames spreading, taste the smoke as it smothers my throat. I can hear myself shout to the figure trapped inside and see them scramble beneath the ancient bench press. Were they the target or did whoever set the fire seek to destroy what lay beneath once and for all?

At the front of the building the ground is heavy, churned over by a thousand footprints in the past week. My shoes sink into the mud, and I step back onto the gravel pathway. The sky is bright blue, the air crisp and fresh and, my hands deep in my jacket pockets, I wander among the crumbling gravestones. I follow the path to the top of the cemetery before turning through the trees back to where I entered the churchyard on the night of the fire. I walk slowly beside the iron railings, which divide the cemetery from the St

Marnham playing fields, before stopping beside a canopied oak tree. Two flat, red granite headstones are surrounded by a sprawling holly bush, its berries now a bright orange. Both graves are lovingly tended but upon one of the stones rests a neatly tied bouquet of blue flowers. I step off the path and read the simple inscription etched upon the grave.

JACK CASH, TREASURED HUSBAND
OF ANGELA, DEVOTED FATHER TO DANI.
REMEMBERED EVERY DAY.

Beside the grave of Dani's father is her mother's.

ANGELA CASH, BELOVED WIFE
AND ADORED MOTHER OF DANI.

Dani rarely reveals the suffering she has encountered during her relatively young life. I know she lost her mother at an early age but the more recent loss of her father still saddens her. Working with her at the start of the year, I could see how much her dad meant to her and the huge impact he had on her life. In the time I spent with her, I often thought how much she uses her natural brightness to hide all she has endured.

I follow the path back through the graveyard to the front of the church. I'm about to walk in the direction of the vicarage when I see Emily Withers step off the number 29 bus.

'Mrs Withers,' I call. She appears not to hear me but when I call a second time, she stops.

'Ben, I'm so distracted,' she says. 'Such a sad time.'

'I'm sure the discovery of the body has come as quite a shock to both you and Reverend Withers.'

'Adversity is there to test us I suppose.'

'Indeed,' I say, a little awkwardly. 'I heard the police believe the body was hidden during the construction of the building.'

'It appears so.'

'I was hoping I might catch a quick word with your husband. Is he home?' I ask, taking a step towards the vicarage.

'I believe he's at a meeting with the fire station commander. He's keen for the church to further support the fire service fundraising efforts, in acknowledgement of last week's events.'

'They're deserving of all our thanks,' I reply.

'As are you, Ben.'

I smile. 'I'm glad nobody was hurt and that the fire didn't spread. I don't think I saw you that evening?'

A motorbike races down the Lower Haddley Road and into the woods towards St Marnham. The noise it creates allows Emily to wait before answering my question.

'Such terrible machines,' she says. 'Shall we walk through into the vicarage garden?' Emily leads me along the side of the road, before passing through a narrow gate and into a neatly tended walled garden. 'On the evening of the fire, I enjoyed a pleasant supper with an elderly parishioner. When I stepped off the bus, the fire service had already extinguished the flames. However, with the smoke still so dense, I returned directly to the vicarage to protect my chest.'

'Understandable,' I reply.

'I then watched briefly from an upstairs window, simply to assure myself nobody was hurt. I spoke directly with the police the following day but sadly I wasn't able to tell them anything they didn't already know.'

We walk slowly around the pretty garden, Emily showing me the careful work she has carried out over so many years. We sit together on a raised stone bench, positioned above a grate connecting the garden to St Stephen's ancient crypt.

'I was hoping to ask your husband about the original construction of the community centre,' I say.

Emily nods before glancing towards the churchyard.

I continue. 'When I last spoke with him, he mentioned most of the building work was done by a couple of lads from Haddley.'

'Did he?' she replies, frowning.

'I realise it was a long time ago, but do you think he'd still have a record of the boys' names?'

'Adrian's not a great one for keeping records.'

'I feared not,' I reply. 'I just thought I'd ask.'

I'm about to step away when Mrs Withers continues. 'I'm surprised Adrian told you that; that it was boys from town who built the community centre. My recollection is the construction work was carried out by a building firm named Baxters, based in East Haddley. You may have heard of them?'

The name vaguely rings a bell. I nod and wait for her to say more. 'At that time, the business was run by a woman named Betty Baxter. She was a member of our congregation, but lamentably no more.'

'She passed away?'

'Oh no, she's very much still alive. She retired to the coast, I believe. Together with Adrian, she led the fundraising efforts for the community centre, and I'm given to understand made a considerable personal donation towards the total cost. Her firm oversaw the construction. Any boys involved were no more than labourers.'

'Most generous of her,' I reply, smiling. 'And most helpful of you.'

CHAPTER 19

Standing in the dimly lit corridor, Dani raised her hand to knock. As she did, DS Barnsdale stepped past her and turned the door handle on the chief inspector's office door.

'It's fine to go straight in,' she said, opening the door. 'We're expected.'

'Dani, come in,' said Freeman, half standing as if she were about to move forward to greet her before thinking better of it. Dani watched her slowly lower herself back into her chair. 'Take a seat,' she said, offering her one of the two chairs positioned across from her desk.

With a growing sense of unease, Dani crossed the room, Barnsdale following a step behind her. She took a seat directly opposite the station's senior officer.

'Can I offer you a glass of water, Dani?' said Freeman, reaching forward and filling three glasses.

Dani glanced nervously towards Barnsdale, but her head was down as she straightened an imaginary crease in her trousers. Already Dani knew something was wrong. For almost five years she had worked alongside Freeman and not once during that time had the chief inspector ever addressed her by her Christian name. In the past thirty seconds, she'd done it twice.

Sitting upright in her chair, Freeman picked up a glass of water and took a slow sip. Then, she placed the glass down precisely in front of her before looking directly at Dani. 'I've received the findings from the fire investigation at St Stephen's, along with the provisional forensic report on the human remains. With regard to the fire, significant effort appears to have been made to ensure it remained fully fuelled, with wooden furniture stacked in the centre of the room. This, combined with the accelerant found outside the building, leads to a conclusion the fire was indeed started deliberately.'

'Yes, ma'am,' replied Dani. The senior officer still held her eye.

'The forensic report also provides us with a number of definitive conclusions. The skeleton is of a woman, most likely in her thirties. Her skull was severely damaged, suggesting she was struck either by a series of sustained blows to the back of the head, or her head was repeatedly smashed against a hard surface.' Dani inhaled deeply as Freeman reached forward and took a drink from her water. 'Any conclusion other than it being a vicious and sustained attack is impossible to reach.'

Barnsdale looked at Dani. 'We have to believe the woman would have been left unconscious by either the first or second blow. At that point she would have been unable to defend herself.'

Dani nodded, hesitantly, still unclear as to why Freeman was briefing her directly.

Freeman leaned across her desk. 'Dani, you do understand how DNA profiling works?'

CHAPTER 20

The police car stopped directly outside the front of the station. Pamela had walked past before, and she was certain that was a double yellow line. The female officer climbed out of the front seat and came round to open the rear door. Stepping out of the car, Pamela thanked the officer but couldn't stop herself glancing down at the roadside. She was right about the yellow lines, but she thought it best not to say anything. Perhaps it didn't apply to the police.

She followed the officer up the steps at the front of the building, trying desperately to remember her name. She felt sure it was Karen but for the life of her she couldn't remember her surname. She found it harder and harder to remember names these days but Dr Jha told her that was another thing that came with age.

When the officers had knocked on her front door, she'd been half expecting it. On Monday there'd been no sign of Jeannie walking to school; yesterday morning Pamela had seen her hurry past, with her mother, on the opposite side of the road. This morning, Pamela hadn't looked. Even so, when she opened the door to two police officers, she'd become quite flustered and hadn't really listened to what they'd said. She'd only just cleared her breakfast plates and suddenly there they were standing on her doorstep. Before they could say anything she'd told them she had Jeannie's coat. It was hanging right there in the hallway. You hardly needed to be Vera to work that one out. She'd told them she was worried Jeannie would catch cold without it. It was then they invited her down to the station. Scarcely surprising she hadn't remembered the woman's name.

The reception area inside the police station was much smaller than she'd imagined; a wooden bench, a desk with a sliding glass window and then a door which had to be opened with a buzzer from the reception. She'd always wondered what it was like inside, and she had to admit it was slightly disappointing. She stopped at the window assuming she would need to sign in, but Karen said something to the officer behind the glass and they were buzzed straight through.

Behind the door, the station was bigger and a little bit more of what she expected. Karen led her down a corridor and opened the second door on the left. Interview Room 3. Perhaps 1 and 2 were already occupied. Karen asked her to take a seat at the table and told her she'd be back shortly. This room was exactly as she'd expected. Four chairs at the table, two on each side. Some kind of recording machine at the side of the table. No two-way mirror at the back of the room, but other than that, no surprises. Almost as soon as Pamela had sat down, Karen bobbed her head back round the door and asked if she'd like a cup of tea.

'That would be lovely,' she'd replied, and in no more than five minutes Karen was back with a mug of tea and two sugar sachets. As a rule, she only ever had one sugar, but she thought even Dr Jha would agree this situation called for two. It was time to focus her mind. She needed to be careful not to say something she'd later regret. They would be out to trip her up, to get her confused and to say something she shouldn't. It was easily done – she'd seen it so many times on television – so she had to be on her guard right from the off.

She sipped on her tea and waited. When Karen came back ten minutes later, she stood outside the door and held it open. Pamela was surprised to see a man in a wheelchair enter the room. Karen removed a chair from the table and the man wheeled himself up and introduced himself as Detective Sergeant Mat Moore. Pamela nearly fell off her chair. A policeman in a wheelchair. How would he chase anyone down? Karen formally introduced herself, but Pamela was so distracted she missed her surname again.

'A complaint has been made against you by Ms Kristin Vines in connection with her daughter,' said Sergeant Moore.

Ms, thought Pamela, but she didn't say anything.

'Mrs Cuthbert, did you take Ms Vines's daughter inside your house?'

'I was worried about Jeannie,' replied Pamela. 'She was having to make her own way to school.'

DS Moore and Karen exchanged a look.

'Jeannie,' repeated DS Moore slowly. 'Who's Jeannie?'

Pamela could have kicked herself. 'I thought that was

the girl's name,' she replied, trying to sound as off-hand as possible.

'The girl's name isn't Jeannie,' said Karen.

There was a pause. Pamela clasped her hands in her lap, rubbing her thumb over the lumps in her palms.

'No,' she said eventually. 'No, of course it isn't. That's me being stupid. I see so many children walking past my window. Sometimes you can't help but give them names.'

Karen seemed satisfied with that answer and smiled. Relieved, Pamela turned her attention to the sergeant. 'When you get old like me, Mr Moore, you get a bit lonely. The days get longer and harder to fill. I enjoy seeing the children walk past my window. Some of them think I'm an old fool but a few of the younger ones will smile and wave.'

'And Ms Vines's daughter?'

'She's such a sweet-looking girl with her bright red hair and pigtails. I see her most mornings and always with Ms Vines,' said Pamela, careful to use the correct title. 'On Friday morning, the girl was on her own and I was concerned. She can't be more than eight.'

'She's nine,' replied the sergeant.

Pamela nodded her head in acquiescence but couldn't stop herself from thinking Jeannie was therefore very small for her age. 'Even so, the girl seemed young to be making her way to and from school alone, along such a busy road.'

'Due to work commitments, Ms Vines had made different arrangements for her daughter.'

'A neighbour was meeting her at the top of the hill,' added Karen.

'All I wanted to do was check everything was okay. I called to her from my front door, wanting to reassure myself and at the same time her offered her a glass of Ribena and a chocolate brownie. I'm sorry if I caused any upset.'

From the corner of her eye, Pamela could see Karen nodding but she knew she needed to keep her focus on the sergeant.

'The girl claims you slammed the front door and kept her trapped inside.'

Pamela furrowed her brow. 'I didn't want her to leave until I could be sure she was safe. The last thing I wanted was her returning to an empty house or perhaps something even worse.'

'You could have called us, if you were concerned,' said Karen.

Pamela gave a short sigh. 'I realise that now. Next time I will know what to do.'

'There won't be a next time, will there, Mrs Cuthbert?' said DS Moore, and Pamela felt like she was a schoolgirl again, receiving a warning in the headmaster's office.

'No, absolutely not,' replied Pamela.

DS Moore issued Pamela with a caution. She didn't really understand what this was, but what she did know was that it meant she could go home straight away. She felt exhausted and when Karen said she could arrange for a car to drop her, she gratefully agreed.

Pamela was buzzed back through the reception door and sat on the wooden bench waiting for her lift. The bench wasn't very comfortable, but she was relieved to be sitting back on the public side of the door. Various people – civilians and police officers – came and went, until a young officer headed briskly for the station exit. It was her hair that caught Pamela's attention – she'd know those soft blonde curls anywhere. Before she knew what she was doing, Pamela was on her feet and the movement must have caught the officer's eye because she stopped at the exit, and looked directly at her. Pamela could see from Dani Cash's bloodshot eyes that she had been crying. For a moment they stood staring at each other. Then Dani turned and hurriedly left the station.

Just seeing Dani set her heart racing. Pamela was desperate to speak to her, but she was equally desperate to go home. The officer behind the glass called to Pamela that a car was waiting outside. As she climbed into the back seat, she couldn't have cared less that the car was waiting for her on a double yellow line.

The uniformed officer pulled the car across the traffic and almost immediately they were heading back up Haddley Hill. When the car stopped outside her home, Pamela already had her house key in her hand. As she stepped out of the car, she called a quick thank you to the officer and on reaching her front door couldn't turn the latch fast enough.

Safely inside, she put on the chain and leaned back against the door. She briefly closed her eyes and let the relief wash over her, safe in the knowledge the police had asked her nothing more. Slowly, she walked into the living room and smiled at the picture of Thomas. Of course, he'd been right and she should have left well alone. She moved the school portrait of her daughter, Jeannie, so it faced her dad. Jeannie had always loved that picture of her father and a smaller image still stood on her dressing table, upstairs. Jeannie was always so proud of her dad. Twice a year, on his birthday and on the anniversary of his death, they would press the flag the Navy had presented to Pamela and hang it in the garden. After Jeannie went, she'd stopped doing that. It wasn't that she didn't love Thomas as much as ever but the flag was something she'd shared with Jeannie and, without her, it didn't feel the same. She'd always dreamt of Jeannie coming back for her daddy's flag but of course she knew she never would.

CHAPTER 21

'Ben,' says Alice, as she sits beside me at my kitchen island, 'sausage, Yorkshire pudding, peas and gravy is my favourite.'

'Mine too,' I reply, smiling. Alice spins her chair, her legs flying out in front of her. 'Careful,' I say.

'Can I have another Yorkshire pudding?' she asks, grabbing hold of the counter to stop herself.

'Finish the one you've got and then you can have another.'

'I'm going to eat another two!'

'We'll see.'

Alice picks up a piece of sausage and eats it from her fingers.

'I don't see many peas going down,' I say. 'I thought they were your favourites as well?'

'I'm saving them,' is her quick reply. 'Ben, did you cook the sausage and Yorkshire puddings?'

'Yes, you saw me.'

'Do you do all the cooking in your house?'

'Pretty much, yes.'

'Mummy does all the cooking in our house.'

'Don't you help her?'

'Ben, I'm five. I'm too little to do cooking. Sometimes I sit at the table and watch Mummy. I do cooking in my own house in the garden but it's only pretend. I could make you tea.'

'I'll have to come and visit your garden house.'

'I would make you Yorkshire pudding. I used to make Daddy porridge.'

'Did you?' I reply, unsure how to respond.

'But he's gone away now. Max has got two daddies,' says Alice, her thoughts one continual stream, as usual. 'He's got his real daddy and then he's got Nathan who sometimes lives at his house but not all of the time. Nathan built him a house in a tree out of real wood.'

I smile. 'Nathan is good at building things.'

'And he's good at running. And he's really strong. He can pick up me and Max at the same time.' Alice pauses. 'It's not fair Max has got two daddies when I haven't got any.'

'No,' I reply, quietly. 'But Nathan isn't really Max's daddy.'

Alice sits quietly for a moment, and I can see her thinking. She looks up at me. 'And Max hasn't got a Ben,' she says, before moving her hand across and resting it on top of mine.

Looking at her I have to bite my lip. 'No,' I reply. I lean across and hug her.

'Ben,' says Alice, 'can I have another Yorkshire pudding now?'

Laughing, I step down and open the oven door. 'Two left,' I say, pulling out the tray.

'Both for me!'

'One each,' I reply, dropping them on our plates. 'Would you like some more gravy?'

'Yes, please.' I light the gas and give the pan a quick stir. 'I'll have it on my pudding and on my sausage, please.'

'Why not eat some peas while I'm heating it up?'

Alice quickly scoops a spoonful of peas in her mouth and blows out her cheeks.

'Eat them properly.'

'I am,' she replies, peas spilling out of her mouth.

'What would your mummy say?' I ask, coming to the island and pouring warm gravy on her plate.

'On my Yorkshire pudding!' cries Alice, as if her life depended on it.

'I am!' I reply, with equal urgency. I pour some gravy on my own plate before putting the pan back on the hob.

'Do you want me to cut your pudding up for you?'

'No, I can do it,' replies Alice, before quickly eating three more mouthfuls. 'Can we play a game now?'

'When you've finished your meal.'

'I have finished,' she says, jumping down from her chair and running across to rummage in the cupboard at the back of my kitchen. '*Guess Who?*' She pushes the box onto the island before clambering back up onto her chair.

An hour later, Alice is jumping on the battered sofa that sits in the corner of my kitchen. 'Just one more game, Ben, please,' she says.

'You're the queen of *just one more game*,' I reply.

'But I've won three games and you've won three games,'

she says, pointing her finger at me. 'The winner of the next game gets the trophy.'

'Your mummy will be waiting for you at home. I promise we'll play again next time.'

I step down and reach for Alice's coat, which hangs from the back of a kitchen chair. As I do, there is a rap on my front door.

'There's somebody at your door, Ben,' says Alice. Immediately, she jumps down off the sofa.

'You stay where you are.' I pass her her coat. 'Can you manage to put it on yourself?'

'Of course. I am five.'

I quickly make my way out into the hall. 'Who is it?' calls Alice, as I approach the front door.

'I don't know, I can't see through doors,' I shout back. I open the door to find Dani Cash moving away from my house.

'You've got company, I shouldn't have come,' she says, as soon as I open the door. She takes another step back down the path. 'I'm sorry, I really shouldn't have come. I don't know what I was thinking.'

'Dani, wait,' I say, quickly moving outside. I see the redness in her eyes. 'Please, wait,' I call, reaching out to her.

She stops. 'I just needed to talk to somebody.'

'Come inside,' I say.

'Is it Mummy?' shouts Alice, from the kitchen.

'No!' I reply, turning my head to call to her. 'Have you got your coat on?'

'I really have caught you at a bad time,' says Dani. 'I should go.'

'No, honestly, you haven't. It's Alice, my goddaughter. She only lives three doors down. I was about to take her home.'

'I remember her.'

'Give me two minutes,' I say.

'Only if you're sure?'

I step aside and invite Dani into my hall. Slipping off her jacket, she lets out a heavy sigh.

'Are you okay?' I ask her.

She shakes her head. I wrap my arms around her and briefly hold her close. From the corner of my eye, I see Alice peeping from the kitchen door, her eyes wide. I step away from Dani.

'Alice, coat, now,' I say sharply, and I hear her scamper back into the kitchen. 'I'm sorry,' I say to Dani.

'Don't be. She reminds me a little of me,' she says, as we walk together into the kitchen.

'I'm ready!' says Alice, standing on the sofa, arms outstretched, coat fastened. I scoop her up and carry her out of the back door. 'I'll be back in two minutes,' I say to Dani as we leave.

Walking up the alley between my house and Holly's, Alice leans forward and cups her hand around my ear.

'Ben, is Dani your girlfriend?' she asks in a stage whisper.

I smile as I whisper back that no, she is just my friend. She looks at me with a quizzical stare. Then I whisper to her, 'Is Max your boyfriend?'

'No!' she exclaims, and squeezes her arms around my neck.

CHAPTER 22

When I walk back into the kitchen, Dani is sitting in the corner of the sofa with her coat back on.

'Ben, I shouldn't have come,' she says. 'I'll be fine, honestly. I've just had a bad day.'

'You look anything but fine to me.' Dani closes her eyes. I can see she's exhausted. 'Take your coat off and I'm going to pour us a drink.' I open my fridge door. 'I can offer you a glass of Pinot Grigio,' I say, 'although it's been open for a couple of months. Or, alternatively,' I continue, bending to the cupboard under the island, 'I have some Japanese whisky courtesy of Madeline Wilson.'

'I'll take a chance on the Pinot Grigio,' replies Dani, holding her coat in her lap, 'as long as you're having one.' I tend not to drink much alcohol but reach for two glasses.

'I really am sorry,' she says.

'For what?'

'Landing on you like this. Mat's out celebrating his first day back at the station, but I needed to talk to somebody who would understand.'

I hand Dani a generous serving before sitting across from her on the sofa. 'What's happened?' I ask.

Dani stares blankly out into my back garden and takes a long sip from her glass before she answers. 'The woman buried beneath the community centre was killed with great force, by a number of sustained blows to the back of her head.'

'I heard. Really horrible.'

'They've managed to get DNA samples from the skeleton, and there's a match on the system.'

I lean forward. 'Okay,' I say, slowly, and when Dani doesn't continue, I ask, 'Do you know the person they found the match to?'

Dani's voice trembles. 'The DNA matches to mine.'

For a moment I struggle to understand what she's saying. 'But how . . .' I begin, but before I can say anything further, Dani brushes the tears from her eyes and says, 'The woman buried under the community centre was my mother.'

I sit back, stunned. 'Your mum?' I reply, trying to make sense of it. 'But that body must have been there for . . .'

'Nearly twenty-three years,' says Dani. 'I was four years old when she died.'

I don't know what to say. I know first-hand what it is like to have the trauma of your past reawakened so suddenly. My own mum died over a decade ago, but the shock earlier this year of discovering she'd been murdered made her death once again both real and immediate. I know there are few words that will help Dani right now.

I go to put my arm round her, but she holds up her hand to stop me.

'I feel numb,' she says. 'I keep thinking about how much she must have suffered.'

'Don't,' I reply. 'It doesn't help, and it won't give you any answers.'

Dani drains her wine and places her empty glass on the floor.

'Can they be certain?' I ask.

'Ninety-nine per cent. The police hold my DNA from when I signed up.' She lifts her legs onto the sofa, wrapping her arms around them. Curled in the corner, she looks at me. 'Before today, I always believed she died in a house fire. My childhood home was destroyed. There are times now when I can still taste the smoke.'

'Do you want to tell me what happened?'

Dani grips her legs tightly. 'I only know what I've been told. It was Christmas Day. Sometime around two in the morning, a fire broke out downstairs. We didn't have a smoke alarm. I suppose they were less common than they are now. My dad came into my room, lifted me out of bed and wrapped me in my duvet. He stood with me at the top of the stairs, but the smoke was too thick to go down. Whenever I smell smoke, even now, I'm back wrapped in my penguin duvet.'

Dani pauses. I can tell she's summoning the strength to continue with her story.

'My mum had already gone downstairs, but the fire had taken hold so badly that my dad was left with no choice but to carry me back into my bedroom. He climbed out onto the small flat roof at the back of the house. People must already have been out in the street and one of the neighbours helped us escape down a ladder. We were so lucky.'

'And your mum?'

'She was found at the bottom of the stairs. Her body was so badly burnt, she was unrecognisable. But I know now that wasn't my mum. Until last Thursday, my mum's body was never near any fire.'

I shake my head, leaning forward. 'So it was another woman who died at the foot of the stairs?'

I break off when I see the terror in Dani's eyes.

'There must be an explanation, but right now Freeman is positive there's only one. She's convinced my dad killed them both.'

Four

'I felt so certain this is where he would want to be, lying beside the wife he adored.'

THURSDAY

CHAPTER 23

I'm woken by the buzzing of my phone. In the darkness, I scramble across and grab it from the table at the side of my bed. Half opening my eyes, I see it is not yet six and my boss is already calling. I answer.

'Madeline?'

'I'm at the hospital with Sam,' she replies quickly, fear in her voice. 'They think it's a heart attack.'

I sit up in bed. 'How bad is he?'

'I don't know yet. He was brought in in the middle of the night. They're still running tests.'

'But he's going to be okay?'

'They haven't told me anything.'

Madeline isn't somebody to worry over nothing. I can hear her concern for her father in her voice.

'Are you in Isleworth?' I ask.

'Yes.'

'I'll be there as soon as I can,' I reply.

'No, there's no need.' There's a softness in her voice I rarely hear at the office. 'I just wanted somebody to talk to.'

'He's going to be fine, I'm sure of it,' I say. 'Sam's indestructible; he'll probably outlive us all.'

Madeline breathes deeply. 'I'm scared, Ben.'

'I'm on my way.'

I first met Sam Hardy when, as a twenty-one-year-old, I knocked on his office door at the *Richmond Times* and asked him for a job. We stood in his office, and as I introduced myself I had the immediate impression he already knew who I was. It was a little more than twelve months since my mum had died and, during that year, I'd somehow managed to graduate from Manchester University. After her death, I'd withdrawn from many of my friends but had thrown myself into my politics course. When I received my degree, I'd said it was in honour of my mum. The summer I graduated, I came home to Haddley and began planning a year-long trip that would allow me to travel around the world. In the three months I had at home before leaving, I needed to find some work.

I always felt Sam took pity on me when I knocked on his office door that Monday morning. He would have known my name since I was eight years old and I've no doubt part of him was intrigued by the idea of having me work at his newspaper. But, despite his playing the gruff, old-school editor, I soon learned that, deep down, Sam was a bit of a softie. He didn't have any jobs going, but he said that if I wanted to hang around and learn how a local paper was put together each week, he was fine with that. I had few other options, so I said yes. That afternoon, Sam despatched me to the home of our local MP who had been caught up in an expenses scandal. I came back with a photograph of the MP drinking vintage champagne in a garden pergola paid for by the taxpayer. Sam sat with me late into the evening writing up the story, and two days later, it was my very first byline. Although we had agreed on three months' unpaid work experience at the end of the first week, Sam gave me two hundred pounds in cash and did the same at the end of each of the following twelve weeks.

A year later, when I again returned to Haddley, I applied for a junior reporter's job at a national newspaper, at the time edited by Madeline Wilson. Madeline had started her own career as a junior reporter at the *Richmond Times*. She'd taken her mum's surname, determined her success would be based on her own merit, not who her father was. When I made my application, I'm sure Sam gave me a glowing reference and perhaps put in a call to his daughter to help me on my way.

The early-morning roads through west London are quiet. Along the Lower Haddley Road, when I'm held at a red light, I reach for my phone and send a quick message to Dani.

Hope you were able to get some sleep

I pause before adding:

Thinking of you.

The light turns green, and I drop my phone back down onto the passenger seat. I pass a milkman out delivering for Milk & More and as I do I glance across at my phone. I can see Dani has read my message.

She still hasn't replied when I turn into the hospital car

park, where I'm able to find a spot directly in front of the main building. A watery sun is beginning to rise as I cross from my car towards the front entrance. Approaching the main building, I hear a voice I instantly recognise.

'I'm not pushing you any further. What kind of fool do you take me for?'

'Maddy, don't be like that.'

'I've told you not to call me Maddy.'

I stand on the opposite side of the road and watch as Madeline and her father leave the hospital. She pushes his wheelchair to the side of the exit before walking on alone.

'You can't just leave me here,' calls Sam.

'You are perfectly capable of walking across the road,' she shouts back, continuing towards me.

'Can't you just push me inside the bus shelter?'

Madeline turns to face her father. 'The nurse said hospital procedures dictate that you are wheeled out of the front of building and that's exactly what I've done.'

'But not to be abandoned before we've even passed the tobacconist.'

'It's a newsagent,' replies Madeline, raising her voice again. 'They don't sell cigarettes.'

'You'll wake all the other patients, shouting like that.'

'You're not a patient!'

Sam starts slowly edging forward, pushing the wheels of his chair with his hands. He gains momentum and starts to roll towards the road.

'For Christ's sake, Sam.' Madeline grabs hold of the chair before manoeuvring her father over the crossing.

'You're looking better than I expected,' I say to him, as they approach.

'Chronic heartburn,' replies Madeline. 'Up until nearly two o'clock this morning with his racing buddies. Eating and drinking all night. Whisky and cheese at one and then he's surprised when he thinks he's having a heart attack.'

Sam reaches up and touches his daughter on her hand. 'I don't like the look of those clouds. You couldn't push me under the bus shelter, could you? As long as I can keep dry, I'm happy to wait for the next bus.'

'No need for the bus,' Madeline snaps. 'My car can drop you.'

Sam smiles at his daughter. 'Only if you're sure.'

'Ben, I'm calling my car, you can ride into the office with me.'

'Mine's parked right there,' I say. 'Why don't the three of us grab a coffee and then I can drop Sam home?'

'A little breakfast would be nice,' says Sam. 'Something just to settle my stomach.'

'Don't push me,' says Madeline. She walks towards the car park and then turns. 'Are you two coming?'

Sam smiles at me, gets to his feet and together we follow. I click open the car doors.

'Maddy, why don't you go ahead and jump in the back?' says Sam.

Madeline turns to him. Her eyes flare as if she were dealing with a young journalist's inaccurate reporting, but she says nothing.

Driving into Richmond, Madeline's eyes remain firmly

fixed on her phone. I turn to Sam. 'Glad you're feeling okay.'

'Strong as an ox,' replies Sam. 'That's what the doctor said.'

'I'm sure he didn't,' says Madeline, always listening.

'Let's stop at Rich Café, by the bridge,' says Sam. 'They know me there. I'll be able to get us a table.' In the rear-view mirror, I see Madeline roll her eyes. Sam turns to his daughter. 'And they do the best full English in Richmond.'

'Don't think I'm going to stop you. If you want to keep killing yourself it's no skin off my nose.' I turn off before Richmond Bridge and park at the back of the block of flats where Sam has a top-floor apartment. 'Perhaps you might even manage to walk the two minutes home after breakfast,' says Madeline, stepping out of the car.

The dawn clouds are clearing and with the sun shining on the river, we risk an outdoor table. We order coffees and when they arrive, Sam adds milk to his Americano.

'Any more on the body under the church?' he asks.

'It was the community centre,' I reply, knowing Sam is already fully aware of almost every aspect of the story. In the week since the fire, he's called me daily, chasing the inside scoop. When I tell him the murdered body is the wife of a decorated police officer, and somebody he knew well, he realises the story will become a national one. And so does Madeline.

She quickly looks up from her phone. 'Don't tell him anything more,' she says. 'He'll steal our story.'

'Maddy, as if my little local rag could compete with your behemoth,' replies Sam.

Raising my eyebrows, I turn to Madeline and she smiles. 'Okay, we'll share. But if you try and get the jump on us, I'll . . .' She points her finger at her father, 'I'll . . . tell Mum!'

We all laugh. 'How is your dear mother?' asks Sam.

'Glad to be nowhere near you. Somewhere in the south of France the last time I heard.'

'A long distance from us all – what a relief. Now,' says Sam, clapping his hands, 'who killed Angela Cash?' I see his eyes light up in the same way as Madeline's do when she scents a story. 'Buried under the floorboards for more than twenty years.' Sam narrows his eyes. 'The original story was she was killed in a house fire?'

'Forensics show her body was never anywhere near any fire, not until last Thursday night.'

'Bludgeoned to death by her detective chief inspector husband?' asks Madeline. 'Just what the Met Police commissioner needs right now.'

I nod.

Our waiter returns to take our breakfast order.

'Full English for me and another Americano,' says Sam, before anyone else can get a word in.

Madeline clicks off her phone and places it face down on the table. 'He'll have scrambled eggs, a slice of smoked salmon, granary toast – very lightly buttered – and skimmed milk with his coffee.'

The waiter looks at Sam, uncertain.

'She's in charge.'

'And I'll have the same,' says Madeline.

'Make that three,' I add.

'The police think Jack Cash is their man,' I say, as the waiter steps away.

'You're not certain?' asks Madeline.

'Too soon to say.'

'Why go through the masquerade of appearing to bury your wife in St Stephen's cemetery unless you're the one who killed her?' asks Sam, before answering his own question. 'I'll tell you why. At some point he'd have to explain where Angela was, so why not have a funeral that ties everything up nicely with a ribbon on top.'

'If that's the case, who's buried in her grave?'

'Perhaps nobody,' says Madeline.

'Somebody was definitely killed in the fire,' I reply.

Sam nods. 'I remember it. Christmas Day night, a real tragedy.'

'Jack Cash must have known who he was burying,' says Madeline.

'Unless he knew who had killed her and couldn't say,' replies Sam.

'Blackmail?'

'A lot of cops get caught up on the wrong side of the line.'

The waiter returns with our breakfast. Sam eyes his food with suspicion when it's placed in front of him.

Madeline looks at her father. 'Don't say anything.'

'I wasn't going to,' replies Sam, squirting brown sauce across his plate. 'It all looks very tasty,' he continues, forking his eggs.

'What else do we know?' asks Madeline.

'I spoke with Emily Withers yesterday—'

'The vicar's wife?' says Madeline, interrupting. 'I met her years ago, not long after Nick's murder. I was researching an article about the impact on the local community and asked her for an interview. She invited me to meet with her at the vicarage but gave me virtually nothing. She was more interested in what she could learn from me about her fellow parishioners.'

'And what did she learn?' asks Sam.

'From me? Not to waste my time,' replies Madeline, smiling at her father.

'She was a little more forthcoming yesterday,' I say. 'She gave me the impression she was very happy to point me in the direction of the firm who originally built the community centre.'

'Who was that? asks Madeline.

'A local firm based in East Haddley, owned by a woman named Betty Baxter. I thought I'd try and get in touch with her, fix up a meet and see if she can tell me anything about the construction.'

A broad grin breaks over Sam's face. 'If you can get Betty Baxter to talk, she'll tell you a hell of a lot more than that.' He pushes his salmon to one side and squashes his eggs between two slices of buttered toast, then seizes his makeshift sandwich from his plate and gets to his feet. 'Maddy, leave some cash on the table,' he says. 'We've got work to do.'

CHAPTER 24

'Are you sure it's in there?' asks Madeline, as Sam rummages through a stack of upturned plant pots. He's searching for the key to unlock his garage door.

'Of course, I am,' he snaps back. 'I always leave it here.'

'Perhaps last time you didn't. Or it has been taken; I can't imagine it's the most secure place in the world.' We are standing beside a row of sixteen single garages, one belonging to each of the flats in Sam's small riverside apartment block. Weeds make their way up through the tarmac driveway and greying white paint is slowly peeling from the doors. Madeline casts her eyes around and looks at her watch. 'Sam, surely all your old editions have been digitised. That would be so much quicker. Ben, can you do something?'

'Possibly,' I reply, knowing we do have online access to past editions of the *Richmond Times*.

'We're here now,' says Sam. 'Better to access the actual archive.' He strains to lift a pot housing a half-dead fir tree. 'Ben, can you see under there?' I quickly crouch down and grab the garage key.

'Told you it was here,' says Sam, taking the key from me and opening garage number three.

'I thought you were flat nine?' asks Madeline, as her dad pushes the key into the lock.

'I am,' he replies. 'I rent this garage from Mrs Wasnesky in exchange for me buying her dinner and two bottles of wine at the Cricketers twice a month.'

Madeline turns to me and raises her eyebrows. 'Sounds like a good deal all round,' she says.

'I'm in,' says Sam, twisting the handle. He lifts the door from the bottom, its rusty hinges squeaking as it rolls back.

'For Christ's sake,' says Madeline.

Together, the three of us stand in front of a wall of fading newspapers.

'Every edition since October 1973.'

'They're a bloody fire hazard. One spark and you'll take down the whole block.'

'The one thing I will give your mother credit for is she always said you'd make a great health and safety officer.'

Madeline grimaces at her father before he squeezes between two stacks of newspapers and disappears inside the garage.

'I don't think we'll find anything here, Ben,' she says, again looking at her watch, 'but a policeman's wife beaten to death, an unknown body buried in St Stephen's church-yard . . . This could be a great story.'

'I want to find the truth for Dani's sake.'

'Don't give me that,' replies Madeline.

I smile. 'Perhaps I can find a great story along the way.' I try not to think what I'll do if Jack Cash does turn out to be guilty; how Dani will feel about me if I ever publish a story about her father's murderous past.

'I might put in a call to the Met commissioner,' says Madeline. 'I'm sure she'd love to give us a quote.'

'I bet she would.'

'I'm pretty certain she hates me already, so it's not like I'd be burning any bridges. Why don't you take a few days to dig around? We can always push back the podcast recording.' Madeline draws out her phone and checks the time. 'Right, I need to be back in the office for a meeting at eleven. You couldn't make sure he gets back inside, could you?'

'Leave him with me,' I reply. 'I'll delve a little further into his memory if I can.'

'That's a dangerous place to go.'

Moments later, Sam re-emerges from his archive, triumphantly holding a brown-edged newspaper in each hand. 'My filing system is better than anything you will find online. It's all in here,' he says to Madeline, tapping the side of his head as he does.

'I'm sure it is,' she replies. 'That's my car,' she continues, looking towards the road. 'Promise me you'll behave yourself. I'll call you tonight.'

'Love you, too,' calls Sam and Madeline turns to blow him a kiss as she walks off. We watch her car pull away.

'Give me two more minutes, Ben,' Sam says, before disappearing out of sight. 'There are a couple more editions I need to find,' he shouts from deep inside his archive.

While Sam ferrets around Mrs Wasnesky's garage, I

stand on the driveway and flick on my phone. I hope to see a message back from Dani but there is nothing. I start to message her again, wanting to know how she is holding up, but halfway through my message I stop, and delete what I've written.

Sam soon re-emerges and closes the garage door. After he pushes the key beneath a different plant pot to the one he insisted he always kept it under, we cross towards the back entrance of his building. An older woman is dropping a bag into one of the green recycling bins.

'Still on for lunch tomorrow, Sam?'

'Absolutely, Connie,' he replies. 'Usual time?'

'Lovely. I'll meet you out front.'

Sam and I step inside, and he presses for the lift.

'Mrs Wasnesky?' I ask.

Sam smiles. 'Mrs Wasnesky gets dinner. Mrs Shields gets lunch. Always important to have friendly relations with your neighbours.' As we ride the lift to the top floor, he turns to me. 'I read your articles on your mum's death. The story is so tragic, but it was great journalism.'

'Thanks, Sam,' I reply, praise from your first boss somehow always carrying more weight. My eyes drift towards the floor before the doors open in front of us.

Sam touches my arm. 'You're wasted on Madeline's little website,' he says, leading the way down the corridor towards his apartment.

'We topped thirty-three million users last week.'

'Users,' he mutters derisively, before opening the door to his home.

The stench of stale alcohol, burnt tobacco and overly ripe Stilton fills the room. 'Bloody hell, Sam,' I say. 'You really did have a good night.'

'If you don't mind opening the door to let a bit of air in,' he says, gesturing in the direction of the balcony.

I do as instructed, stepping past the dining-room table, which is still covered in playing cards and poker chips.

'We left in a bit of a rush,' he says, picking up the remains of a wheel of cheese, its middle scooped out.

I slide back the patio door and a breeze blows up from the river. I walk around the room collecting half-drunk glasses of port, while Sam sweeps the poker chips into a banker's case and gathers up the playing cards.

'Grab a seat, Ben,' he says, when the table is clear, and as I do he lays out four faded editions of the *Richmond Times*, each of them more than twenty years old.

NOT GUILTY! is the headline splashed across the 24 June edition, published just six months before the fire at Jack Cash's home.

Beneath the headline is a photograph of a middle-aged woman standing outside Richmond Crown Court, her arms held triumphantly aloft, a grin stretching from ear to ear.

'That's Betty Baxter, more than two decades ago,' says Sam.

Behind her on the steps of the building is a small but chaotic crowd, seemingly made up of well-wishers and journalists.

'She was pretty well known?'

'Everybody knew Betty, she was a real local character,' he replies. 'She and her sister inherited a fairly insignificant little business from her father and Betty turned it into a household name across Haddley and Richmond. Most people knew Baxter's DIY Warehouse and, if not, Baxter's Builders Merchants. She placed two half-page ads in the paper every week, accompanied by a photo of herself. *Nobody beats Betty on price; Betty's best for building; Betty's best for bargains; Betty's best for bathrooms.*'

'I get the idea,' I say.

Sam smiles. 'She was the face of that business, a real local success story, or so it seemed. But then the rumours started. I heard them long before most people had a clue about any of it.' He points to the newspaper in front of me. 'None of this came as a huge surprise.'

I read the opening paragraphs of Sam's report:

After a two-week trial, local businesswoman Betty Baxter and her sister Charlie were yesterday acquitted of all charges in relation to their alleged conspiracy to supply Class A drugs.

The Crown Prosecution had argued large quantities of heroin and cocaine were smuggled into the country hidden inside floor insulation, wallpaper products and breathing aspirator masks, all destined for the Baxter family business. Haddley police maintained Ms Baxter, 48, who manages the business, had masterminded the scheme.

Standing outside Richmond Crown Court, Ms Baxter told reporters: 'After months of furtive surveillance, Jack Cash and the Haddley police force launched a raid upon my family home and business premises. Regardless of the fact they failed to find one single shred of evidence, they still insisted on pursuing a baseless and vendetta-driven prosecution. They are the ones who must be held to account, although right now all I want to do is go home and hug my young son, Bertie.'

'Battle lines drawn with Jack Cash?' I say.

'For the next twenty years,' replies Sam. 'Jack took a zero-tolerance approach to drugs and instilled the same in his officers. He might have lost this case, but he had no intention of backing down. Once he was running the station, it became his obsession, turned him into a one-man vigilante. Jack was determined to get Betty, but he never did.'

'Why no conviction in this case?' I ask.

'Jack pushed ahead too soon. It was his mistake. He never had enough evidence to make a conviction stick. Not for the last time, he was humiliated.'

I read on.

Police raids failed to produce quantities of drugs beyond small amounts of cocaine, which the defence successfully argued were for purely recreational use. Regardless, Haddley police pressed ahead with their prosecution. The police and Crown Prosecution Service argued evidence downloaded from mobile phones and computers demonstrated significant supply of narcotics from across Europe. In court, the defence contended this evidence related to the import of building supplies, not drugs. Only one message, discovered on the phone of Charlie Baxter, 37, referred directly to drug purchases. Her solicitor claimed that, as a regular frequenter of the London nightclub scene, Ms Baxter would often allow others to freely use her phone.

Sam points to a figure at the back of the crowd on the front-page photograph. 'That's Charlie Baxter,' he says. 'She was a loose cannon, much less savvy than Betty. The drugs in the house were hers and it was her phone message that the police tried to hang everything on. Betty never forgave her.'

During the raid on the home of Betty Baxter, police made a discovery of in excess of £100,000 in cash, the money hidden among several boxes of Christmas decorations. The defendant claimed that as an avid antiques collector, it was necessary for her to have cash available at all times.

To cheers from well-wishers, Betty Baxter concluded by saying she was looking forward to returning to work as soon as possible and that Betty was open for 'business as usual'.

I turn to Sam. 'She was guilty, I take it?'

'Is the Pope Catholic?' he replies. 'Betty relished rubbing Jack Cash's nose in it. A case like that should have been an easy win for him. By then, so many people were asking where her money came from. How many cans of paint can one business sell? But Jack was too hasty, perhaps even exaggerated what evidence he did have. Either that or Betty saw him coming. Over the next two decades, he worked damned hard to keep drugs off the streets of Haddley and after Angela's death that became his life, but he could never catch Betty.'

'And now?'

'The building firm's still there, although I don't think she has much to do with day-to-day operations,' says Sam, with a chuckle. 'Before he retired, Jack rolled the dice one last time. He was desperate to convict Betty, charged her with ferrying drugs across county lines but the case collapsed long before it reached court. Somehow he'd failed to learn that with Betty every piece of evidence needed nailing down. History had come full circle. That last investigation showed Jack was still making the same mistakes as twenty years before. In all honesty he was past it, while Betty was spending most of her time by the coast enjoying her ill-gotten gains. Jack quit pretty soon after – or so the official line went – and a year later he was dead. Drank himself to death.' Sam looks at me and says, 'A lesson to us all.'

I turn back to the front page of the paper to read the closing paragraphs of Sam's original article.

Asked to comment, Jack Cash for the Metropolitan Police gave the following statement outside the court:

'Drugs have a devastating impact on people and communities. They affect all our lives and many of our families but particularly the young and vulnerable. I believe we had a strong case but on this occasion, we have failed. However, we will continue to ensure those susceptible to exploitation are protected, and to seek the convictions of those who wreak such destruction upon our community.'

Haddley police later confirmed no further prosecutions would be sought at this time.

Sam places a second newspaper in front of me. It is an edition dated Wednesday 22 December, only three days before the Christmas Day fire at Dani's childhood home.

'Turn to page five, or it could be page seven.' I flick through the pages, glancing at the headlines on pages five and seven before stopping on page nine.

'Okay, page nine,' says Sam, smiling. 'I can't be expected to remember every little detail.' His mind is as sharp as ever.

A photograph of the newly opened St Stephen's community centre covers most of the page. A group of young children with bright smiling faces, dressed in Christmas hats, sits around two giant trestle tables, both laden with party food. A banner draped across the room announces the grand opening of the new community facility, 'to be enjoyed by all'.

Standing proudly at the back of the room are Emily and Adrian Withers. Alongside them is Betty Baxter.

CHAPTER 25

On her way into work, Dani stopped again at the flower stall across from the station and picked out some brightly coloured yellow roses. In the tiny kitchen, where officers brewed tea and coffee throughout the day, she found an old glass biscuit barrel hidden at the back of a cupboard. As she cut the stems from the roses and did her best to arrange them in the barrel, her mind drifted to the woman who'd spoken to her yesterday in reception. There'd been an expression of recognition on her face when she looked at Dani. But no matter how much Dani racked her memory, she couldn't place her. Did her face look vaguely familiar? During her five years in the force, Dani had met so many Haddley residents it was impossible to remember them all. Filling the barrel with water, she smiled to herself as she thought how it was always the town's older residents who remembered and appreciated police officers.

Dani walked through into the unit and placed the bright yellow flowers on the corner of her desk. Simply breathing in their soft lemon scent lifted her spirits. The flowers were her mum's favourite, or so her dad had always told her. Logging on, she stared aimlessly at her screen, unable to concentrate. The fire in her childhood home once again so fresh in her mind, she hadn't been able to sleep, haunted by the same images. Her dad wrapping her in her duvet before he carried her out of the back window. And the woman lying dead at the bottom of the stairs.

She glanced across the office. Mat wheeled himself into the room before engaging in conversation with two uniformed constables. Both laughed at something he said. She dropped her eyes, but he'd already noticed her and pushed himself towards her.

'You were out of the house early this morning,' he said, manoeuvring his wheelchair alongside her desk.

'I'm surprised *you* even made it in. It must have been after two when I heard you come home.'

Mat shrugged. 'So many friends wanting to welcome me back, buy me a drink. Lucky I don't get hangovers,' he said. 'Lots of rumours about you. I hear you were in and out of Freeman's office again yesterday afternoon.'

'Can we talk about that when we're at home,' she replied, 'assuming you are coming home at a reasonable hour tonight?'

'She offering you a promotion already?'

'Nothing like that,' said Dani.

'You weren't the only one having a meeting with her yesterday,' continued Mat. 'She called me in to see her.'

'Really?' Dani unzipped her bag and reached for the key for her desk drawer.

'Aren't you interested in what she said?'

'Of course, I'd love to hear about it but why don't we talk when we get home tonight?' replied Dani.

'Her expectation of me getting a result from next week's reconstruction is pretty much zero,' replied Mat. 'Can you believe that?'

Dani pressed her temples, a dull ache sitting behind her eyes. 'Why don't you wait and see what happens? If you open up some leads, you'll have the pleasure of proving her wrong. You win on both fronts.'

'I tell you, Dani, she's already made up her mind. If she could, she'd pull the plug right now.'

Thinking of the speed with which Freeman had concluded that her father was guilty, Dani realised to her surprise that she knew how Mat felt. 'All you can do is keep plugging away.'

'Her only interest is in the cost. She and Barnsdale have got effing nowhere over the past twelve months and now all she wants to know is how much money I'm spending. That tells you all you need to know.'

'I'm sure she's under pressure.'

'She should try sitting here.'

Dani rested her head in her hands and felt guilty for thinking how glad she'd be when next Monday was over. She looked up at Mat. 'Don't pin all your hopes on the reconstruction,' she said. 'It has been a year.'

'Perhaps it would help if I had my wife's support.'

'You always have, one hundred per cent.'

'Sometimes, I think you're as bad as Freeman. It would suit you just fine if I gave up now.'

'What's that supposed to mean?'

'Your move into CID? A close examination of events from last year might well have a negative impact on your career.'

Dani shook her head. 'Mat, that's not fair.'

He looked away and for a moment was silent. 'She's already talking to me about what I might do next, as if Monday won't lead to anything. You'll never guess what she wants me to do.'

'Tell me.' Dani glanced at her phone and smiled at a message from Ben. She liked the way he checked up on her.

'Lead a diversity and inclusion project. For the next three months, that's all I'm to do. She's agreed it with the borough commander. Seemingly, I'm the ideal person to lead the review for the whole region. Race, disability, gender, sexual orientation. I'm to review them all, determine if we are offering a nurturing environment and make recommendations accordingly.'

Dani saw Barnsdale enter the far end of the room and, knowing her superior officer wanted to meet with her, edged her chair back from her desk. 'At least she's offering you something relevant and high profile,' she said to her husband.

'It's not police work,' he replied.

Dani got to her feet. 'You have to be realistic,' she said, quietly. 'It's not going to be easy for Freeman to find you a role in CID.'

'She wants a programme where every officer has their own personal inclusivity goal.'

'It's something she's passionate about.'

'I've told her no. It's work for police staff, not a serving officer.'

'You never thought it shows how seriously she takes both it and you?' said Dani, leaning forward.

Mat opened his mouth to reply but Barnsdale had appeared at Dani's desk. 'Shall we have ten minutes?' said Barnsdale. She didn't acknowledge Mat, and Dani was relieved at the opportunity to escape the conversation. 'Grab your jacket and we'll pop outside, so we're not interrupted.'

The detective sergeant pressed the button to open the rear doors and Dani followed her into the car park. Together, they walked across to the old bus shelter, still used by a few colleagues for an occasional cigarette.

'How are you holding up?' asked Barnsdale. 'Yesterday was a tough day for you.'

'Listening to CI Freeman, I'm worried minds have already been made up,' replied Dani, sitting beside Barnsdale in the nicotine-stained shelter. 'I get the impression she wants the case tidied away as quickly as possible—'

Barnsdale interrupted her. 'Dani, you have to accept the murder of the wife of a decorated former officer is not a good look. CI Freeman is under enormous pressure. It might have been twenty-plus years ago—'

'Twenty-three years this Christmas,' replied Dani.

'But we can't have this hanging around for months on end. It needs to be resolved and then we can all move on.' Barnsdale twisted on the plastic seat, moving to face Dani. 'I know this is incredibly difficult for you, Dani, and we will do everything we can to support you. But we also have a duty to fulfil, and you have one, too. It's time for you to stop being Jack Cash's little girl. You need to accept what happened and support what's right for the Metropolitan Police.'

'And what is that? Rushing to convict an innocent man?' replied Dani. 'I guess it's very convenient my dad's dead – so much easier to dump everything on him.' Dani realised she was shouting and stopped.

The two women sat in silence until Barnsdale continued. 'I will lead a full and comprehensive investigation, but you need to be realistic. How could anyone else have disposed of your mother's body beneath the community centre without your father being complicit?'

Staring at the yellow walls of the bus shelter, Dani didn't respond.

'One of the things I need to try and do is build a picture of your mother and her life. Can you tell me if there were any other family members she was particularly close to?'

'Not that I know of,' replied Dani.

'I know this isn't easy, but I may need to interview you next week.'

'I can tell you now, there is very little I can remember about my mum.'

Barnsdale hesitated. 'I need to understand more about both your parents.'

Dani faced her superior officer. 'Can I speak to Freeman directly? I want to be reassured she's open to all lines of enquiry.'

'I don't think that's a good idea,' replied Barnsdale. 'Why don't you take a couple of weeks off?'

'I'd rather be here,' said Dani.

There was a pause, before Barnsdale, her tone a little firmer, said: 'You can take it as compassionate leave. Come in tomorrow for the briefing on the reconstruction, since I understand you're needed on that. But after that, you can sign off for the next two weeks.'

Dani stared at her. 'Are you suspending me?' she asked.

Barnsdale gave her a thin smile. 'Only if you force me to.'

CHAPTER 26

I hold a mug of Sam's extremely strong coffee and read the 12 January edition of the *Richmond Times*. It is a report on the funeral of Dani's mum.

'I'm surprised to find it tucked away at the bottom of page six,' I say, turning to Sam as we now sit on his small balcony overlooking the Thames. In the bright late-morning sun, his eyes are dropping. 'Sam?'

'Don't worry, I'm still with you,' he replies.

'You did have a long night.'

'Might have a little doze once you've gone,' he says. 'There wasn't a huge amount to say about the funeral. Small gathering at St Stephen's, Reverend Withers said a few words, a couple of hymns and then they took her outside to be buried.'

'Or not,' I reply.

'Indeed.'

'Did you go?'

'To the funeral? No, didn't seem any point. I sent a junior reporter to stand in the shadows but only because it was Jack Cash's wife.'

I reach down for the final newspaper Sam brought up from Mrs Wasnesky's garage. Its publication date is Thursday 6 January.

'Thursday publication?'

'Extra days holiday for Christmas,' replies Sam, smiling. 'There's a small paragraph on the front page and then a couple more paragraphs on page five.'

Investigators believe faulty Christmas tree lights were responsible for the deadly fire that hit Haddley in the early hours of Boxing Day. Angela Cash, 31, lost her life when fire swept through her Haddley Hill home. Her husband, Detective Inspector Jack Cash of the Haddley police, 41, and their four-year-old daughter, escaped through an upstairs window.

'You read the fire report?' I ask.

'What makes you think that?'

'Because you say faulty Christmas tree lights were responsible for the fire.'

'Isn't it always tree lights? My guess is that's what we were given by Haddley police, but I didn't write the report.'

'You didn't?'

'I spent that Christmas on my own and my only gifts were two bottles of Lagavulin single malt courtesy of my beloved daughter. But the even greater gift she gave me was agreeing to join her mother for five days in the Swiss Alps. Coming from my former in-laws, there was zero possibility of that invitation ever being extended to include me.' Sam briefly opens his eyes and winks. 'When I heard about the fire, I felt sorry for Jack Cash, of course I did, but I had my own shit to deal with. Whoever wrote about the causes of the fire would have been the same junior reporter I sent to the funeral.'

I turn to page five and read on.

A spokeswoman for the London Fire Brigade hoped this tragic accident would serve to remind all members of the community to be fire aware at all times of the year. She said smoke alarms saved lives and she hoped to see the day when every London home was fitted with one.

A statement from the Metropolitan Police said they were supporting DI Cash and his family at this difficult time.

A neighbour of the Cashes told the *Richmond Times*, 'We are all so very sad. Jack and his daughter are a delight, and we are all doing everything we can to help. It's a miracle the fire didn't spread any further but the response from the fire brigade was outstanding.'

I hand the paper to Sam, and he glances over the article. 'Doesn't tell us much,' he says. 'Little more than a couple of cobbled-together statements. You can tell we pulled the paper together between Christmas and New Year. I hope I sacked the reporter.'

I smile. 'The story didn't warrant more coverage?'

'As a rule, it probably would've but with Christmas the paper was published nearly two weeks after the fire. Most people would have already heard about it. Even in local news, two weeks later and people have moved on.'

'There was nothing fresh to say?'

'Why would there be? It was a tragic fire, made worse by the fact that it was Christmas Day. Not much more for us to cover. I guess we spoke to the investigators involved but over Christmas everybody takes time off. And I don't just mean journalists. Police numbers would have been limited and the fire investigators were probably operating with a skeleton staff,' he replies, resting his head on the back of his chair.

'If you're looking to hide a murder,' I say, leaning forward and turning to face Sam, 'it seems to me Christmas Day is the perfect time.'

Sam opens one eye and looks at me. 'Nobody would have known that better than Jack Cash.'

CHAPTER 27

Dani drove slowly past the stone gates that guarded the entrance to St Stephen's church. She glanced across before continuing past the vicarage and turning up the tiny side road that ran behind the cemetery. Pulling onto the grass verge, she stopped her car beside the rust-covered side gate. This was where she and her dad would enter the churchyard when they came to visit her mother's grave. He'd called it their own secret entrance and as a child she'd often imagined herself entering a magical garden. It was here, a month after his retirement, that she had found her father virtually unconscious.

On that spring afternoon, she'd parked her car directly behind his before walking up to his driver's side window. When she'd tapped on the window, his head had lolled forward against the steering wheel. She'd tried the door handle but found it locked.

'Dad, open the door,' she'd said.

He'd flopped back against his headrest. She'd taken a step back and looked at her father through the window. In only four weeks, he'd become an old man. A drunken old man. His silver-grey hair had become yellow. The smiling eyes she so loved appeared drained.

Dani had knocked again on the window. 'Dad, you're going to have to unlock the doors and let me in.'

Jack's head had dropped forward, before quickly jerking backwards. When his head hit the rest, his eyes sprang open. She could see he was struggling to focus.

'Dad, it's me. Please try and unlock the doors.'

He'd slouched forward again, somehow managing to click the locks open as he did.

'I can't believe you drove in this state,' she'd said, before turning to see an empty whisky bottle on the back seat, 'although I guess you kept drinking once you got here.' Seeing his eyes droop closed, she'd felt desperate. She wanted to help him but didn't know how to. Knowing she needed to get him back to his home in Clapham, she'd decided to try and move him to her car.

'Can you twist your legs out?' she'd asked.

'Honestly, I'm fine to drive,' he'd replied.

'Don't be ridiculous.'

'Not a single officer in Haddley police would dare pull me over.'

'That might be true until you kill somebody.'

'I'm a professionally trained driver.'

'Dad, swing your legs out,' she said, sharpening her tone. It worked. Jack Cash had done as he was told and, supported by his daughter's arm, slowly shuffled to the neighbouring car.

Heading into Clapham, Dani had cut through the back streets before stopping outside the Victorian terrace, which had been her home for most of her childhood. Unable to find her dad's keys, she'd walked around to the back of the house. Inside the small garden shed, she'd found the stack of plant pots and hidden inside the sixth one down was a spare door key. Always the sixth pot down, her mum's birthday. The same place since Dani was eight years old.

After helping her dad upstairs, she'd left a large glass of water and a packet of Nurofen on his bedside table. He would need them in the morning. As she'd closed his bedroom door, she'd promised him that she'd call back in a couple of days, but he'd already fallen fast asleep.

Two days later, after finishing her early shift, she'd arrived at her dad's house in the middle of the afternoon. After calling a quick hello to a neighbour, she'd made her way to her dad's front door. Pressing his doorbell, she was aware of a nervous flutter in her stomach. What condition would she find him in?

'Dani!' he'd said, quickly opening the door and throwing his arms around her. 'Come in, come in.' He'd ushered her through to the living room. It was a mess. Papers were scattered across the sofa, strewn across the floor. 'Sit down wherever you can find a space.' Jack had gestured vaguely about the room.

Dani had perched uncomfortably on the piano stool, next to the instrument that had been largely untouched since she'd quit lessons after moving to secondary school.

'You're looking much brighter,' she'd said.

Her dad was clean shaven and his hair neatly parted.

'I am much brighter,' Jack had replied. 'I can promise you that. When you said I needed a new focus, you were absolutely right.'

Dani had picked up two folders from the top of the piano. 'Where did these come from?' Leafing through the pages, she repeatedly saw the royal blue crest of the Met Police.

'The new CI might not like it, but I've still got some friends in Haddley.' Dani had stared at her father. 'Don't look at me like that,' Jack had said to his daughter, pushing some papers aside to make space for himself to sit down. 'They're my cases, so I'm entitled to read the files. Don't worry, I won't be asking you to get involved.'

Dani had recognised immediately that arguing with her father was pointless. 'What is it you're looking for?'

'I'm the first to hold up my hands and say I made a mistake. I went after Betty with charges that were never going to stick. I should have learned my lesson from twenty years earlier. But the more I look at it now, the more I'm convinced she knew I was coming after her again.'

'Dad, there was no evidence then and there's still no evidence now. You can read those files as many times as you like but that won't change.'

'Somebody tipped her off and the county lines were closed down. If I can prove that—'

'Stop. You've given your whole life to fighting drug crime. You need to let others pick up the fight.'

Dani's words had failed to register with her father.

'They've been waiting for their chance to drive me out. I don't trust any of them.'

'Who don't you trust?' she'd asked, bewildered. 'What are you talking about, Dad?'

'The Met, the secret influencers.'

'The secret influencers!' Dani had laughed. 'Dad, listen to yourself.'

To her surprise, Jack had rounded on her with fury etched across his face. 'Don't you dare mock me, not until you've done your forty years.'

Then he'd stormed from the room, leaving Dani surrounded by the mass of documents.

After that, Jack didn't mention Betty Baxter to her again, and although Dani didn't raise it with him, not wanting to give oxygen to his obsession, she suspected it hadn't disappeared. Then, in the late summer, six months after her father's retirement, Jack had invited his daughter for a Saturday evening barbecue. Her shift had overrun and, as she'd stepped off the train at Clapham Junction, she'd imagined him bemoaning the fact that their steaks were overcooked. She'd hurried her way out of the railway station and up the hill, before turning into Lavender Gardens. Arriving at the house, she'd headed straight into the back garden and was surprised to find it deserted. She'd lifted the lid on the barbecue and seen it was still to be lit. She'd tapped on the back door, wondering if her dad had fallen asleep, and when she received no reply had peered in through the living room window. Endless papers were stacked on the top of the piano and scattered across the floor, but there was no sign of her father. She'd moved to the kitchen window. The sink was piled high with dirty plates. Unwashed pans were still on the stove and the milk had been left out on the small kitchen table.

Just as she was pulling out her phone to call him, he'd staggered around the side of the house and into the back garden. His right eye was blackened and swollen, a line of blood dripping from his cheek onto the blue cotton V-neck sweater she'd bought him for his last birthday.

'Dad! What's happened? Come and sit down.' She'd led him to a garden chair.

'It's nothing, don't fuss,' Jack had replied. 'I got caught in an argument with a bloody lorry driver and before I knew it he jumped out of his cab and laid one on me.'

'Give me your key, I'll get you an ice pack.' Jack had handed her his key and she'd unlocked the back door. 'What were you getting in a fight with a lorry driver for?' she'd called, but her father didn't answer.

There was no ice pack in the freezer, but Dani had returned with the steaks which were meant to be sizzling on the barbecue, and a damp cloth. She'd dabbed her father's eye, and Jack sucked air between his teeth.

'Put your head back,' she'd continued, laying a steak across her father's beaten eye. 'Hold that in place. It might help with the bruising.'

Jack had done as he was told, and after a minute or two, Dani tried again. 'Dad, what was the argument about?'

Jack had shuffled uncomfortably in his seat. 'Nothing, really. Idiot completely overreacted, said I was following him.'

Dani felt her stomach sink. 'So were you following him?'

Jack had refused to say anything more. He'd stumbled into the kitchen, returning moments later with a bottle of whisky and two glasses.

'Just to take the edge off,' he'd said, opening the bottle.

Watching her father's hand shake, Dani had known that by the end of the night he'd have drunk the bottle.

CHAPTER 28

Late in the afternoon, I sit alone on the wooden bench at the side of St Stephen's church. I watch Dani push the wrought-iron side gate that leads directly into the cemetery. The grass around the gate is overgrown and at first the gate refuses to move. She pushes again and it squeaks open. Engrossed in own her thoughts, she's yet to see me. The wind from the river is bitter and she pulls her jacket close; her blonde bobbed curls are whipped about her face as she makes her way to the graves of her parents.

I head along the gravel path until I am standing behind her. She is engrossed in her thoughts. I watch her clear the small bouquet of fading blue flowers from her father's red granite grave. She wraps the dying flowers in paper before gently resting new blooms on the tomb.

'Hello,' I say, quietly.

Dani turns and smiles softly. 'Sorry I'm late. I always try to bring him his favourite blue irises.

'How're you doing?' I ask. It's a stupid question.

Dani sighs. 'For so many years, I came here to sit with my mum, to tell her my deepest thoughts.'

'It's a lovely spot.'

'It was my dad who found it. He knew the church. This is where he married my mum, and when she died, he discovered this little corner. He was the one who planted the holly bush. It reminded him of Christmas. I felt so certain this is where he would want to be, lying beside the wife he adored.'

We are silent for a moment before Dani begins to follow the path that winds through the churchyard. 'It was a spot my dad created for me,' she continues, as I walk beside her. 'For me, as a child, this was the place where my mum lived. It sounds stupid saying it out loud, but somehow my dad kept her alive for me.'

'Not stupid at all.'

'When I was small, we would often stay for hours. I'd run through the gate at the bottom of the cemetery, down to the river and then back up to tell my mum about the swans on the towpath, or the boats racing on the water.' We walk on, the path tracing the route of the riverbank before we approach the community centre. 'On my ninth birthday, my dad took me and a group of school friends to the coolest pizza restaurant in Clapham – cool to a nine-year-old. Over lunch, he spun tales of great detection, car chases and criminal wrongdoing. He was like a celebrity to the kids in my class. After lunch my dad and I came to the cemetery and for the very first time I told my mum that when I grew up I was going to be a police officer, just like my dad.'

'He must have felt very proud.'

Standing in front of the burnt-out building, Dani turns to me. 'Ben, my dad was a lot of things. He was an old-school copper and I'm sure there were times when he crossed the line. He might have done some things he shouldn't have but whatever Freeman and Barnsdale say, as long as I have breath in my body I will never believe he killed my mum. You have to help me prove them wrong.'

CHAPTER 29

Dani and I turn away from the community centre and follow the path along the side of St Stephen's church.

'Somebody killed my mum,' she says, 'and somebody else is buried in my mum's grave.'

I understand her need to know the truth, but I also know she needs to be ready for whatever that might mean. 'It's a mistake to set out to prove somebody else wrong,' I say.

'I know.'

I wait for her to say more, but when she doesn't I say, 'Tell me about your dad and Betty Baxter.'

Dani stops at the side of the church. 'How did you know?'

'Let's just say I've already started doing some digging,' I reply, and Dani briefly smiles, aware now I'm ready to help her. 'Incidentally, it was Baxter who built the community centre.'

'Throughout his career he went after her, and I'm sure rightly so. But, in the last year of his life, once he'd retired, she became an obsession. Honestly, I thought he just couldn't let go of the fact that he'd lost – he never could stand losing. I told him I was bored of his rants, but he refused to let go.'

'What drove him?'

Dani tells me Jack believed he'd made a mistake at the end of his career, preventing him from finally convicting Baxter.

'Had he made a mistake?'

'Emotions cannot drive a police investigation. His desperation got the better of him. Somehow for my dad it had become personal and that never works.'

'Did he miss something?'

'He was convinced she was shipping drugs across county lines, that she was using kids as a means of ferrying them to her customers. He gambled everything on flipping whoever it was supplying the kids, but he could never get to them.'

'Might he have been right?'

'He probably was, but it's not always about being right. Results are important but so are how we get to them.' Dani breaks off, before adding, more quietly, 'Sometimes it's about being realistic.'

We walk to the front of St Stephen's and leave through the churchyard gates. We stand beside the Lower Haddley Road.

'Have you read the fire report from last week?' I ask.

'I haven't seen the details,' Dani replies, 'but you were right about someone starting the fire deliberately.'

'Was there a knife discovered in the remains of the building?' Dani looks at me blankly, so I continue: 'There was a knife, jammed beneath the gym equipment. That's why whoever it was went to the community centre.'

'I don't remember any mention of a knife, but I could have missed it.'

'It would be very helpful to get a look at that report,' I say, smiling.

'Officially, I'm suspended,' says Dani, 'but leave it with me.'

'Thanks. I know how hard this is for you, but whatever you need, just say.'

Dani is quiet for a moment before she says, 'I was so young when my mum died, my memories of her are only fleeting. Sometimes I think I can still remember how it felt to be with her, her simply holding my hand. That last Christmas morning, I was so excited – what four-year-old isn't? My stocking was overflowing but the one thing I can distinctly remember was my bright red scooter with a giant pink bow. That afternoon, racing up and down the paths in Haddley Hill Park, it was just me and her.' Dani swallows, and closes her eyes. 'My mum deserves the truth, Ben. Freeman has already made up her mind, wants the case closed as quickly as possible. But I owe it to my mum to find out what really happened.'

Dani briefly kisses me on the cheek before turning and walking towards her car. I stand and watch her disappear down the narrow road at the side of the cemetery. As I do, I think of the clippings Sam shared with me this morning.

The 22 December edition of the *Richmond Times* reported the grand opening of St Stephen's community centre.

Angela Cash was already buried beneath the newly completed building.

Whoever Dani remembers from Christmas Day, it wasn't her mother.

Five

'I've often thought I could have told her anything. I could have made Thomas whoever I'd wanted him to be.'

FRIDAY

CHAPTER 30

'Leave some for the rest of us,' said Jason Grace, as his youngest son filled his cereal bowl to the brim.

'There's another box in the cupboard,' said Amy, her back to her husband while she made her son's sandwiches for lunch.

'I don't like mayonnaise,' called Ted, craning his neck to inspect what his mother was doing.

'I thought you did?'

'It makes them go soggy.'

Amy sighed but spread only butter on the bread. 'Archie,' she called, crossing to the doorway to shout up the stairs. 'Do you want a sandwich making or are you buying your own?'

Archie ran down the stairs and stormed into the kitchen. Leaning across the table, he shouted in Ted's face. 'Keep away from my stuff, you little runt!'

Ted flinched and leaned back in his chair. He could smell Archie hadn't brushed his teeth.

'Easy,' said Jason.

'He's taken my black hoodie,' yelled Archie. He grabbed

hold of Ted's shirt. 'I've told you; you can only use my stuff when I say you can.' He shoved Ted against the table, spilling milk out of his brother's cereal bowl.

'Archie!' came his mother's voice.

'It's miles too big for him, he's just trying to wind me up,' Archie said, dragging a chair out from the table and staring at his brother. 'What have you done with it?'

Ted looked up at his mum but said nothing. She walked to the back of the kitchen and pulled the hoodie out of the pile of clean washing. 'Here,' she said, pushing it into Archie's chest. 'Freshly laundered after being left on your bedroom floor.'

Archie took the sweatshirt and wrestled it over his head.

'Do I get a thank you?'

'Thanks,' Archie mumbled to his mother.

'And Ted?' said his father.

Archie glared across the table. 'Sorry,' he said, 'but if I catch you again—'

'Leave it, Archie,' said Amy, snapping.

Archie looked at Ted. 'You know what I'm talking about.'

Ted swallowed hard before turning away. When he caught his mum's eye, she smiled.

Archie reached for a piece of toast and took a quick bite. 'I'll buy a sandwich,' he said, before downing a glass of juice. He reached for his rucksack on the back of his chair, stuffed his football boots inside and fastened his trainers to the back.

'My wallet's by the front door,' said Jason. 'You can take a tenner if you like.'

Ted saw his mother turn and look directly at his father. She said nothing.

'Don't worry,' said Archie. 'I've got money. And I'm working tonight so I'll be back late.'

Ted looked up from his cereal. 'Working again?' he said, quietly.

'Afraid so,' replied Archie, his tone softer now. 'Always a job to be done at the boathouse.'

'I wanted to play football after school.'

Archie looked at his brother. 'We'll play tomorrow morning. I'm only working a half day this Saturday.'

Ted sighed. He watched Archie drag his best football from beneath a chair in the corner of the room before flicking it up and catching it.

'Not inside,' said Jason.

Archie rolled his eyes at Ted. Ted half smiled but couldn't help wishing his brother was coming straight home after school. He leaned forward and finished his cereal. As he did, his brother crossed the kitchen and pushed his football into Ted's arms.

'Lose it and I will kill you,' said Archie, ruffling his brother's hair before calling goodbyes as he ran from the room.

Amy poured herself a cup of instant coffee before coming to sit at the table. The front door slammed.

'You're too soft on him,' she said reproachfully to Jason, then, as Ted started to push his books and sandwiches into his school bag, 'There's some fruit in the bowl.'

'We can afford to feed our own family,' said Jason. Ted

looked in the fruit bowl but turned his nose up at the blackening bananas.

'Yes, and I'll make him a sandwich,' Ted heard his mother reply.

He sat on the floor and pulled on his school shoes. Out of habit, he felt for his phone, usually hidden in the inside pocket of his bag. But the pocket was empty.

'Give me five minutes and I'll walk you to school,' said Jason.

Ted grinned. 'I'll wait for you outside.'

When the door slammed behind him, Ted stopped and looked towards the foot of the steps. His brother was waiting for him. Ted's stomach turned and he walked slowly down. When he reached the bottom of the steps, Archie pressed his hand on his chest.

'I told you, you could have your phone back after a week, and a deal's a deal.' Archie reached into his back pocket and handed Ted his phone. 'But next time it's a month. And if I ever catch you sending a message like that again, I really will kill you.'

Ted stared up at his brother.

'Understand?' said Archie.

Ted swallowed, then he nodded. For a moment he wondered whether he shouldn't ask the question, but he couldn't help himself. 'Are you scared?' he whispered.

'Scared?' Archie laughed and shook his head.

But Ted knew he was lying. He sat on the bottom step and watched his brother run across the lane and onto the common. Once Archie was nothing more than a dot in the distance, Ted clicked the button on the side of his phone. The screen flashed into life. He hesitated, but then began typing out a new message.

It's Ted. Please help.

His finger shook as it hovered over the send button.

CHAPTER 31

At eleven o'clock last night, I sent my revised podcast manuscript to Madeline. Writing about my own mum's death left me thinking about how I'd felt at the start of the year, when I'd been desperate for answers to questions unasked for too long. I wanted the truth for my mum and understand completely how Dani feels now. A little after midnight, Madeline replied to me with further edits, and we agreed to meet for coffee in Richmond this morning.

Following the path across the top of the common, I look towards the home of Jason and Amy Grace, a home they have occupied for the past five years. The house stands on a corner plot, with views extending down towards the river. While their home is impressive, Jason has told me the upkeep is vast and the cost can be overwhelming. As I approach, I see Archie and Ted together in the Graces' driveway. It's plain to see how much Ted idolises his brother. Watching them together has at times felt like watching a piece of my own life.

When I reach their driveway, I see Archie charge across

the narrow lane that runs in front of their home. I raise my hand to greet him, but his head is down and he doesn't see me. I call his name but he doesn't reply. I stand at the end of the driveway where Ted now has his head buried in his phone. I call to him. He looks up, startled, and jumps to his feet, thrusting his phone into his school bag. He mumbles a reply before running up the steps and disappearing into the house.

I turn back out onto the lane. Halfway across the common, Archie is passing the narrow and overgrown entrance to the woods. I look towards him and for a moment find myself gripped. Keeping him in view, I move slowly back towards my own house. When the number 29 bus pulls up on the Lower Haddley Road, I stop again. Two older teenagers step off the bus and I see Archie greet them with a fleeting fist bump. Beyond them stands the soaring bell tower of St Stephen's. The church's bright blue stained-glass windows and its heavy oak door are as grand and imposing as ever. Only a stray strip of blue and white police tape, trapped on the railings and fluttering in the breeze, suggests any interruption to the church's tranquil existence.

I look back at the three teenagers, now crossing towards the river. Archie follows the two older boys, his rucksack thrown over his shoulder. And it's then that I realise what made me stop. Hanging from the back of Archie's rucksack is a pair of bright orange trainers.

CHAPTER 32

Dani stood alone at the back of a packed incident room. She watched Mat wheel himself from behind his desk and position himself directly alongside the station's senior officer. When Chief Inspector Freeman stepped forward to address the unit, everyone fell silent.

'Twelve months ago, our whole team here in Haddley was shaken to its core. We suffered an attack at the very heart of this department. But not for one moment did I ever doubt the strength and resolve of this unit nor of the officers that make it the very best team in London. Today, I couldn't be prouder to be able to say the simple words, DS Mat Moore is going to kick off our briefing.'

Cheers echoed around the room and Dani saw Mat's chest swell with pride. Freeman grasped hold of his hand to officially endorse his return. The chief inspector knew what people wanted, Dani thought, she had to give her that.

'A huge thank you to everyone here for welcoming me home,' said Mat, 'but now it's time to get back to business. Hopefully by now each of you is fully aware of your roles for Monday. The reconstruction will take place at the same time as last year's attack. The supermarket will be decorated as it was on Hallowe'en. Those of you assigned to conversing with members of the public, please remember not only to ask them if they saw anything that evening but also if they know anybody else who might have.'

Dani looked at her husband. He'd let his blonde hair grow longer. She hadn't noticed before, but it had a gentle wave running through it. She only ever thought of him with a close, military crop. When was the last time she'd really looked at him?

'Following up on those names –' Dani realised Mat was still speaking '– might allow us access to key witnesses who have been previously missed or overlooked. PC Higgins will retrace my footsteps for the cameras and PC Fidler those of DC Cash.' DS Moore paused and stared across the room at his wife. Dani held his gaze but her skin prickled as the eyes of the unit turned upon her. 'Detective Constable Cash,' he continued, still looking at his wife, 'will join me in speaking to the media as required. I'm pleased to say we will have television coverage from BBC London, Sky News, GB News and London Live. The local press has promised us front-page coverage and I'm sure a number of the rolling twenty-four-hour so-called news sites will pick up the story.' Dani stared down at her shoes and waited for Mat to continue. 'Thank you to everyone who worked so hard in making this happen. I am determined we will still make arrests in this case.'

Hearing the intensity in Mat's voice, his absolute commitment, Dani felt a fleeting flush of pride. It was something she hadn't heard for so long, but listening to him rally his colleagues, she recognised this was where he belonged.

Mat edged his chair backwards as CI Freeman again stepped forward. 'Thank you, DS Moore,' she said. 'We all want to see a result on this. You've had an incredibly tough year and we all appreciate and welcome your return.' Freeman smiled and firmly gripped Mat's shoulder. Dani saw him flinch. She knew how much he would have hated the senior officer's touch.

'Along with the return of DS Moore, it's also been a challenging week for Detective Constable Cash. I'm sure most of you will be aware by now that the body discovered under the fire-ravaged community centre was that of Angela Cash, DC Cash's mother. All of our sympathies, of course, go to Daniella and her family at this difficult time.'

Once again, Dani stared at the floor, only lifting her head when Freeman continued her address. 'DS Barnsdale will lead the immediate investigation of that case and we are expecting a swift resolution.'

Watching Freeman leave the room, Dani grasped her hands together, the nails from one hand digging into the back of her other. As the unit went back to work, Dani returned to her desk, snatched hold of her bag and pressed the silver button to exit. Walking through the rear doors, leaving the unit where she had spent so much of her life, her heart sank. Hearing the doors close behind her, she realised they were closing on her home.

CHAPTER 33

Having agreed a final set of edits to the podcast script with Madeline, I catch the train back to St Marnham station. From there, I follow the narrow footpath that runs across the top of the woods, before winding its way through to Haddley Common. Often it becomes overgrown, and I have to push aside thorny branches before I emerge onto the southern corner of the common.

Victorian villas line the quiet lane and the first house I reach is the Graces' family home. I pause, staring at it, thinking about the trainers I saw hanging from Archie's rucksack. What happened at this house on the night of the fire? Did Archie run through the woods, directly back to his home? Did someone help him? And late in the night, did Archie go back and retrieve the knife?

I cross the common, passing my own home, and walk down onto the Lower Haddley Road, glancing briefly at St Stephen's before turning away from the river. I cut through the weaving side streets of my hometown, until I arrive on Haddley Hill. I stand opposite a small row of terraced houses. Nestled in the middle is a house clearly distinct from each of the others. The houses to either side are weathered with age but this house's façade is relatively modern. Its bricks are a brighter red, its window frames are plastic, not wood, and its front door is finished with a synthetic sheen. It's Dani's rebuilt childhood home.

I cross Haddley Hill Road and follow a narrow passageway that leads to the back of the house. Dani's old home is built to the same design as the rest of the terrace with a small upstairs bedroom jutting out above the rear kitchen below. I imagine Jack Cash, Dani tightly held in his arms, clambering out of the bedroom window; a neighbour's ladder helping them flee the fire.

When I return to the front of the house, I find the last of the schoolchildren making their way up the hill, heading home in high spirits and looking forward to the weekend. I now pass directly in front of Dani's old home. I glance in through the living-room window. A child's train track covers the floor and toys are scattered across the room. Stepping aside for an older woman as she shuffles up the hill carrying two full bags of shopping from the local mini market, I linger for a moment. I imagine the room as part of Dani's childhood, but then all the horrors that followed flood into my mind.

A shout from across the road snaps my attention back.

'There she is!'

I turn to see a group of four teenage boys running out of Haddley Hill Park. They charge across the road. The woman with the bags of shopping has stopped outside the neighbouring house. She has put both bags down on the pavement and is rummaging for her house key.

'You crazy old biddy,' shouts one of the boys, as the four run towards her.

'You're like a paedo, you are,' another cries.

The woman doesn't move; her eyes are wide with panic. One boy sprints forwards and yells directly into her face. 'You make me sick!' Then he grabs one of her shopping bags and empties it upside down onto the pavement. The boys scream with laughter, taunting the woman as she tries to bend and retrieve her shopping.

'Mince pies!' howls another boy, grabbing a box of the cakes and throwing it at the woman.

'No wonder she's so fat,' cries another. 'Are you going to use those to lure in some other little girl?'

I run up the street. 'Back off,' I yell at the boys. They take a step back and stare at me. 'Now!'

I bend down and begin scooping up the woman's shopping.

'She's a pervert,' one of the boys shouts.

'Get out of here!' I shout back. The boys head down the road, hurling abuse as they go. I turn to the woman. She is still clutching her box of cakes. 'Can you find your keys?' I ask quietly. Her hands shake so violently she's unable to unzip the side pocket of her shopping bag.

'I can do that for you,' I say.

Once the door is unlocked, she takes my arm and I help her slowly inside her home.

CHAPTER 34

'Let me make you another cup of tea,' says Pamela, as we sit together opposite her bright living-room fire. On her lap, she is still clutching a framed photograph of her daughter, Jeannie.

'I should probably get going,' I reply.

'Nonsense,' she says. 'I owe you far more than one cup of tea.' I smile, before she adds: 'And you must have another mince pie. I always say, it's never too early for a good mince pie. And these are so deep filled.'

'They are very nice.'

'That's settled, then.'

Pamela props up the photograph on the small table beside her chair. She crosses the room and heads into the kitchen. I can hear her running the tap to put the kettle on to boil. 'Won't be a minute,' she calls, coming back past the living room door. 'I'm just going to pop upstairs and put my slippers on.'

Pamela has told me of her interview at the police station. She explained her only intention was to try to help the girl, who has always reminded her so much of her own daughter. I feel certain she was well intentioned, but Pamela is a woman whom the modern world has slightly passed by. Looking around her living room, I imagine she grew up at a time when neighbours still looked out for each other, took an interest in one another's families. It would have seemed the most natural thing in the world to her to check in on somebody else's child. Not any more.

I reach for the picture of Jeannie. It's a school photograph, Jeannie with her hair pulled back and her school tie neatly knotted. I'd guess it was taken when she was in her mid-teens. There are other pictures of her dotted around the room but in each one she is younger. The school photograph of Jeannie reminds me of the one I have hanging in my hallway of my brother. In the same way as Nick, Jeannie feels frozen in time. I hear Pamela coming back down the stairs and when she walks into the kitchen, I go and stand in the doorway.

'Can I ask what happened to Jeannie – your Jeannie?'

Pamela busies herself with the kettle. 'She was such a daddy's girl, although that sounds such a silly thing to say.'

'Why's that?' I ask. 'Lots of girls are close to their fathers.'

'Jeannie never met her father, but she idolised him nevertheless.' Pamela picks up the teapot and walks past me into her living room. 'You bring the cakes.' She puts the teapot down on the table before bending forward to turn down the fire. 'It soon gets so warm in here, even with my rattling old windows.' I watch her settle back into her chair. She looks directly at me. 'I encouraged her in that. Thomas was such a good man. He's been gone more than forty years but I still talk to him every day.' I realise Pamela must have lived a very lonely life.

I look across at the small set of bookshelves. Taking pride of place is a photograph of a man in Royal Navy dress military uniform. 'May I?' I ask.

'Please do,' replies Pamela, her pride in her husband still evident.

I stand and reach for the image. 'He looks like quite an imposing figure.'

'He was already a lieutenant commander and would have gone much further. He might look a little daunting, but to me he was a kind-hearted softie. I don't suppose you would expect me to say that about a military man. Pass me your cup.' Pamela leans forward and picks up the teapot. 'I'll let you add your own milk. Of course, when I say I talk to him every day, I do just mean his picture. I don't want you thinking I'm completely bonkers.' I laugh before Pamela adds, 'Not yet, anyway.'

'Thomas was killed?'

'So many people recall it as such a joyous time. We're told to remember it as a time of national celebration.' Not understanding Pamela, I shake my head. 'You're too young,' she says. 'The Falklands War. A triumph for Mrs Thatcher and for the nation.' The contempt in her voice is barely concealed. 'But we lost good men. Very good men.'

Her voice drops away and she stares down at her teacup.

'That must have been so hard, losing someone you loved so deeply and to have people celebrating around you.'

'I was invited to all kinds of ceremonies. I'm still invited to memorials. I don't go,' she says, turning up her nose. 'Military types. Jeannie and I had our own ways of remembering, our own commemoration. Twice a year, we'd hang her dad's flag in the garden – once for his birthday and once for the anniversary of his death.' Pamela pauses and sips on her tea. 'I was pregnant when Thomas's ship left Portsmouth, although I didn't realise it at the time. That was the last time Jeannie was with her father. As she grew older, I'd tell her all kinds of stories about him, the fun we'd had together, how wonderful he'd been to me. I've often thought I could have told her anything. I could have made Thomas whoever I'd wanted him to be, given Jeannie whatever father she might have wished for, but I didn't need to. He was my hero and as she got to know him, he became hers as well.'

'She was lucky that you could share him with her.'

'He'd have told those boys where to go, just like you did. You're my new hero, Ben,' says Pamela, laughing. 'Come on, have another cake.'

I do as I'm told.

'Thomas became such a hero to Jeannie; in time it became impossible for me to compete. I think she became disillusioned about the reality of life. She's fifteen in that picture. Not long after she started going out and a couple of years later, she met a boy. He was older than her, by one or two years, and he got her mixed up with the wrong crowd.' Pamela stares out towards Haddley Hill Park. 'Jeannie wasn't the first and she won't be the last. She started taking things, experimenting, easily done. Once she started, she soon spiralled downwards. I tried to help, gave her money. I suppose you'd tell me that was stupid.' I shake my head. I can see Pamela searching for her words, almost hating herself for saying them. 'She got more and more angry. Argued with me, stole from me. In the end, there was nothing more I could do to help her.' Pamela runs her thumb over the worn fabric on the arm of her chair. 'Every night for two years, I left a light on in the hall. I couldn't live with the thought of her coming home to a dark house. I always hoped, once she sorted herself out, she'd come back for her dad. And his flag.'

Pamela reaches across to a small cupboard that sits beneath the front window. She opens the cupboard door and carefully lifts a neatly folded Union Jack flag. She comes to sit beside me on the sofa.

Placing the flag on her lap she says: 'This is the Union Jack that covered Thomas's coffin. It gave Jeannie a real connection to her dad. It's the one thing I hoped might bring her back to me, but it never did.' As she smooths her hands across the flag, Pamela lifts her eyes and looks at me. 'I know it's stupid, but I couldn't bear the thought of that little girl from St Catherine's going the same way. I know I will never see my Jeannie again.'

There is a bang against the adjoining wall so loud that it sounds like a train carriage has collided with it. It's followed by the raised voices of children.

Pamela rolls her eyes. 'They're new,' she tells me. 'They said hello on the day they moved in but we haven't spoken since. That'll be six months ago. Three children under five would be my guess. Must be quite a handful. If I'm honest a bit of noise doesn't worry me too much. It can be nice to hear other people when you're on your own. Good job really – that wall's paper thin.'

'I thought this was a Victorian terrace?'

'It is,' replies Pamela, 'but that house was rebuilt, more than twenty years ago. Never been the same. Cowboy builders.'

'Why knock it down?' I ask, hoping Pamela might tell me about Dani's childhood home.

'There was a terrible fire, destroyed the house. We were lucky the whole street didn't go up in flames. The fire brigade were outstanding. I'm still thankful every time I see a fire engine pass.'

'Was anybody hurt?

Pamela reaches for her cup of tea. 'You know what, I might just have another of those mince pies.' I offer her the plate. She picks up a pie and peels back the foil before carefully taking a bite. 'These are terrible for crumbs,' she says.

'But very tasty,' I add.

Pamela puts her pastry down on the plate beside her. 'A woman was killed. Angela Cash was her name. A bit like the family that lives there now, I met her when she first moved in. I think we even had a couple of coffees, but after that I barely saw her.' Pamela stops. She takes another bite and then sips her tea. 'Angela was trapped in the fire. Tragically, there was nothing they could do to help her.' Pamela slowly gets to her feet. 'I think half a pie is enough for me. Any more for you, Ben?'

'No more for me, that was lovely,' I say, holding up my

hands. 'Let me help you clear.' I pick up the plates before following Pamela back into the kitchen. Part of me wants to tell her Angela Cash is the body buried beneath the community centre, but I decide not to. I want to wait to see if she will volunteer anything further herself.

Pamela stands by the kitchen sink and runs the hot tap. 'I'll just give these a quick rinse,' she says, as I sit at the small, wooden table.

'The fire must have been a difficult time for everyone on the street?'

'Terrible,' she replies, her back still towards me. 'It was some comfort that at least the father and daughter were safe. The little girl would have been four, almost five. I used to watch her through my back gate, running up and down the alley. Such a pretty little girl, her hair a mass of blonde curls and startling blue eyes. Sometimes she'd pop her head around the gate and whisper hello. I often felt like scooping her up and having her all to myself.' I look at Pamela. 'Somehow it seemed she needed a little bit of looking after,' she adds, before moving away from her sink and reaching for a towel hanging on the kitchen radiator. She begins to rub the plates dry.

'How did they escape the fire?'

'The father carried the little girl out of a back bedroom window, I believe. The tragedy might have been far worse. They were both so lucky. After that they moved away.'

'Do you know where they went?'

'I can't remember if I ever knew. Like I said, I barely knew them.' Pamela drapes the towel back across the radiator.

'It's all such a long time ago. I hope the child has forgotten it by now.'

'I'm sure she has,' I say.

When I get up to leave, Pamela walks with me to the front door of her home. Standing by the door, she hugs me and quietly thanks me again.

'Any more trouble from those boys,' I say, 'don't hesitate to call the police.'

'I won't,' she replies, waving me off as I walk down Haddley Hill.

CHAPTER 35

Pamela closed her front door, dropped the latch and turned the key. She walked back into the living room, picked up Thomas's flag and carefully returned it to the cupboard beneath the window. On the shelf below the flag was her photograph album and, encased in its pages, the memories of her life. She pulled out the album and eased herself into the armchair by the window.

Flicking through the pages, she couldn't remember the last time she'd looked at some of the pictures. Thomas, and then Jeannie, both looking so young, never ageing. She flipped the pages forward until she found the photograph she was looking for.

The Filey boating lake.

A beautiful warm summer's day. Such happy, smiling faces.

Her, Dani and Jack.

She sat for a moment and let her hand gently rest on the image. If only Jack were here now, he'd know what to do. She brushed a tear from her eye before pressing the album closed and returning it safely to the back of the cupboard.

Six

'I was always under the impression that somehow he thought he could fix her. You can't fix a person like that.'

SATURDAY

CHAPTER 36

Adrian Withers silently closed the front door of the vicarage. A sharp frost underfoot broke the morning stillness as he moved along the path towards St Stephen's. His breath filled the cold air and, feeling the chill, he began to button his long winter coat. Majestic in the church's stained-glass window was a bright blue cross, illuminated by the rising sun. Reverentially hanging his head as he passed, the vicar walked quickly through the church's heavy wooden door and stepped inside.

Briefly he stood, admiring the light as it poured across the nave. Then, as he moved to one side and lit a small candle, his teachings briefly filled his mind.

The candle bringing light to the darkness of life, illuminating the spirit of truth.

Lighting a candle as a moment to remember the dead.

A chance to reflect upon your own life.

He said a silent prayer before rapidly moving on. Tomorrow, it would be two weeks since he'd last led church services. Two weeks of gossip among the congregation. He hated to think what people were saying about the discovery of a body on church property.

Hastening towards the vestry, located at the far east end of the church, and concealed behind the altar, a shiver ran through him. He wrapped his scarf tighter around his neck and pulled his coat closer. The door to the vestry had a habit of sticking, and so he leaned his shoulder firmly against it. Inside, the room was damp and cold. As ever, money was tight. He only fired the church heating on days with services. He bent down, flicked the switch on the electric fire beside his desk and adjusted the setting to light a second bar. The vestry was a tiny room, housing little more than his desk, a filing cabinet and an old wooden dining chair for visitors. At least that meant it would soon warm through.

With the small, raised lead window at the back of the room offering little light, he pulled the brass chain on the faux antique banker's lamp, which sat on the corner of his desk. Beside the window was a splintered wooden door, furnished with heavy black iron hinges and a rusting mortice doorknob. Lined up along the bottom of the door were three heavily worn, cushioned prayer kneelers, each one frayed around the edges. He had rescued them from the front pew at a time when the church had had money for replacements. Although not perfect, they did a good job in keeping out some of the chill wind, especially when it blew up from the river. He picked up two of the kneelers and stacked them one on top of the other, beneath the window. Gripping hold of the window ledge, he stood on the kneelers, pulled himself up and tried to peer out.

Through the heavily marked glass, he was frustrated he could see almost nothing. He stepped down and carefully moved the third kneeler onto the old wooden dining chair before reaching for the iron bolt at the top of the rear door. He had to twist the bolt from side to side but, once he had, it slid easily down. He pulled back the iron bar that hung across the middle of the door and turned the handle. Gently, he eased the door ajar, being careful to duck his head as he twisted himself through the gap. In the small outdoor vestibule, he was shadowed by an iron gate at the back of the church. The gate was chained with a heavy padlock, and he had no idea if the key still existed. He stood to the side, knowing the gate's arched stone frame kept him hidden.

Staying concealed, he watched a figure slowly make its way around the side of the church towards the burnt-out community centre. After a moment, he edged forward out of the shadows to observe his wife more closely. He could see her looking into the space where the woman's remains had been found.

In silence he waited while she stood unmoving beside the sham grave. Her phone still clutched in her hands, she appeared deep in prayer. The strength of her Christian conviction had always been so much greater than his own. Was she praying for forgiveness – and if she was, was it for herself or for Luke? Throughout their son's life, Emily had always defended and protected him. When he'd dropped out of college, she'd welcomed him back into their home; so much so that Withers had felt obliged to line him up with odd jobs around town. Some decorating, helping with the refit of a restaurant on the high street kept him busy, but all of the work came as favours from parishioners. Withers hated when the same parishioners then asked after Luke each Sunday morning, when he knew his son lay hungover in bed.

During that time, Emily had grown to enjoy having Luke at home. That was until she'd discovered packets of pills stuffed in the pocket of his jeans. Perhaps all Withers had needed was that excuse. His argument with his son was so ferocious it had almost been physical. Two days later, Luke was gone. He had not seen him since. In the two decades that followed, he hated himself for not missing his son once.

Emily had tried to find ways to keep in touch. She'd sent gifts for his birthday and for Christmas, but Withers had seen them returned unopened. She still had a phone number for Luke and had messaged three times since the discovery of the body. She was yet to receive a reply.

As they'd climbed the stairs to bed last night, Withers had said to his wife: 'Have you thought perhaps he doesn't want to be contacted? He's never tried to reach us.'

'He's our son,' was her only reply.

This morning, when she began to type a fourth message and he told her she had to stop, he'd seen the anger in her eyes. He didn't care. It had to end.

After several minutes, Emily eventually made her way to the rear of the burnt-out building. Losing sight of her and feeling certain she would remain occupied for some time, Withers snuck back inside the vestry and bolted the wooden door behind him. Carefully, he dragged the two cushioned kneelers back from beneath the window to their place at the base of the door. Then he lifted the third kneeler onto his desk before turning it over and slipping his hand inside a tear in the base. He moved his fingers until he felt the cold, metal key and quickly removed it.

Twisting the key in the filing cabinet's lock, he looked briefly in the top drawer before bending down and sliding opening the bottom one. At the back of the drawer was a stack of old sermons, kept from the days when he would pen his weekly address in full. He rapidly flicked through the sheets and found a couple of brown envelopes. Surely there would be something in one of them? But when he opened them up, he discovered them both to be empty.

His anger and frustration spilt over. He kicked the cabinet door, swearing as it slammed closed.

CHAPTER 37

I press the door buzzer for Sam's flat for a third time. This time I hold it down.

'Enough already, I'm coming,' says his voice over the intercom.

Realising I needed to speak to Betty Baxter about more than the simple construction of the community centre, I called Sam yesterday evening. He readily agreed to join me on a trip to the coast.

I return to my car, parked in front of Mrs Wasnesky's garage, and wait. After another five minutes, Sam emerges through the back door of his building and climbs in beside me.

'Bloody hell, it's freezing out there,' he says, as he reaches forward and turns up the heat.

'Make yourself comfortable,' I reply, before pulling out of Sam's drive and turning away from London.

'Is that the actual time?' he asks, pointing towards the clock in the middle of the dashboard. 'I don't think I've seen eight o'clock on a Saturday morning this century.'

'The sea air will do you good,' I reply.

Sam removes his seatbelt and begins fumbling beneath his seat.

'What are you doing?'

'Looking for the handle. I need to angle the seat back.'

'There're three buttons on the left-hand side, by the door.'

'Very fancy,' he replies, and begins fiddling with the adjustments to his seat. 'Maddy is paying you too much.'

'Are you settled now?' I ask, when he finally stops sliding his seat backwards and forwards.

'What time are we stopping for breakfast?'

'I've brought you a coffee,' I reply, pointing to one of the two cups in the middle arm rest.

'I'll have to have food, Ben. And you're buying. I've had to cancel lunch with Connie to come on your little road trip.'

'At least you can save your strength for tonight and Mrs Wasnesky.'

Sam laughs. 'I've told her I'll be at the Cricketers by seven.'

'I'll do my very best to have you back in time.'

The roads out of London are quiet. Before long, Sam and I are racing around the M25 and then out towards the Suffolk coast. To keep Sam happy, after an hour, I pull into a Starbucks coffee shop to buy him breakfast.

'We can't get a fry-up here,' he says. Stepping out of the car, I turn to him and raise my eyebrows. 'Don't give me that,' he continues. 'Maddy overreacts, always has. You should know that by now. I told you yesterday, the doctor says I'm as strong as an ox.'

'I'll buy you a toasted sandwich,' I reply, and Sam follows

me inside, where we are served by an assistant who moves quickly between us and the drive-through window.

'Can I get another couple of sachets of brown sauce?' says Sam, readying himself for his sausage bap.

'She can't hear you,' I reply, picking up our breakfast. 'She's talking into her headphones.'

Sam rolls his eyes and reaches across the counter, helping himself to his sauce. We sit together at a small table in the corner of the restaurant.

'Is it possible Angela Cash might not have been quite the person we thought she was?' I ask.

'What kind of person did we think she was?' replies Sam, unwrapping his sandwich.

'A loving mother, adored by Jack?'

Sam shrugs. 'Who told you that?'

'Dani,' I reply, hearing a defensive tone in my own voice.

'Correct me if I'm wrong, but Dani was not yet five when her mother died?' I nod as Sam sinks his teeth into his breakfast sandwich. 'So, in reality, Dani didn't tell you that, her father did. Or that's what he told *her*.' I drink my coffee and Sam wipes off the sauce running down his chin. 'Jack was well known across the borough. Every now and again, he'd point me in the right direction on a story, and equally I might help him out with a friendly article. Occasionally, we'd have a pint together. He always talked about his daughter, never his wife.' Sam finishes his breakfast. 'Not bad,' he says. 'What made you ask about Angela?'

'I got chatting to an old neighbour of hers.'

'Just by chance?'

I smile. 'Something she said gave me the impression she didn't necessarily see Angela as the perfect mother.'

'Any reason for her to lie?'

I can't think of one and I don't reply.

Sam twists in his chair and reaches into the pocket of his anorak. He turns back around and passes me a folded page of the *Richmond Times*. 'Something was bugging me last night,' he says, 'so, I went back down to my archive.'

'You've got lights in there?'

'Don't you start, or I won't help you. Two months after Betty Baxter's trial, her sister was arrested again.'

'Charlie?' I ask.

Sam nods as I fold open the page. He points to just two lines in the *In Your Neighbourhood* section.

Local businesswoman, Charlie Baxter, of Riverside Gardens, Haddley, was arrested on Thursday evening outside the Wandsworth nightclub, Heaven. She has been charged with possession of a Class A substance.

'She'd been snorting lines of cocaine in the club,' says Sam. 'What happened?'

'Quantity was small. I think she paid a fine and that was the end of it.'

'Except?' I say.

'Two weeks later, I was drinking at the Cricketers. She came over to my table, shouting her mouth off. I could tell she'd had a few. She told me Jack Cash was harassing her, that he was a bully, and maybe I should investigate his family and see how he liked it.'

'She was talking about Angela?'

Sam nods. 'She told me if I ever wanted to speak to Angela the best place to find her was at the Watchman, as she was drunk at the bar almost every night.'

'What did you do?'

'Nothing.'

'Why?'

'Jack asked me not to.'

CHAPTER 38

The smell of crusty, artisan bread made Pamela's mouth water. The stall holder wrapped two loaves and brought them around to the side of her stall before slipping them into Pamela's basket. Pamela handed her a crisp note and wished her a successful day.

St Marnham's Saturday-morning farmer's market was becoming crowded. Pamela squeezed passed a child's buggy and crossed to the dairy stand. Two packs of butter and a nice chunk of strong Cheddar. While the assistant wrapped the cheese, Pamela looked across at the preserve stand. Dr Jha's husband was serving a young, red-headed woman two jars of gooseberry jam. He put the jars into a small bag before bringing them around his stand to place them in the woman's backpack. As he did, Pamela watched him let his hand fall across the woman's arm. Then she saw him touch his hand against the woman's. Pamela quickly gave the man at the dairy stall his money and walked in the direction of preserves.

'Good morning, Edward,' she called, waving briskly as she walked past. He stepped quickly away from the woman, a guilty move if ever she'd seen one. 'Lovely day,' she said, and he half waved back as she marched past. She certainly wasn't buying anything from his stand today.

By now, the October sun had melted away the early-morning frost. The sky was bright blue and, relishing the warmth of the sun on her face, Pamela decided to make her way home along the river path. The towpath soon filled up, dog walkers and cyclists out in force, but they didn't worry her. She liked to see people enjoying themselves and as she approached Haddley she sat briefly on a bench to watch the rowers making their way upriver. After a short rest, she continued on her way until she reached St Stephen's church.

Turning away from the river and towards the Lower Haddley Road, she walked up the side of the churchyard. With the burnt-out building to her side, she kept her eyes forward. Blocking her path was a bright blue and yellow police sign.

WE ARE APPEALING FOR WITNESSES
CAN YOU HELP US?

Pamela read further down the police request for any information relating to the previous week's fire.

WERE YOU IN THE AREA AT THE TIME?
DO YOU HAVE DASH CAM FOOTAGE?

She wasn't sure what dash cam footage was. There was a number to call, in the strictest confidence.

She walked on, pausing beside the main gates at the

entrance to St Stephen's. Looking around, she could see no sign of life; no lights on in the church, no visitors parked in the church car park.

Rarely did she visit St Stephen's. Although it was only small, she had forgotten what a pretty church it was. She imagined the bells ringing loud from the tower, well-wishers gathering outside in the colourful garden. That was where she and Thomas had stood for photographs after celebrating their wedding. Such a happy day. Her happiest.

She walked on until she arrived at the opening that led directly into the cemetery. Resting her hand on the gate, she looked across the church grounds once more and assured herself they were deserted. Then she looked towards the vicarage. Did she see a brief movement at a side window? She took a step back onto the road. A car, coming through the woods from St Marnham, sounded its horn. She jumped forward and, finding her hand on the gate, moved inside the cemetery.

Feeling certain she was alone, she began to walk between the graves. She struggled to remember the last time she had been here. She recognised some of the names etched in stone and thought of how many people she had seen come and go in Haddley over so many years. She hurried along the winding path at the top side of the cemetery, soon spotting some dark green leaves and bright orange berries. Stepping off the path, about to cross towards the holly bush, she looked again at the upstairs vicarage window.

A pair of dark eyes were locked upon her, watching her every step. Pamela shuddered. She turned, hurried back down the path and out of the cemetery.

CHAPTER 39

We speed through the open Suffolk countryside, the roads becoming increasingly narrow as we wind our way towards the coast. I slow for a tractor before accelerating away and finally crossing a small bridge to be met by a road sign welcoming us to Southwold.

It is approaching the middle of the day and the town's Victorian high street is busy. Locals jostle with tourists, all moving between butchers, bookshops, the marketplace, as well as numerous cafés in this gentrified coastal town.

'Pleasant place to retire, assuming you can afford it,' says Sam, as we walk towards the sea.

'Have you got the address?' I ask, and Sam hands me a scrap of paper from his pocket. I type the address into my phone. 'You do think she'll see us?'

Sam smiles. 'For old times' sake if nothing else.'

'You were close to her, despite everything?'

'I wouldn't say close, but in our business sometimes we can't be too choosy about who we're prepared to talk to.'

'True, but you were pretty certain, at some level, that the Baxters were dealing?'

'I never did Betty any favours, but we might have shared an occasional glass of whisky. She could be good company.' There is a glint in Sam's eye, but he offers nothing more.

I look at the map on my phone. 'Five minutes' walk,' I say, as we continue down the high street. 'We can cut along the seafront.' I turn to Sam. 'Did you apply the same principle to Angela Cash – that you weren't there to make judgements?'

'After what Charlie Baxter had said, I could've looked for a story.'

'But Jack Cash asked you not to pursue it?'

'As journalists, we all make choices.'

'And Jack gave you some nice story leads. You scratch my back?' I say.

Sam sighs. 'That's a bit harsh. You'd have gone after Jack's wife, would you?'

I meet his gaze. 'I'm not saying I would, but if there *was* something, maybe what she actually needed was help.'

'Ben, I'm not responsible for putting her in the foundations of that building. It wasn't my job to sort her out but, equally, me looking for a story to splash across the front page wouldn't have helped much, either.'

'You needn't have worried – three months later, she was dead.' For a moment we walk on in silence until I say to Sam, 'I'm sorry. It's Dani I want a different ending for.'

He waves me away, telling me not to give it a second thought before he stops and peers down a narrow side street.

I grab hold of his arm. 'We're not stopping for fish and chips now!'

'I'm thinking about the journey home. They're the best in town. It says so!'

I laugh and, as seagulls screech overhead, I drag Sam on towards the seafront. 'Fill your lungs,' I say, as the wind blows in from the North Sea.

Sam zips his coat and pulls up his hood. 'Bloody freezing,' he mutters. 'Why would anybody live here in the winter?'

I flick on my phone. 'Three minutes and we're there.'

The Georgian home of Betty Baxter stands in private grounds, with hilltop views out to sea. With its symmetrical windows and heavy black front door, it is what might traditionally have been called a gentleman's residence. Standing with Sam at the end of the sweeping driveway, I reflect on the old adage of crime not paying. Looking at this place, it most certainly does.

We walk up the driveway, where a black sports Range Rover sits outside the front of the house. We are met by a voice calling to us from across the garden and turn to see a man tending the precisely manicured lawn.

'Can I help you with something?' he asks, approaching us before we can reach the house. 'If you're looking for the Promenade, it winds its way back out in front of the house.

Sam steps forward and meets him with an outstretched hand. 'Sam Hardy,' he says. 'We're here to see Betty.'

'Geoff Horsfield,' replies the man, equally robust. 'Do you have an appointment?'

I follow Sam onto the lawn. When I stand next to Horsfield, who is closer to Sam in age than me, he towers over my six-foot frame. His giant forearms suggest he is employed to do a little bit more than light weeding.

'I'm an old friend of Betty's from way back,' says Sam.

'Is she expecting you?' is the polite but firm response.

'We were enjoying a day by the coast, and I knew Betty would be furious if we didn't stop by and say hello.' I have to admire Sam's persistence and his bravery, as he takes a step closer to the imposing Horsfield. Sam drops his voice. 'I knew Betty well, in Haddley.'

Horsfield is unmoved. 'I believe she has a full diary today; sadly, no time to travel down memory lane.'

'We'll just knock and say hi.' As Sam speaks, Horsfield steps sideways and positions himself between us and the house. 'I could call her first,' suggests Sam, pulling his phone out of his pocket, 'but I'd worry she may find that a little odd. I'd hate to put you in an awkward position.'

Horsfield doesn't respond. I'm sure he knows as well as I do that Sam's bluffing. I'm about to drag Sam back when the front door of the house is thrown open. Leaving the door open, a young man, dressed in a grey hoodie with tracksuit trousers, runs across to the Range Rover and fires the engine.

I turn to Horsfield. 'Can I ask who that was?' I say, as the car reverses rapidly out of the driveway and races towards the high street.

'Old friends of Ms Baxter yet you don't know her son?' he replies.

'Bertie?' says Sam. He turns to me. 'Appears we're not the only ones enjoying a day trip from Haddley.'

CHAPTER 40

'You've just caught me, detective,' said Adrian Withers to DS Barnsdale, as he pulled the door to St Stephen's closed behind him. 'I'm working on my sermons for tomorrow and thought I might take a stroll through the woods to contemplate. I find it a very peaceful place.'

'I won't detain you any longer than absolutely necessary,' replied Barnsdale. To Withers's dismay, she had parked her police vehicle directly in front of the church. He decided it was best to say nothing. Barnsdale continued, 'I was passing and had a couple of questions I was hoping you might be able to help me with.'

'I'll do my very best,' he replied, his attention briefly caught by a woman hurriedly leaving the cemetery and crossing onto Haddley Common.

'Perhaps we can walk around the outside of the church,' said the officer. 'It's such a beautiful old building.'

'Ah, yes, of course,' Withers replied, focusing his attention back on the detective. 'I understand the body under the community centre has been identified?'

'Yes,' she replied, after a second's hesitation.

The detective's response told Withers he had caught her off guard and that pleased him. 'You must remember, Haddley is a small community. News like that spreads fast. Jack Cash's wife. Quite a turn-up for the books.'

'You knew Detective Inspector Cash? I was hoping you might be able to help me with some background information.'

'I encountered him through my church work. As you're no doubt aware, the church shares several charitable interests with the police. We like to do our bit to support all the services and your colleagues have always reciprocated in supporting our efforts.'

He knew the detective was fishing and said nothing more. For a moment there was silence until Barnsdale stopped and faced him. 'And his wife? Did you know her as well?'

'It's all such a long time ago.'

'I understand they were married at St Stephen's.'

The detective had done her research. It was to be expected, he thought. 'That's true, yes,' he replied. 'I'd say six or seven years before the tragic fire that . . .' He stopped and he looked directly at Barnsdale. 'I was going to say the tragic fire that killed her but, of course, we know now . . .'

'We're still investigating,' replied Barnsdale.

'If I recall, their wedding was one of the first I conducted here at St Stephen's. She was younger than him, of course. I'd guess at ten years, but it may well have been more than that. In many ways they were a surprising match.' Withers could see he had the detective's attention. 'I think we'd agree that DCI Cash was somebody who was married to his work. Wouldn't you say so, DS Barnsdale?'

'I only worked with him briefly, when I first came to Haddley.'

'You're not local?'

'No.'

The detective offered nothing more, so Withers continued. 'There were very few officers as committed as Jack Cash. His marrying Angela came as quite a bolt from the blue. I believe she'd worked as a civilian employee for the police, but only for a relatively short time.'

'Do you recall the wedding day itself?'

'Weddings all share many similar characteristics,' he replied. 'However, standout at theirs was the large congregation. I'd imagine officers came from far and wide to fill the church, although I was never convinced we would all be reunited for a silver wedding celebration.'

'What in particular makes you say that?'

'Just an inkling, detective. When you've seen as many couples on their wedding day as I have, you start to get a sense of which ones are going to last and which ones sadly may flounder. There were a lot of pressures on that marriage. One couldn't help but wonder if Jack had hoped for a family and, perhaps fearing that opportunity might have passed, grasped the opportunity when it came along. Not necessarily the ideal foundation for a long and prosperous marriage.' Withers paused. 'Was it six years it lasted before Mrs Cash's tragic passing?' The pair reached the back of the church and looked across at the burnt-out building. 'Such a nasty business.'

'In the years after the wedding, were Mr and Mrs Cash regular church attendees?'

'I'm sorry to say I could probably count the occasions on which they joined the congregation on just one hand. DCI Cash's attendance tended to be limited to his work. I don't think his wife ever attended again after their wedding. And, I may be wrong, but to the best of my recollection I don't believe their daughter was ever christened. For a Christian service, we would normally require church attendance but, if I'd been asked, I'm sure I would have made an exception for Detective Cash's baby daughter. Do you have family, detective?'

'No,' was Barnsdale's reply, and the pair walked on in silence.

'Of course, I would see DCI Cash on quite a regular basis, in the years following, visiting the cemetery with his daughter,' Withers began again. 'When she was young they would spend some considerable time here, tending to her mother's grave.' He stops, and frowns. 'Though, of course, it couldn't have been her . . . Is it possible Jack Cash, one of the true talents of the force, simply had no idea his wife wasn't the one buried beneath that headstone?'

Barnsdale ignored him. 'One last question, reverend,' she said.

'Yes, detective?'

'Mrs Cash's funeral?'

'Births, marriages and deaths, they all pass my way. I remember nothing out of the ordinary with Angela Cash. Whisky and egg sandwiches in the community centre. Jack was most stoic, didn't shed a tear. But then, some people don't. Everybody's different, wouldn't you agree?'

Barnsdale nodded and thanked the reverend for his time. Withers crossed to the vicarage, stopping to watch the detective's car enter the traffic on the Lower Haddley Road. Seeing the postman approach his home, he took three quick steps forward and collected the morning's stack of letters.

Inside the vicarage hallway, he flicked through the pile of mail. Another collection of parishioner peeves accompanied by a letter from Haddley Council. He put the complaints of his congregation to one side and opened the council's letter. Reading its contents made his heart sink. He walked slowly through into the parlour where he found his wife completing her morning crossword.

'Back so soon?' she asked. 'Are we to have only a truncated sermon in the morning?'

'I got distracted,' he replied. Withers dropped the letter down onto the table. 'Planning application on hold,' he said.

'To be expected, I suppose,' said Emily, only now looking up from her newspaper. 'Patience is a virtue.'

Withers turned away from his wife and went back out into the hallway. He walked through into the sitting room and looked out at the burnt-out shell. Without planning permission, the land was worthless. He was becoming desperate.

CHAPTER 41

Deliberately entering at the rear of the building to avoid the desk sergeant's eye, Dani scanned her security pass and made her way to her desk. Just as she'd hoped, early on a Saturday afternoon, the CID office was deserted. Quickly she logged on and waited nervously for her system to come to life.

While waiting, she unlocked her desk drawer, pulled out her notebook and reread the statement she'd made following Mat's stabbing, although she'd read it so many times, she could recite it almost word for word. Then, she reached across her desk and picked up the briefing document Mat had prepared for Monday's reconstruction. In every word, she could feel his determination to achieve a positive result. Her fear was he had somehow convinced himself making an arrest would change his own condition, and she couldn't help but wonder if he also believed it might change theirs.

Last night, after the success of the incident room briefing, Mat had arrived home in a genuinely good mood. At his suggestion, they'd shared a Chinese takeaway. When they'd opened a bottle of white wine, Dani had almost relaxed. For once, they felt like a normal couple. For two hours their conversation had been calm and, at Barnsdale's expense, they'd even managed to laugh. Returning to the station had given Mat a belief he could still pursue a career in the police. Dani knew his identity was built upon reviving his career as a successful officer and, if nothing else, she wanted to help give him that.

She clicked on her email and was relieved to find the two fire reports she'd requested. She flicked through to a second screen and found the forensic report on her mother's body. She paused before clicking on one last file – the chaotic collection of documents her father had amassed during the final year of his life. After his death she had uploaded them onto her system but, until now, she'd never been able to face reading them. She hovered her mouse over the file before quickly clicking and sending them all to print.

The unit remained deserted but that didn't stop her walking rapidly across the room to stand beside the ancient printer and wait for it to come to life. As she loaded more paper, something her fellow officers appeared incapable of doing, she heard the door to the kitchen creak open. Her stomach turned when she saw Karen Cooke enter the room.

'I didn't expect to see you here today,' said Cooke, moving immediately towards her.

'I thought I'd come in while it was quiet,' replied Dani. 'I've a couple of things to finish off for Barnsdale.'

'She does love her paperwork,' said Cooke, watching as the printer began to churn out Dani's reports.

As each page printed, Dani reached for her documents and folded them over. 'She definitely does.'

'I heard you're going to be off for a couple of weeks,' said Cooke, following Dani back to her desk, 'taking some personal time.'

Dani was no longer surprised at Cooke's intimate knowledge of the station. 'That's right,' she replied, pushing the documents into an envelope. She reached for Mat's briefing document and, along with the envelope, slipped it into her bag. 'Time for me to get out of here,' she said, hoping her tone sounded breezy.

Cooke stood in front of her desk. 'I want you to know your dad was the best officer I ever worked with,' she said. 'Everybody wants to get to the truth about your mum, for your dad's sake as much as anything. He was a good man.' Cooke smiled at Dani. 'If you need to get away quickly, I can switch everything off here.'

'Thank you,' said Dani, getting to her feet and looping her bag over her shoulder. Perhaps she had misjudged Cooke. 'Karen,' she said, as she stood by the exit, 'there's something I've been meaning to ask you about the fire at the community centre.'

'Go ahead.'

'On the night of the fire, when you followed Mr Harper back inside the building, did you see a knife jammed beneath the gym equipment?'

Cooke shook her head. 'Everything happened so fast,' she replied. 'When we went back inside, Mr Harper moved forward but then the floor cracked, and we exited as quickly as possible. My main aim was to get us out safely. He mentioned a knife, but I didn't see anything, I'm afraid. Do you think it's significant?'

'I'm not sure,' replied Dani, 'but thanks.' She hit the button to leave but then stopped and turned back to face Cooke. 'Karen, one other thing,' she said. 'It's something stupid, I'm sure ...'

'Go on.'

'You and Mat interviewed an older woman on Thursday morning? I saw her out front. There was something vaguely familiar about her.'

'Mrs Cuthbert?' replied Cooke. 'I'd say she committed no greater crime than being a bit lonely. Mat cautioned her, but I think it was something and nothing. I'm sure she didn't mean any harm. Sweet old thing, really.'

Dani nodded but was still unable to place the woman. 'You don't remember where she lives, do you?'

'Yes, I brought her in. The row of terrace houses on Haddley Hill, directly across from the park.'

CHAPTER 42

At the side of the bus shelter that faced the back of the police station, Dani stopped. She turned and looked back towards the old building – a place that had been more of a home to her than any other throughout her life. Never had she imagined finding herself on the outside. Standing alone in the car park, for the first time she felt some of what her father must have felt when he walked away from Haddley police for the final time. He'd given more than any other serving officer, but during the last year of his life he'd found himself deserted by many of his former colleagues, the people he thought were his friends.

The morning after Jack had staggered home with his eye blackened and his nose bloodied, Dani had returned to Lavender Gardens. It had been almost lunchtime when she'd arrived but, finding no sign of life, she'd gone around to the garden shed, counted down to the sixth pot and let herself in. An empty whisky bottle had stood on the kitchen table and, alongside it, a second bottle already half drunk. Her heart had sunk. She'd made her way upstairs and into her dad's bedroom.

'What time is it?' he'd asked, stirring when she'd opened the door.

'Almost noon,' she'd replied. 'It's very stuffy in here. Shall I open some windows?'

'Don't you do anything,' he'd snapped back.

'I'll give you five minutes to come round,' she'd replied. 'I've some paracetamol in my bag downstairs if you want them.'

Her dad had grunted a response. She'd stepped back out of his room and crossed the landing to the bedroom that for so many years had been hers. Pushing open the door, she'd stared at the wall in front of her. Gone were her posters of Harry and Liam, and her collection of penguins no longer stood beneath the window. Instead, she was met by a wall covered with hundreds of surveillance-style photographs. A giant whiteboard, filled with more images and scrawled-on dates, blocked the window.

Dani had stood in front of the wall. Pictures of container ships were pinned alongside photographs of heavy goods trucks; images of lorry drivers stepping from their cabs outside a builder's warehouse were repeated over and over. Turning to the whiteboard, she'd seen hundreds of photographs of the same woman. Each image had a barely legible date and location scribbled beneath it. Arrows criss-crossed the board in seemingly random directions. She could make no sense of what she was looking at. To her, it appeared little more than the scrawls of a madman.

A noise behind her had caused her to turn quickly. 'Dad. You startled me.' She'd looked at her father standing in the doorway – his crimson-blue eye swollen closed, his white T-shirt turning grey and his tracksuit trousers ill-fitting and worn. 'What is this?' she'd asked.

'Keep away from my investigation,' he'd replied, growling at his daughter. 'I've told you, this has nothing to do with you.'

'For Christ's sake, Dad, look at you. It wasn't just any truck driver you got into an argument with, was it? It was one of these you were spying on. This is Baxter's warehouse. What the hell are you trying to prove?'

Stung, Jack had barked at his daughter: 'This is my investigation. I'll deal with it.'

'Deal with it? You're no longer a serving officer and this isn't an investigation. This is harassment.' Dani had walked over to the whiteboard. 'This is Betty Baxter, isn't it?' she'd said, while looking at repeated images of the woman entering and exiting her home. 'And who's that?' she'd asked, pointing at numerous pictures of a younger man.

'Her son, Bertie,' Jack had replied, before angrily stepping into the room and turning the whiteboard away from his daughter. 'I told you, this has nothing to do with you.'

Dani had inhaled, summoning all her patience. Then she'd reached for her father's hand. 'Dad, this has to end.'

CHAPTER 43

The front door to Betty Baxter's home has been left open by her son. Sam makes a move towards it but Horsfield is after him in an instant. A giant hand lands on Sam's shoulder, stopping him in his tracks. But before any kind of exchange can take place, a voice calls from the doorway of the house.

'Sam Hardy. You I was not expecting.'

We all turn to see a woman with a silver-grey bob, wearing a fitted black dress and a simple pearl necklace. Cigarette in hand, Betty Baxter looks like a woman from a different age. With a virtually imperceptible flick of her hand, she dismisses Horsfield. He turns and walks slowly back to the front of the garden and the shoreline.

Sam crosses the path in front of the house. 'You know me, full of surprises,' he replies, before stepping up to the door to greet Betty with a kiss on the side of her face.

'I assume you're going to tell me you were just passing?'

'Of course,' says Sam. 'And how could we not drop by?' He turns briefly towards me. 'May I introduce Ben Harper?'

With the feeling of being presented to royalty, I nod my head and step forward. Betty Baxter takes my hand.

'Mr Harper, I've heard so much about you. You're an interesting character.'

'Thank you,' I say, unsure how else to respond.

'Are you coming in?'

Betty shows us into her drawing room, where light pours through the floor-to-ceiling windows and two sofas face each other beside a grand fireplace. Sam and I take a seat on one; Betty sits opposite us.

'Was that Bertie we saw leaving?' asks Sam, unzipping his anorak and dropping it over the back of the sofa. 'He seemed to be in quite a hurry.'

'Carla,' calls Betty, in a calm voice. A woman appears instantly and Betty points towards Sam's coat. After picking up the anorak, the woman stands and waits for my jacket. 'Three glasses, please, Carla,' says Betty, and the woman leaves the room. Betty leans forward and fixes her eyes on Sam. 'A little like you, Sam, he just dropped by. How's your daughter? I don't read her kind of news, but people tell me she's doing quite well.'

'Thirty-three million users last week. Ben works on her site.'

'Indeed.' Betty arches an eyebrow at me but says nothing. Carla returns with a silver tray and offers us each a glass of champagne. 'I hope you'll join me,' says Betty, raising her glass to Sam. 'Old friends and old times.' She turns to me. 'And new ones, of course.'

Sam quaffs his champagne and says, 'Bertie runs the family business now, I take it?'

'We work together. I like to keep my eye on things but he's on the ground in Haddley. Every generation likes to make their own mark, and Bertie's no different. He's keen to expand but we all need to learn the ropes first.' Betty's face is taut. 'Still, I'm lucky to have such a thoughtful son.'

'How is business?' I ask.

'We've had a successful few years; the building trade never seems to slow.' Betty sips her drink and looks towards me. 'Always another renovation needed and, with such loyal clients, we've flourished.'

'It was a building job from a few years ago we were hoping to ask you about,' says Sam.

'I'd never say subtlety was one of your greatest strengths, Sam,' replies Betty, laughing. 'I'm only sorry it takes an act of arson for you to come and visit me.'

'You've heard about the community centre?' he asks. 'You always did have a knack of keeping yourself well informed.'

'A near tragedy, averted by Mr Harper, I understand. A boy owes you his life.' Betty now fixes her eyes upon me. 'He and his parents must be hugely grateful.'

'The boy is yet to be identified,' I reply.

'I see.' Betty nods her head.

'I assume you know a body was discovered in the foundations of the building?'

'Intriguing, isn't it, Ben?' replies Betty. 'Just the kind of mystery you like.'

Clara appears again and refills Sam's glass. I've barely touched mine.

'And you'll have heard who the body is?' asks Sam.

'Enlighten me.'

I look at Betty and try to gauge if she does already know. The look of expectation on her face seems genuine.

'Angela Cash,' replies Sam, a grin creeping across his face.

Betty leans back and arches her spine. 'One thing I'll say about you, Sam Hardy, is you always found a way to surprise me.' She drinks from her glass before placing it down precisely on the highly polished marble table that divides us. 'I never thought she was right for Jack,' she says, shrugging and clicking her polished fingernails.

'You knew her?' I ask.

She turns towards me. 'Only by reputation. If I was being charitable, I would say Jack and I enjoyed a professional relationship. People will tell you all kinds of things, Ben, but I will tell you, he harassed both me and my family for over twenty years. He was bad for Haddley and I was glad when he was forced to retire.'

'Forced?' I reply.

Betty raises her hands. For the first time she shows a flash of anger. 'He came after me and my family one too many times. Even the Metropolitan Police could see his last set of charges were a crock of shit. He did us all a favour in drinking himself to death.' Her venomous tone reverberates about the room.

'And his wife?' I ask Betty.

'That was a long time ago, but I was always under the impression that somehow he thought he could fix her. You can't fix a person like that. I should know. For a while, I tried to do the same with my sister.'

I remember what Sam told me, about Betty never forgiving Charlie for the trial. 'Do you still see Charlie?'

Betty tilts her head. 'I've always believed if you work hard, you'll get your due rewards. I took a rundown, back-street business and built it up by sheer hard graft.'

Sam snorts.

'I did that, nobody else,' she continues. 'I wanted to help Charlie, of course I did, she was family. But she was both stupid and greedy. That's a dangerous combination. You don't compete with family, ever.' Betty's voice is hard, but I press her.

'Did you see Charlie again, after the court case?'

'Everyone makes mistakes, but the stupid ones never learn. She tried to steal a share of my business and that was never going to happen. She wanted what I had. I never saw her again. And I never missed her.'

Sam leans forward and drinks his second glass of champagne. 'What we're trying to understand, Betty, is why would anyone want to destroy that old building now?'

Betty laughs. 'Sam, why the hell would I know that?'

'Maybe because it was you who built it,' he replies.

Betty holds up her finely manicured fingernails. 'Who told you that? These hands have never done a day's hard labour in their life. The most I ever did was oversee a few minor building projects, which I think we did in this case.' Betty turns back to me. 'As a rule, supplies were our game, some lovely profit margins.'

'But you did help fund the building?' I say.

'Only after much pitiful pleading from Adrian Withers.'

'You knew him well?'

'Purely as an occasional member of his congregation, nothing more,' she replies. 'But, when one is fortunate enough to be able to give a small something back, one carries a certain obligation.'

'Yes, but who actually built the damn place, Betty?' asks Sam.

She looks at him quizzically. 'I'd have thought you'd have already asked Adrian Withers?'

'He told us a couple of lads from town.'

Betty sniffs. 'If you call his son a lad from town, then I suppose that's true.' Betty looks at Sam and sips her champagne. 'You look surprised. The reverend was desperate for the lad to be working so we used him on a few jobs. I don't remember his name, although I'm sure it was something biblical.'

'Luke,' I say.

Betty nods but keeps her focus on Sam. 'Not long after the building was complete, I believe he disappeared; vanished without a trace, not seen in Haddley since. Another refill, Sam?' she adds, smiling.

Seven

'If you are given to gluttony, put a knife to your throat. And he who utters lies will perish.'

SUNDAY

CHAPTER 44

It's still dark when I open my front door early on Sunday morning. The trees in Haddley Wood bend beneath a strong autumn breeze with fallen leaves swirling around the common. Instantly I question the wisdom of my decision to take an early-morning run. I pause in my hallway before taking a deep breath, grabbing my keys and forcing myself outside. In a vain attempt to keep warm, I sprint across the common, soon slowing when I realise my pace is one I cannot hope to maintain. At a steadier speed, I cross the Lower Haddley Road and with dawn only now beginning to break, decide to continue along the roadside where street lamps light my way. I turn up one of the town's narrow side roads and begin my run up Haddley Hill.

I woke early, with my head full of thoughts of the breakfast I'd arranged with Dani. I feel increasingly fearful the mother she remembers so lovingly may be very different to the woman who was married to Jack Cash. Through Pamela Cuthbert and Betty Baxter, I'm beginning to draw a portrait of a woman who was anything but the adoring mother of a four-year-old girl. Placing their memories alongside those of Sam, I realise I need to understand more of who Angela was in life before I can hope to unravel her death. Last night, I thought eagerly of our breakfast. Now, as I think of what I need to ask Dani about the family she so treasures, my appetite gives way to anxiety.

I reach the top of the hill and loop around the park before beginning a steady descent back towards Haddley Bridge. In my mind I replay the conversation Sam and I had with Betty Baxter. Could her animosity towards Jack Cash have caused her to act against his wife? And how would it have been possible for anyone to hide a body in the building's foundations without Luke Withers being aware of it?

Two empty buses stand idle as I approach the bridge. Across the river, the rising sun glints off the giant glass tower block and, with a bright day dawning, I decide to take the river path back to Haddley Common. I follow the steps down on to the embankment where I find the first of the boathouses coming to life. Shuttered doors are hauled open while early-morning crews carefully begin to carry boats down to the water's edge.

I make my way along the towpath, passing a number of smaller boathouses yet to open. St Stephen's bell tower stands proudly in front of me, and I slow to a walking pace as I approach the narrow road that turns back up towards the common. I'm about to pass the back corner of the cemetery when I notice a figure lingering outside the last of the boathouses. The man, dressed not for rowing but instead in a long, dark winter coat, ducks behind a tarpaulin-covered sailboat. I take a step back onto the river path and watch him move between the upturned boats racked outside the redbrick building. Standing beneath the building's first-floor balcony, he rattles the padlocked door. When it won't give, he stoops again, concealing himself between two sailboats.

I wait beside the wall that separates the small Neptune Boathouse from the neighbouring building belonging to Haddley Grammar School. It isn't long until a second figure emerges from the back of the building. I instantly recognise Archie Grace from his bright orange trainers. He walks directly to the entrance of the Neptune Boathouse, unlocks the heavy padlock and slips inside. He leaves the door ajar and, seconds later, the older man steps out of the shadows, hurries forward and follows him into the building. Once he's inside, the door slides closed behind him.

I step between upturned boats, moving closer to the boathouse entrance. Climbing onto the boat racking, I look through a narrow window above the door. There is little light inside with the only brightness coming from a phone illuminating the shadows in the far corner of the room. I jump down and reach for my own phone. I'm about to go inside when I hear footsteps returning to the door. I press myself back against the side of the building as the door slides open. I edge forward and watch the Reverend Adrian Withers scurry away, crossing quickly back to St Stephen's church.

Still standing by the boathouse door, I can hear Archie speaking inside. I strain to hear what he is saying but it proves impossible. I take a step forward, slide the door open and silently step between the boat racks. Almost immediately, Archie ends his call and I step out of the shadows.

'Archie,' I call, holding up my phone's torch to light the back of the room. Panic flashes across his face. 'What's going on?' I ask. Trapped in the far corner, he has nowhere to go. I take a step forwards. 'I want to help you, but you have to level with me first.'

His body stiffens and he clenches his fist.

I keep talking. 'Don't be stupid. I know it was you in the community centre on the night of the fire. You were hiding a knife.' In his eyes there is a flicker of recognition, but he says nothing. I take another step towards him. 'I know you're scared. You messaged me for help. Let me help you now.'

But before I can come any closer, he flies forward, crashing into a boat rack and sending it hurtling towards me. I'm knocked off my feet as a four-man racing boat tumbles down on me. I cover my head. Archie leaps forwards and, trapped against the racking, I can only watch as he sprints for the door.

I clamber over the fallen boats and chase Archie out onto the embankment. He is already sprinting away towards Haddley Bridge. Glancing over his shoulder, he sees me and stops.

'Archie,' I say, panting for breath and holding up my hands. 'I just want to—'

'Leave me alone,' he screams, and I'm struck by the terror in his eyes. 'Leave me alone, or they will try to kill me again.'

CHAPTER 45

'The fire was an attempt to kill Archie Grace?' asks Dani, as we sit across from each other at a small corner table inside the Coffee Canteen on the Lower Haddley Road.

'That's what he thinks,' I reply, and explain to Dani that it was Archie I freed from the burning building.

'But why kill a fifteen-year-old child?'

'He's got himself mixed up in something he shouldn't. When I saw him this morning, he looked terrified. We know he was in the community centre for a reason.'

'The knife.'

Finishing my first cup of coffee, I nod, and glance across the busy café towards our waiter. He approaches our table, and we order breakfast. When he walks away, Dani reaches down into her bag.

'I took these from the station yesterday afternoon,' she says, passing me an envelope. 'Fire and forensic reports.'

'Great. Any mention of the knife?' I ask, eagerly rifling through the pages. I begin to scan through the documents but catch Dani's eye. I put the papers face down in front of me. 'I'm sorry,' I say. I must remember this isn't simply a great story; it's Dani's family.

'That's okay. I did ask for your help,' she replies. 'No mention of the knife. Are you absolutely certain it was there?'

'One hundred per cent. Archie was scrambling backwards in the fire, either to hide or retrieve the knife. When Cooke and I went briefly back inside, the blade reflected off the light of my torch.' I continue to read through the fire report.

'I even asked Cooke yesterday,' says Dani.

'And?'

'She didn't see it.'

'It was there, and somebody took it,' I reply. 'Archie almost got himself killed for it. There has to be a reason.'

As I open the original fire report on the destruction of Dani's childhood home, our food arrives.

'I see your diet is as unreconstructed as ever,' she says, as I ask for brown sauce to go with my scrambled eggs and sausage.

Eating breakfast, we are suddenly fifty years older, enjoying the simplicity of a Sunday morning. We both smile at a young couple with a newborn baby sitting at a neighbouring table.

'No mention of Christmas tree lights,' I say, again reading from the original fire report. 'Only embers escaping from an open fire in your living room.'

'What does that mean?'

'It might be nothing,' I say, still reading. 'Empty Christmas boxes were the first to catch alight, and then the living room furniture provided the fuel.'

I explain to Dani how, at the time, the local press reported the fire was due to faulty Christmas tree lights. I have a nagging feeling it was easier for Jack Cash to leave that report uncorrected. While we finish our breakfast, I share with Dani the newspaper cuttings from the *Richmond Times*, as well as the details of the meeting Sam and I had with Betty Baxter.

'What did you make of her?' asks Dani.

'She's incredibly poised, only let her guard slip once and then for no more than a split second. She didn't like it when your dad went after her that last time.'

'But he had nothing on her.'

'Something touched a nerve. She was angry.'

'He pulled together so much random information in the last year of his life. Perhaps I should go through it again, but I'm not convinced I'll find anything.'

'Why did that final prosecution fail?'

'The county lines link. He gambled on finding the source of the kids but never did.'

'Then that's what he was looking for. And it's what we need to find.'

Dani is silent for a moment.

'What?' I ask.

'What if we find out he was right? And I didn't believe him?'

I shake my head. I know too well how dangerous 'what ifs' can be. 'You did what you felt was right at the time,' I say. 'That's all anyone can do.'

Dani nods. 'Did you learn anything else from Betty?'

'Reverend Withers's son built the community centre.'

'I didn't even know he had a son.'

'Long since fled this parish, if he's even still alive. I'd love to try and track him down.'

'I can't go back to the station again,' she replies, drinking the last of her coffee. 'Yesterday was a risk.' She pauses. 'But I could ask Karen Cooke.'

I shake my head. 'No.'

'Why? I think she wants to help.'

'I don't trust her,' I reply. 'If the forensics team didn't find the knife, then somebody else did. On the night of the fire, the only other person who knew it was there was her.'

CHAPTER 46

'That's a big leap,' says Dani. 'I've had my run-ins with her in the past and I don't like the way she behaves around the station, but she's a decent officer.'

'Somebody wanted that knife out of the way for a reason.'

'That doesn't mean it was Karen.'

'Doesn't mean it wasn't.' I smile and after a moment ask Dani if she will still attend Monday's reconstruction.

'It's important to Mat. Somehow I need to find a way to help him recapture the old life he loved.'

I reach across the table and take hold of Dani's hand. 'I understand that but what about you?'

'Right now, Ben, this is me,' she replies, pulling her hand away from mine as the waiter comes to clear our table. From her tone, it's clear she doesn't want to discuss this any further.

I lean back in my chair. 'I walked up Haddley Hill yesterday afternoon,' I say, 'to take a look at your old house.'

'It's not really my old house. After the fire, it had to be completely rebuilt.'

'You never went back?'

Dani shakes her head. 'I think it was too hard for my dad, living with my mum's memory. He loved Haddley but needed some distance. I was five when we moved to Clapham.'

'I met the woman who lives next door,' I say, looking at Dani. 'I think she was there when you were.'

'I don't remember her,' replies Dani, edging her chair back.

'Could she have been the neighbour who helped you out of the fire? She was right next door.'

'I suppose she might've been, but my dad never talked about it,' says Dani, getting to her feet and avoiding our conversation. I watch her walk across the room and stand by the counter at the café entrance.

'I've ordered you another coffee,' she tells me when she returns moments later.

'After you'd moved to Clapham, from that point on was it always just you and your dad?'

Dani nods. 'All I wanted was for my mum to come home but that was never going to happen. So many times, I'd put an extra plate out for dinner and tell my dad it was for Mummy when she came home. In the end, I think he thought it was easier just to leave it.'

'I'm sorry.'

'Don't be. It was something we shared, keeping my mum alive, making her feel real. She was everything to him and she doted on me.'

I hate seeing Dani's unflinching belief in all she tells me. Unpicking her childhood memories is not something I want

246

to do but, if I'm to uncover who killed Angela Cash, I fear I have to.

'You and your dad must have made your own memories, just the two of you?'

'We had the police. That was how we connected; that, and our memories of Mum. Even as I got older, a lot of what we did together was about Mum – visiting the cemetery, remembering her birthday, little Christmas rituals, going back to the same small seaside town for our one week of holiday each year.'

I smile. 'Where was that?'

'A place called Filey, on the Yorkshire coast. My mum found it years before and suggested to my dad we go. I wouldn't have been more than two or three the first time we went. It was a kind of old-fashioned place, but it was our place.'

'And you kept going back with your dad?'

'Only for the next twenty years! We ate fish and chips on the seafront, walked along the cliff tops and each year made a point of hiring a boat on the boating lake. We had a photograph of the three of us in a pedal boat – my mum holding me, me eating ice cream and my dad frantically pedalling. The picture was lost in the fire.'

I can see how much the connection means to Dani. 'You must have lost so much.'

'I still have the memory.'

The waiter returns with our fresh coffees and, as I sip on mine, I can't stop myself thinking everything Dani knows about her mother came from her father. And I worry any memories she did have of her mum were shaped or remade by her dad in the years that followed. Jack Cash wanted her to cherish Angela, to create a bond between mother and daughter, but did that bond ever really exist?

Holding my cup tightly in my hands, I lean forward. 'As a child, I can remember visiting Hampton Court maze,' I tell Dani. 'Me and Nick and my mum and dad. Ice cream covered my face and ran all the way down my arms to my elbows. I chased around the maze but fell and scraped my knee. It bled a bit but nothing serious. My lip trembled when my mum wiped it clean, but I soldiered on. I clambered back into my buggy and my mum and me raced my dad and Nick to the middle of the maze. We won and when we did my mum hugged me so tight, I can still feel it.'

Dani leans forward and our hands touch. 'That's a lovely thing to remember.'

'My mum loved that story,' I continue. 'It was one of the few occasions the four of us were together, and happy. I don't think I was even two years old, but it feels as if I can remember it like it was yesterday. It was her memory.'

Dani leans back in her chair, resting her face in her hand. When I look at her, I remember what Pamela said to me about her husband. For her daughter Jeannie, she could have made Thomas into anything she wanted him to be. I'm beginning to realise that is exactly what Jack Cash did with Angela.

CHAPTER 47

Dani walked slowly up the high street, passing in front of the police station before crossing the Upper Haddley Road. Rather than cutting through the park to reach her home, she continued along the roadside and stopped at the top of Haddley Hill. She looked across at the neat row of terraced houses. The house with the bright façade felt suddenly so familiar, and a sense of grief overwhelmed her. For a few minutes she stood there, thinking about her mother – bludgeoned and buried beneath the community centre – her father, dead from drink and grief for the job he'd given his life to. What had happened in this house that she couldn't remember?

Her attention was caught by a light turning on in an upstairs window of the neighbouring house. As she turned to look at it, an image flashed in her memory: a small bedroom, its walls covered with giant posters. Then, as quickly as it came, the image was gone. Unnerved, she moved away and hurried into the park, the wind fresh in her face. Her mind turned again to the final months of her father's life.

'The weather will be bloody awful,' Jack Cash had said to his daughter, as she'd loaded their bags into the back of her car.

'Dad, we're not going for the weather. It's Christmas and I'm not spending it cooped up at home, just the two of us. A couple of days away will do us both good.' Dani knew she had to get her father away from Haddley and all that consumed him. She could see his inability to let go of his past was slowly destroying him. 'Anyway, it'll be nice to have someone else worrying about the cooking.'

'I always enjoy the cooking.'

'Get in,' she'd replied, opening the car door. 'You enjoy the cooking because I do all the hard work.'

'Only because you like to take charge. Your mum was just the same, never wanted me getting in her way.'

Dani had smiled and, although two days before Christmas the traffic out of London was heavy, she'd enjoyed the drive with her father. They'd stopped halfway for coffee, her dad adding a tot of whisky to his.

'Irish coffee,' he'd said to her, and for a brief moment she saw the crinkle in his eyes light up his face. 'It's Christmas, after all.'

Driving into Filey, they played the same game they'd been playing since their very first visit. As they rounded the bend into town, and a glittering expanse of blue came into sight, Dani yelled 'I see the sea!' at the same time as Jack. In the end they'd agreed to call it a draw.

Pulling up outside their hotel was like coming home – the sun shining on the bay, the waves rolling onto the sandy beach, flags fluttering outside the whitewashed hotel.

'Smell that sea air,' her dad had said.

Dani had linked her arm with Jack's and together they'd looked out across the bay.

'I'd love to live by the sea,' she'd said, as they'd walked onto the neatly kept lawn at the front of the hotel.

'You'd miss London too much.'

'What makes you say that?' she'd replied, nestling into her father's side. 'The traffic, the pollution, the crime! What's to miss?'

'Whatever you might think, you love your job and you're pretty good at it. A couple of weeks away and you'd be bored stupid. You like the buzz of people around you. Your mum was just the same. I always told her she'd miss the city too much.'

Dani had pushed the curls back off her face. 'Can't you see me running a small station by the sea? I'd know everybody in the town, be on top of all of the local gossip and on hand to deal with the occasional skirmish.'

Jack had smiled. 'Mark my words, within a few days you'd be desperate to get back to Haddley.'

'Just like you always were?' Leaning against the clifftop railings, Dani had turned back to look at their hotel. Together with her dad, she had visited the same hotel every year for two decades. On each trip, long before the end of the week, she could remember her dad making phone calls back to Haddley Police Station, itching to be back at the place that was his real home. 'Let's go inside,' she'd said.

Christmas Eve had been wet. Late into the evening, Dani and her father had sat together sharing a bottle of Pinot noir.

By the warmth of the fire, he'd turned to her and said, 'I guess this is what retirement is meant to feel like.'

She'd smiled. 'Some of the time.' He'd topped up their glasses before she continued. 'You've earned the chance to let go.'

Jack shrugged. 'What if I don't want to let go?'

Curled in the fireside chair, Dani had tucked her legs beneath her. 'Then why did you retire? Was there no way you could have stayed in the fight?'

'Every day, for forty years, I saw the damage drugs did to people's lives. They're a scourge but it's impossible for us ever to be rid of them. I was never stupid enough to think I could fundamentally change that but on every single day of those forty years, I did my damnedest to make a difference. Betty Baxter and her family were only ever one part of the problem. I knew that but it didn't stop me doing everything I could to slow her down. After I'd tried that last time to get her . . .' Jack paused '. . . and failed, I made it clear to all concerned my plan was to go harder than ever. That's when the pressure started.'

'Because of your determination to go after the Baxters?'

'Not just the Baxters. I wanted more resource, more police on the street, a visible presence outside every bar on the high street. I had a very loud voice but everything I wanted cost money. Gradually at first but with an ever-increasing volume, the message back was it was time for me to step down, that Haddley needed a different approach. Needed somebody more like Freeman.'

'Dad, I love that you fought for so long and never gave up. But now, however unfair it seems, you have to walk away.'

Jack had looked at his daughter. 'What if Betty was the one who forced me out?'

'What do you mean?'

'Think about it. Getting rid of me suited her just fine. I caused her nothing but aggro. If she had somebody on the inside—'

'Dad, stop!' Dani had shouted. The woman behind the bar had looked towards her and she'd raised her hand in apology. Dani had leaned closer to Jack and dropped her voice. 'You can't go on like this,' she'd said, her voice quiet but firm. 'I've looked at all of your photographs and supposed evidence. You've got nothing.'

Like a scolded schoolboy, Jack had looked away and for a moment they'd sat in silence. When the waiter came to offer them a nightcap, Dani told him she was done for the night. Her father ordered himself a double whisky.

'Please don't stay late,' she'd said, and kissed Jack on the cheek.

By the middle of the following morning, Christmas Day celebrations had begun. Drinks were followed by a traditional lunch and then more drinks. Together, Dani and Jack had reminisced, both enjoying the day in their own way. In the late afternoon, Dani persuaded her father to join her on the seafront. The air was cold, with a strong wind blowing across the bay, but the sky was clear – perfect for a walk. Christmas lights lit the town, twinkling through windows on almost every street.

'Your mum loved Christmas,' Jack had said, when they turned back along the promenade. 'Taking you to see Father

Christmas, I think she was even more excited than you. Buying you presents, wrapping them for your stocking. Anything to make you happy.'

Dani had smiled. 'How can I help you be happy?'

'You don't have to worry about me.'

'I do worry.'

'I'm a survivor.' Jack had paused before saying, 'But I do have to keep going.'

Beneath the Christmas street lights, Dani had looked at her dad's ageing face. 'Let somebody else go after Betty Baxter while you still have time.'

'My whole career, she found me waiting for her at every single turn. After all I've been through, and all I've done . . .' At the top of the cobbled landing, where the fishing boats were moored for the day, Jack had stopped. 'I have to get to her. She can't win.'

Dani had stepped forward and wrapped her arms around her father. He'd rested his head on her shoulder and she'd hugged him tight. When they'd broken apart, he was sobbing.

CHAPTER 48

When I step outside into the fading evening light, the peel of church bells reverberates across Haddley Common. I bend to give Alice a farewell hug, having spent the afternoon with her and her mum. I promise to visit again later in the week. I walk down the road towards my house, but my attention is caught by a small gathering on the far side of the common.

When I head towards them, I see Amy Grace standing with her husband Jason and their youngest son, Ted. With them is PC Karen Cooke. I catch Jason's eye.

'Everything okay?' I call.

'Archie's missing,' he replies.

'He didn't come home last night,' adds Amy, panic evident in her voice. 'He went out yesterday afternoon, said he was meeting friends from school before finishing up some jobs at the boathouse.'

'He's got a part-time job cleaning up after the crews,' adds Jason.

'Mrs Grace, we'll talk to the rowing crews to try and establish if Archie did go to work yesterday,' says Cooke, 'but more often than not in cases like this, the child returns home before the second night. Archie probably stayed over with friends, experimented with a few drinks and today was a bit hungover and a little embarrassed. Fifteen-year-old boys are achingly predictable.'

'I said I didn't like the boys he was hanging out with.' Amy isn't talking to Cooke, but to her husband. 'Some of the boys I see him with, I'm not even sure they are still at school.'

'He plays football with a whole bunch of lads,' says Jason to Cooke.

The police officer nods. 'Mrs Grace, perhaps you have contact details for some of the boys? Often it's useful to try calling friends as a first step.'

'I've no idea who they are.'

'That's not a problem. We can speak to Archie's school in the first instance. I'm sure they will be able to help us with some contact numbers.'

'Perhaps Ted knows some names?' I say, turning towards him. His face flushes bright red and he puts his arm around his father's waist. Jason looks down at him and Ted shakes his head. 'Are you sure, Ted?' I press.

'He said he didn't know any!' Amy snaps at me.

'I only want to be certain,' I reply. I look again at Ted. 'I often see you all out playing football on the common. I've seen you with the older boys.'

'Ted?' says his father.

'I don't know any of their names,' he replies, his voice almost inaudible.

'Let's start with some phone calls,' says PC Cooke, ushering Amy and Jason back in the direction of their home.

'Constable Cooke, I couldn't have just one minute before you head off, could I?' I call.

'I'll catch you up,' she says to the Grace family, before turning back to me. 'Mr Harper?'

I explain that I saw Archie at the boathouse this morning and share my certainty he was the boy who ran from the burning building. 'He believes his life is in danger.' Cooke listens closely. I want to see if she tries to contradict me. 'On the night of the fire, I believe there was a knife in the community centre. That knife is now missing.'

'It's still only twenty-four hours since Archie was seen by his parents,' she replies, choosing to ignore my comment, 'and less than twelve hours since he saw you. We will continue to make enquiries.'

CHAPTER 49

With the church bells issuing their final summons, I follow a small but devoted Sunday evensong congregation towards St Stephen's. At the entrance of the church, I'm greeted by an enthusiastic member of Reverend Withers's flock, who, spying fresh blood, seizes hold of me. Remaining hidden at the back of the church is not an option and I'm eagerly escorted to an empty front-row pew. Taking my seat, I glance behind me and realise I'm under close scrutiny from regular attendees. Self-consciously I hang my head, a schoolboy prayer hazily coming to mind.

A hand rests upon my shoulder. I flinch and sit upright. 'I didn't take you for a regular church goer,' breathes a voice in my ear.

I look over my shoulder and smile at Sam. 'I could say the same about you.'

'It was a fine evening. I thought a walk in the fresh air would do me good,' he replies. 'Always nice to offer support to the local clergy.'

I twist in my pew. 'How was your evening with Mrs Wasnesky?'

Sam grimaces. 'Her granddaughter made a surprise visit. Madeline ended up joining me at the Cricketers for fish and chips.'

'Nice to have some father–daughter bonding time.'

'Not quite what I'd planned.'

Over Sam's shoulder, I catch sight of a figure silently entering the church. She walks up the aisle and takes the front pew adjacent to me. Sam looks towards her before leaning forward, closer to me. 'Always looks a little cowed,' he whispers, as Emily Withers sits in silent prayer. 'Madeline's going to have a dig around to see if she can find out what happened to the son, or where he might be now.'

'If she finds him, let's keep it between us. If he's chosen to keep himself hidden for such a long time,' I say, 'there must be a reason.'

Sam nods his head in the direction of the pulpit and I turn to face the front of the church. Dressed in long white robes, Adrian Withers has made a theatrical entrance. Standing motionless, he waits for his congregation to fall silent. Then he raises his palms and, in response, the congregation rises obediently.

I'm distracted by a noise at the rear of the church. The heavy wooden door creaks open and Amy Grace creeps nervously into the empty back-row pew. Briefly she kneels to pray but while others stand, she takes her seat. As she holds her prayer book, I can see her hands shake.

Withers conducts his assembled worshippers through brief

prayers before the choir leads in the singing of psalms. While the organist extends the final note, Withers turns his hands palm down to seat his followers. Raising my eyebrows, I risk a glance back towards Sam. From the corner of my eye, I catch a smirk break across his face.

'Our very own religious impresario,' he whispers.

Withers steps up into his pulpit. From his elevated position, he contemplates his congregation. He waits again for absolute silence. In response, Sam lustily clears his throat and the reverend's gaze falls reproachfully upon him. Sam coughs again. I chance a look back in his direction. He is reclining in his pew, his arms folded, looking directly at the vicar. Withers shifts his gaze away from Sam and he begins to speak.

'Beloved brethren, ordeals are sent to try us, to challenge the strength of our convictions and resolve. However painful it may be, we are forced to recognise tragedy and destruction have alighted on the very land upon which St Stephen's stands. Our spiritual home, the place we hold most dearly, has been assailed by evil.'

I look across at Mrs Withers. Her head is bowed, her hands clasped tightly together. Her husband continues his sermon.

'A man's wrath has overtaken him, consumed him with madness until he performed the evillest of acts.' Withers pauses. 'Murder. A sin we must always deem the most vile, the most unpardonable. That this heinous crime occurred so many years past is of no consequence to us. This deeply sinful act will forever throw a dark shadow over our sacred earth. We shall cast the perpetrator into the furnace of hell; their torment an everlasting fire from which they will never rest, day or night.'

Behind me, Sam sighs heavily. Withers turns in our direction and amplifies his voice.

'How can we ever hope to atone to this wretched victim, a woman from our very own parish? We must begin by ridding ourselves of all our sins. Our repenting must be absolute, and we must seek to live our own lives devoid of sin. We must all now acknowledge our weaknesses, our manifold sins, and our wickedness. It is beholden to each of us to confess them all with a humble, lowly, and obedient heart.

'All around us is sin. We must drive it from ourselves and help guide all our neighbours. We must support them, let them be freed from evil influence. If you are given to greed, you must now find charity within your home. Envy of others will cause only despair. Pride will blind you.'

Withers brings exaggerated fervour to his speech. His moustache begins to glisten under the spotlight of the pulpit.

I look quickly to the rear of the church. The back row pew now stands empty.

Withers's throat tightens. His brow becomes moist and he attempts to loosen his collar.

'Any form of unbridled lust, be it of the flesh or of money or power, will consume you. If you are given to gluttony, put a knife to your throat.

'And he who utters lies will perish.'

CHAPTER 50

He could feel the moisture running down his burning cheek. He pulled his sleeve over his hand and slowly raised it to his face.

His heart was racing.

His sermon concluded, Adrian Withers resumed his seat next to the pulpit.

He needed to escape.

Forcing himself to breathe, he could hear the sound of the curate's voice wretchedly attempting to bring life to the gospel, but he heard not one of the words. The sound of the choir washed over him and they had scarcely sounded their last notes before he was on his feet. Avoiding all the members of his congregation, he walked swiftly around the altar and headed for the seclusion of the vestry.

Once inside he closed the door, extinguishing the deep tones of the organ, before hurriedly removing his robes and messily hanging them on the peg behind the door. Briefly he sat behind his desk, bending to flick the switch on the small electric fire. Then he reached for his wallet and looked inside – a single twenty-pound note.

Quickly, he was back around his desk, stooping to pick up the padded kneeler that concealed the key for his prehistoric filing cabinet. He found the slit in the fabric and inserted his hand all the way to the back. Nothing. He felt into the corners. A wave of panic swept over him. He traced his fingers around a second time, but he couldn't find the key.

He closed his eyes and forced himself to take a calming breath. He needed to slow down. He let his fingers carefully trace their way through the soft filling and, a moment later, he felt the cold metal.

His heart jumped. Pulling the key out of the cushion, he blew off the dust before slipping it into the filing cabinet's rust-covered lock. The key turned with a creak. He knelt and pulled open the bottom drawer. Hidden behind a sermon he had delivered for Lent almost a decade ago was the white envelope he had secured earlier. Simply holding the envelope in his hand, he felt his anticipation rise.

He crossed back to his desk. Taking his seat, he felt the warmth from the fire starting to fill the room. He leaned back in his chair, reminding himself always to savour the moment. He cleared a space on his desk, pushing aside countless letters; parishioners campaigning, complaining, destitute or perhaps all three. What did he care?

With precision, he placed the envelope directly in front of him. He used his fingers to remove the crisp white paper, always so neatly folded, from inside the package. Using only his thumbs and forefingers, he meticulously opened out the paper.

After a moment, he reached across his desk for his wallet. Trying not to think of the debt it carried, he pulled out his credit card. With delicacy and finesse, he began to cut two thick lines of pure white powder. Once the lines were perfectly drawn, he ran his finger along the edge of the card before pressing it onto his lips. How he relished that tingle. He always thought of that as his aperitif.

He slipped the credit card back into his wallet and pulled out the crisp twenty-pound note. During the afternoon, he'd walked down to the cashpoint at the garage. He always liked a fresh note.

He rolled it into a tight cylinder and slowly leaned forward. He pressed his left nostril closed before beginning slowly to inhale the first thick line. His mind shifted; the world seemed to tilt away from him.

He began to imagine the pleasure the second line would bring, but when the door burst open all he could see were his robes falling from the peg to the floor.

CHAPTER 51

We stand for the final hymn, and I feel Sam rest his hand on my shoulder. I turn my head and he leans forward.

'The reverend is making a very speedy departure,' he says, as our congregation heaps more praise upon the Lord. Sam nods towards Adrian Withers who is hurrying from the pulpit. I watch the vicar, his gowns flowing behind him, disappear into the shadows of the transept. Before the final chorus is sung, he is out of sight. I edge along my pew and step into the side aisle.

Sam moves towards me and reaches for my arm. 'Where are you going?' he asks.

'I've a couple of questions I want to ask him.'

'Not without me,' says Sam, and he stumbles as he squeezes past a pillar at the end of his row. I catch hold of his arm and, for a moment, he rests against me. 'I'm fine,' he says, his voice rising. 'Don't give me that look. I get enough of that from Madeline.'

I smile, and as the music from the pipe organ continues to fill the church, we hastily follow Withers's trail.

'What does the vicar do after a church service?' asks Sam, in a hushed voice.

'I've no idea,' I reply. 'I guess it depends what he feels like doing.'

'Doesn't he have certain duties to fulfil?'

'Who do you think I am? The Archbishop of Canterbury?'

'I just thought you'd know.'

'Why? Because I live across the road from a church? Weren't you raised Catholic?'

'Lapsed.'

'He probably goes and drinks tea with his flock,' I say, as we stand at the back of the altar.

'That's what I mean,' replies Sam. 'Where was he heading in such a hurry? Certainly not to the tearoom.' We find ourselves standing outside a small wooden door. 'That'll be the vestry,' says Sam. 'It's where a vicar keeps his clobber.'

'Worth a try,' I reply. With the organ still booming, I knock sharply and push open the door.

Reverend Withers jerks back his head. His startled eyes stare across at us. Hanging from his nose is a rolled up twenty-pound note.

'That looks like a sizeable toot, vicar,' says Sam. Withers remains rigid as Sam pulls his phone from his pocket. 'Smile!' says Sam.

The camera on his phone flashes brightly.

'I wanted to ask you about your meeting with Archie Grace,' I say, 'but I think you've already answered my question.'

Eight

'I can feel his body shake. I realise I'm shouting at my eight-year-old self for a secret I should never have kept.'

MONDAY

CHAPTER 52

I wake before six. I reach for my phone and flick on the screen. A message from Jason Grace tells me he and Amy have spent the night waiting for news of Archie. There is none and I'm still the last person to have seen him. I reply to Jason, offering some vague words of reassurance, but I'm increasingly concerned. If Archie is dealing drugs out of the boathouse, what else might he be mixed up in?

Jason messages me again, to tell me he's put a notice out on the neighbourhood app asking residents to meet him on the common later in the morning.

I want us to cover as much ground as possible, he writes. Will you join the search?

I'll be there, I reply.

While I type, I can see Dani is writing a separate message to me. I lie back on my pillow and wait for it to arrive. She asks if we can meet at my house at eight. I reply immediately, telling her yes.

At a little after seven thirty, I stand at my front window and look out across the common. Dani's car is already parked at the entrance to St Stephen's. I walk quickly through into my hall, pull on my trainers, grab my jacket and head outside.

Entering the churchyard, I spot Dani walking away from her father's grave. She looks up and crosses directly towards me.

'I couldn't sleep,' she says.

'Long day ahead,' I reply. It's a year since Mat's stabbing.

'Something like that.' Her smile is soft, but I can see her mind is distant.

'You're doing the right thing,' I say, 'in supporting Mat.'

Dani briefly touches my arm but says nothing more. I suggest we walk down to the river. However much she might believe she made mistakes at the supermarket twelve months ago, I feel certain she did everything a good officer could be expected to do. I can't help but wonder if, on that day, Mat Moore charged in; a rash decision costing both him and Dani dearly.

We stand together at the front of the Neptune Boathouse, and I tell her of the discovery Sam and I made the previous evening.

'Snorting in the vestry!' she replies, laughter briefly lighting up her face. 'You never can tell.'

'Couldn't finish his sermon quickly enough,' I say. 'A crisp twenty-pound note dangling from his nose. Worth you speaking to him?'

'We see so much of it. The police wouldn't get involved with a small-scale user.'

'I get that,' I reply, 'but I think it's Archie Grace who's supplying him. This is where they met,' I say, as the boathouse doors open. 'I'd bet any money Withers left here with his stash tucked away inside his coat pocket.'

A women's eight crew carefully carry their boat across the path towards the Thames. We stand aside to let them pass before I lead Dani inside the Victorian building.

'Where are we going?' she asks, as she follows me between the racking to the back corner of the boathouse.

'This is where I saw Archie with Withers yesterday morning,' I say. Oars lean against the wall; two discarded life jackets lie on the floor. A small wooden table is tucked away beneath a bare lightbulb. 'My guess is this is where he does his deals.'

'You spooked him. Your arrival probably meant he left a whole load more customers without their dinner-party fix.' Dani flips over a few boxes and opens a couple of drawers beneath the table. 'Nothing here but if he was dealing he'd almost certainly keep all the stuff with him.'

'Archie is mixed up in something he should never have got involved in. I don't think he's a bad kid, he just ended up in the wrong crowd. A year ago, he was trying out for the school football team and now he's dealing drugs.'

'Ben, it happens.'

I push the table to one side and then lift two old rowing boats that clearly haven't been used in years. The first is rotting and damp, two wooden planks falling to the floor as I lift. The second is dry. Hidden beneath it is an old grey blanket, an empty Sainsbury's sandwich packet and an apple core beginning to brown.

'Archie hasn't gone far,' I say.

Dani walks ahead of me, out of the boathouse and towards the water's edge. She stops at the railings where the water floods the embankment. I stand beside her, and we look out across the river.

'I need to find Archie and speak to him before the police,' I say. Dani smiles and I continue. 'You know what I mean. If Archie is anything, he's a tiny cog in a machine making money for other people.'

'I spent last night going through my dad's old files.'

'And?'

'Nothing we didn't already know. His final case collapsed when he failed to break the source of county lines kids,' replies Dani. 'Once I was done, I dug out all of the *surveillance* photographs he took during his year of retirement. I was up until after three. There are literally thousands of pictures, but I think I found one that might just help us.'

'Go on,' I say.

'Throughout his career, my dad was obsessed with Betty to the extent he became blinkered. I should have realised but even before the end of my dad's career, she was scaling back.'

'Even drug dealers downsize.'

Dani smiles before reaching into her pocket. 'I found this,' she says, handing me a photograph of Reverend Withers stepping out of the derelict community centre. 'Control of Betty's business was passing to a new generation.'

I stare at the image. Leaving the building, directly behind Withers, is Betty's son, Bertie.

CHAPTER 53

On the last day of February, rain had bounced off the bonnet of Dani's car as she sat gridlocked in traffic, slowly creeping from Haddley to Clapham. It was late in the afternoon and it was already dark. She hated long winter evenings and couldn't wait for spring to arrive. A motorbike swerved in front of her, forcing her to slam on her brakes – in the mood she'd been in she'd felt like taking its licence plate.

For the previous ten hours, Dani had stood as part of a police cordon, as a demonstration against rises in local government taxes had become increasingly ill tempered. She'd been spat on, twice. How spitting on her would help reduce the tax burden, she wasn't sure. All she'd wanted to do was head home to her tiny one-bedroom flat in East Haddley and soak in a long, hot bath. If she'd turned off the Upper Haddley Road she'd have been home in ten minutes, but she didn't. She'd promised her dad she'd call round after her shift. She knew he'd want her to stay for dinner, and despite being exhausted, she knew she'd agree. Approaching a year since her father's retirement, he seemed to spend more and more of his time alone. He'd drifted away from his former colleagues; nobody enjoyed his haranguing them over his former cases.

She'd parked outside his house and with the rain still lashing down, had run to the front door. After repeatedly ringing the bell and banging on the door, she'd dashed around to the rear of the house, cursing her dad's increasing absent-mindedness. Rainwater streamed down her back as she counted down to the sixth plant pot before running to the back door and unlocking it.

'Dad?'

She'd grabbed a towel off the kitchen radiator and rubbed her hair dry. The kitchen was spotless; the sink was free of dishes, the worktops gleamed. She smiled. Had her dad actually listened to her for once and employed a part-time cleaner?

She'd called his name again and walked through into the living room. About to call a third time, she'd stopped when she'd seen her father slouched on the sofa, surrounded by his case files. She'd rushed to his side and taken hold of his hand. It was ice cold. When she'd kissed his cheek for the last time, tears had filled her eyes. Linking her arm in his and resting her head on his shoulder, she'd whispered, 'I love you.'

CHAPTER 54

A small group has gathered in the middle of the common. I see Jason Grace standing with his wife. Behind them, Ted is kicking a football back and forth with Max Wright. I walk towards Jason and Amy, and I tell them what Dani and I found in the boathouse.

'Thank God, he's alive,' says Amy. She turns away from the group and starts to run towards the embankment.

'I should go with her,' says Jason.

'There isn't too much to see – an old blanket and some food wrappers. We'll start searching along the river and then up towards the park.'

'Can I leave Ted with you?' calls Jason, already chasing after his wife.

'Leave him with me,' shouts Sarah Wright, Max's mum. 'Have you found him?' she asks me. I shake my head and explain. 'At least that's something,' she replies.

'He can't be far away,' I say, before Sarah calls for her son, telling him it's time for school. Max kicks the football towards the road before racing towards her.

I run across the common to retrieve the ball.

When I reach the ball, I crouch down. Ted walks slowly towards me.

'I guess Max is always kicking the ball away?'

He looks down and shrugs. 'He's quite good, for his age.'

'He's got a good teacher.'

'Maybe,' says Ted, standing opposite me, kicking his feet on the grass. 'I should get going. I think I'm meant to walk with Mrs Wright.'

I nod. 'I'm sure Archie's not far away.' Ted chews on his lip. 'The more I know the more I can help,' I say, reaching for my phone. 'Was it you who messaged me?' I say, showing him the *help* message.

Ted stares at the ground. I pick up his football. 'Why was Archie in the community centre on the night of the fire?'

Ted looks at me, his eyes wide. 'How did you know?'

'I saw him.'

'You can't tell anyone,' he breathes.

'You saw him coming home, didn't you?'

'I was still outside, kicking a ball. I helped him get cleaned up. I showed him how to wash his clothes in the washing machine. He made me promise not to tell anyone.'

'You have to let me help,' I reply. I throw Ted his football.

'Thanks,' he mutters. 'Archie didn't know about the fire. He went to the community centre like he was supposed to and then they set the place on fire. They tried to kill him!'

'Who did?'

Ted clutches his football to his chest.

'Ted?'

'I don't know, I really don't know. The people he works for. Archie's scared.'

'On the night of the fire, did he go back to the community centre, after the fire?'

'No, he was glad to be out.'

'Are you sure?' Ted nods. 'Are you in touch with him now?' I ask.

Ted shakes his head. 'He's not answering my messages and he told me never to call him. After I messaged you, he took my phone. I didn't dare message you again. He's the one who pays for the phone.'

'When you know something is wrong, it's fine to ask for help.' I crouch down again and make Ted look at me. 'You understand that? This is not a secret you should be keeping.' He turns away and I grab hold of his arm. 'Look at me,' I say, my voice rising. 'Never keep a secret if you think something is wrong. Never.' I can feel his body shake. I realise I'm shouting at my eight-year-old self for a secret I should never have kept from my mum. I let go of his arm. 'Go and find Mrs Wright.'

Ted turns and runs across the common. I see Holly leaving her house and walk over to her.

'You look tired,' she says.

'I'm worried about Archie but I'm fine.'

Holly nods, frowning. 'I feel the same. It sounds stupid, but after I dropped Alice at school I stood and watched her through the window.'

'Not stupid at all.'

We walk towards the group gathered in the middle of the common.

'Alice wants to know if Dani might come for tea at her house in the garden?' says Holly.

I smile. 'Alice is persistent. Dani needs to get through the reconstruction, and I need to find out what happened to her mum. After that, perhaps she'll be able to look forward.'

Holly gives me a sideways look, and at the corners of her mouth are the traces of a smirk. 'You know how perceptive Alice is. It's not often she's wrong where matters of the heart are concerned.'

'I should warn Max,' I say, and we laugh. I look towards the road and see Sam walking briskly past St Stephen's stone gates. 'I have to go but I'll come and find you later.'

I stride across to Sam, take hold of his arm and turn him away from the group gathered on the common.

'Morning,' he says. 'What's got into you?'

I don't answer but lead him onto the Lower Haddley Road. Then, when I'm sure we can't be overheard, I say, 'Jack Cash's last case broke down because he couldn't prove Betty Baxter was shipping drugs across county lines.'

'And?'

'What if, by then, Betty was stepping aside, and Bertie was running the show – expanding the family business.' I pass Sam the photograph Dani shared with me. 'And who lined up the kids to ferry drugs?'

Sam grins. 'Adrian Withers.'

CHAPTER 55

Adrian Withers stared out of the tiny window at the back of his study. He'd told his wife he was spending the morning working through parishioner correspondence. He was yet to answer a single letter.

He looked at the burnt-out building across the church-yard. What an eyesore, he thought. The sooner it was demolished the better. He'd received a letter from one of his parishioners proposing the construction of a memorial garden. He'd shuddered at the suggestion and tossed the letter in the bin. He needed to progress the sale of the land as quickly as possible before any such compassionate sugges-tions found a more receptive audience.

He stood beside his desk. Much as he disliked his study, he hadn't been able to stomach the thought of returning to the vestry. Why hadn't he locked the door? What a stupid mistake to make. Had he really been that desper-ate? Contemplating his predicament for the last hour had allowed him to make a decision. He would speak to his wife.

He left his study and walked slowly through into the

parlour. It didn't surprise him to find her still sitting at the table, her crossword puzzle in front of her. When he entered the room, he noticed she had her phone in her hand and appeared to be typing a message.

'Have you made contact?' he asked.

'Adrian,' replied his wife, turning the phone face down on top of her newspaper, 'you startled me.'

'Have you heard something?' he said, nodding towards the phone.

'No, that was nothing.'

'Nothing?'

She looked up at him. 'Nothing,' she replied. 'A message from the electricity company. I don't know why they bother sending them.'

He walked into the kitchen and picked up a cup from the draining board before returning to sit beside his wife.

'I think that'll be cold,' she said, as he lifted the teapot. She returned her attention to her crossword.

'Can you leave that for a minute,' he snapped. She was right about the tea, but he needed something to stop the dryness in his mouth.

Emily glanced up in surprise, but she did as he told her and pushed the crossword away. Withers licked his cracked lips.

'There's something I need you to do,' he muttered.

Recounting last night's events to his wife, as well as a habit ingrained for more years than he dared remember, he saw her recoil in disbelief. That he could live with, along with her obvious disappointment in him and even her religious piety when she briefly closed her eyes in prayer. He drank again from his cold cup of tea before he told her of the debt he'd amassed and his now desperate need for money. It was then he saw her complete disdain for him as a man. At that moment, he realised she held a deep-running contempt for him, one which in all likelihood had existed for many years.

He told her it was his addiction and the desperation it created in him that had led him to begin recommending boys who might work for the Baxters; boys who might be useful to them in distribution and supply.

'You need to understand this affects us both, equally,' he said, as she listened mutely. 'If those two journalists reveal what they saw, I'll lose my job and we'll lose this house. We'll be ruined.' He paused. 'I need you to speak to Ben Harper.'

'Me?'

'You've always been closer to him, supported his family after his brother was murdered, comforted him after his mother died. Surely that counts for something?'

Holding his gaze, she shook her head. 'Tell me about the boys you sent to the Baxters.'

'What?'

'Tell me about the boys.'

'I needed a way to make myself more valuable to Betty. With my limited stipend, we never had much. The situation became almost untenable. I only ever recommended boys with little or no prospects.'

As soon as he said it, he knew it was a mistake.

The whole time he'd been speaking her eyes had never left

him. There was more than contempt in them now, there was something else. Something more unnerving.

Emily picked up her phone and clasped it in her hand. 'Was Luke one of those boys?'

He didn't answer. When she left them room, he called after her, but all he received in reply was an echoing silence.

CHAPTER 56

A year ago, a long shift behind her, Dani's walk towards Haddley Bridge had been swift. In her mind, she'd been planning dinner with Mat. A bottle of her favourite Gavi Italian wine from the gourmet supermarket on the north side of the bridge had topped her list.

Today, her walk was slow. Mid-afternoon traffic already tailed back to the Upper Haddley Road. When she inhaled she could taste the car fumes that clogged the air. At the bottom of the high street, shoppers hurried past her, filling the new bargain clothes shop on the day of its grand opening. Waiting to cross the Lower Haddley Road, she stood and watched a toddler reach up for his mother's hand. When the traffic stopped, she crossed, smiling at the woman as they passed. Moving on, Dani briefly glanced down the river, past the boathouses and onto Haddley Common. When she reached the middle of the bridge, she stopped. There was the shimmering glass tower and, beneath it, the supermarket.

Standing in a vast open courtyard, the soaring building cast a shadow over all that surrounded it. She stood at the side of the bridge and looked down. Twelve months earlier, she'd followed the steps from the bridge directly into the courtyard below. With dusk falling, the faux Victorian streetlights had already illuminated the open space. As she'd headed across the courtyard, her mind had been on dinner and the glass of wine she would enjoy with Mat, so she'd barely noticed the three figures sprinting past her. School kids in ghoul masks ready for Hallowe'en, she'd thought. She could still hear their voices now, shouting as they ran into the store.

She walked forward and stood at the top of the same steps she'd taken a year ago. In the months since, she'd deliberately avoided returning. From the top of the steps, she watched Mat wheel himself across the open space. She gripped hold of the handrail before taking a first hesitant step down. She realised she was terrified.

'Hello,' she said to Mat, when he crossed towards her. 'Everything set?'

'Pretty much,' he replied. 'We've another half hour or so to wait. Keep everything crossed we get all of the media coverage we've been promised.'

'I'm sure we'll get most of it.'

'Have you eaten any lunch?' he asked, after a moment's silence.

'Not much. I wasn't really hungry.'

'I can offer you half a sandwich if you like,' he replied, holding up a bag from the supermarket.

'Thanks.'

'You can share a can of Sanpellegrino fizzy orange as well if you like.'

Dani smiled and together they moved towards the river. She sat on a bench looking out across the water while Mat twisted his chair next to her. As he did, a wheel caught in a broken pavestone.

'I'd offer to help but . . .'

Mat manoeuvred his chair forward. 'I can manage,' he replied quickly, before adding, 'but thanks.' He positioned his chair next to his wife. 'Perhaps I could be a little less churlish at times.'

'It's not easy for me, either,' said Dani, sighing.

'I have to learn to do things for myself. There are times when we're together when I feel like a little kid who needs to be helped with everything.'

'That's the last thing I want. If you don't need my help, that's fine with me. It's the anger and hostility I can't cope with.'

'It's not aimed at you.'

'It feels like it is. It feels like you see me as your enemy, not as your wife.'

Mat slowly raised his eyes. 'I'm angry at the world, and it's too easy for me to take it out on you.' He opened the bag he was holding and split his sandwich in two. 'Paprika shrimp and hummus,' he said, handing Dani half.

'It really is that kind of shop,' she replied.

'Wild chilli crisp?'

'Now you're spoiling me,' she said, taking a crisp and trying to smile. 'I can't feel guilty for ever. I know you blame me. You think I should have acted differently.'

'It was an impossible situation.'

Dani caught her husband's eye. 'But in the same situation, you would have acted differently?'

'Dani, I'm twice your size. I could have taken them down.'

'Exactly. You could have taken them down and you can't forgive me for not doing the same.'

'No, that's not true.'

'Yes it is. In your mind, because I didn't take down three grown men, you blame me.'

Mat edged back his chair. 'Let's not do this now, not today,' he said, but Dani pressed on.

'Part of me will always feel guilty. Every time I look at you, I blame myself. I promise you, I don't need you to make me feel any worse.'

'I'm sorry.'

'I don't need you to be sorry,' she replied. 'For us to have any chance of making this work, I need you to forgive me.'

Mat moved his chair around the bench until he faced his wife. 'After today, let's find some time for you and me.' He took hold of Dani's hand. 'I do love you.'

Dani's smile was rueful. A year ago, when Mat was severely injured, she'd told him she loved him when she knew she didn't. Now, she felt him squeeze her hand as he leaned forward to kiss her cheek. What might her life have been if she'd been honest with him a year ago?

But it was so much easier to lie. She dropped her voice, and simply said, 'I love you too.'

CHAPTER 57

At the bottom of the high street, Pamela stood and peered through the enormous front window of the new clothes shop. Banners hanging from every inch of the ceiling told her everything was on offer at amazing prices. Unrepeatable deals were to be discovered across the rows and rows of clothes racked across the store. A young assistant, standing beside the open door, thrust a leaflet into her hand and told her she could take another 20 per cent off any purchase. The shop did appear quite busy, although it was filled with lots of young mums, each one jostling with a pushchair. To Pamela, it all looked a bit like an old-fashioned jumble sale. She smiled at the assistant before shoving the leaflet back into the woman's hand and saying sorry, but it wouldn't be for her.

When she crossed onto Haddley Bridge she began to slow her pace. She reached the spot where she could look directly down into St Catherine's school playground and stopped. To get a better view she leaned forward over the side of the bridge. It was the end of the school day. Children were rushing out of a side door to race around the schoolyard. She desperately hoped she might see Jeannie, but the children were a fast-flowing mass and she struggled to make out any faces. It made her think she must get her eyes tested. She moved back from the side of the bridge and, looking towards the monstrous glass tower, saw two police constables idly talking. The last thing she wanted was for the police to see her anywhere near the school. Once the number 29 bus had turned towards the common, she quickly crossed to the opposite side of the road.

Pamela had read on the neighbourhood app about the plan for the reconstruction. Each of the officers involved in the original incident were to attend. A year ago, when the stabbing had occurred, she'd gone down to the mini market and bought a greetings card. They only had a small selection, mostly for birthdays, but she'd found a blank one with a simple floral design. She'd decided it would have to do. She'd read about Dani's involvement and had wanted to let her know she was thinking of her. Borrowing a pen from the girl at the checkout, she'd written the card while she was still in the shop. She'd walked straight down to the police station, planning to leave the card at reception, only to find the front door locked. It was early evening so she'd guessed crime must have been done for the day. She'd pushed the card under the door hoping she might eventually hear back from Dani. She never did.

Standing in the middle of the bridge, she looked across the road. She could see the man who presented the local news on television. A strong breeze blew down the river and she smiled at the sight of his hair flying in every direction. He pulled a comb out of his inside jacket pocket and attempted to tidy his parting. How vain, she thought. She was glad she always switched channels to her favourite quiz programme whenever he came on.

She hastened her way over the bridge. Once she was opposite the steps that led down to the supermarket, she waited for the traffic to clear before crossing back over. A small crowd had already started to gather in the open courtyard. She made her way carefully down the steps, which were surprisingly steep and, in her opinion, in need of a good hosing down. When she got to the bottom she turned away from the supermarket as nothing much seemed to be happening yet. There were some seats in front of a podium but the last thing she wanted was to find herself sitting on the front row. She walked a short way along the river to where a woman was sitting alone, looking out onto the water.

'Do you mind if I join you?' she asked. The woman moved to stand. 'Just two minutes, that's all. Please.'

Pamela saw Dani's shoulders rise but when she remained in her seat, she sat beside her and smiled.

CHAPTER 58

Holly and I follow a steady stream of people down the steps from Haddley Bridge and into the open courtyard below. The attendance of police, journalists and a significant number of local onlookers means a sizeable crowd is now starting to build. A television reporter interviews Mat Moore outside the entrance to the supermarket. Behind him are a small number of uniformed officers, each placed to offer support to their colleague. A temporary podium, with a Metropolitan Police lectern, stands in front of the store's main window. Chief Inspector Bridget Freeman is reading through her notes as she prepares to address the assembled media.

We walk towards the supermarket and find ourselves a spot at the back of a small group of journalists listening to the comments of Mat Moore.

'Have you ever spoken to him?' asks Holly, turning to me. I shake my head. 'Can't help but feel for him,' she continues, 'whatever he's like as a person.'

'I've nothing against the man,' I reply, sounding defensive even to myself.

'I never said you had,' says Holly. 'It's impossible to know what exists inside other people's marriages. I should know.'

We listen as Mat Moore asks for witnesses to come forward, even with what to them may appear an insignificant piece of information. Anyone in the vicinity of the attack last Hallowe'en should speak to Haddley police, he says. Members of the public should think of friends or relatives they saw on that evening. Were they behaving strangely or out of character? This was a brutal attack, and the perpetrators remain a direct threat to the public.

Holly and I walk on and find a seat opposite the police podium.

'Afternoon, all,' says Sam, appearing from behind us. 'Room for a little one?' I shuffle up to allow him to sit down. 'Impressive turnout.'

'The police will always pull out the stops when it's one of their own,' I say.

'Taken a while,' he replies. 'They've had twelve months to do this. And, right now, in terms of suspects, it would appear they've got a little less than eff all. I wonder why that might be?' There's a glint in his eye as he speaks.

'You think they've deliberately delayed investigating?' asks Holly, surprised.

Sam shrugs. 'That's not for me to say. What I do know is that it's taken the return to work of a decorated detective, now paralysed from the waist down, to bring any impetus to this investigation. His disillusionment with the force must be palpable. To see such limited interest and momentum from his own senior colleagues for the past twelve months must have only heightened his disillusionment. And as for the impact on his mental health, don't get me started. It would be very easy for him to conclude the Haddley force has become little more than a paper-pushing bureaucracy interested only in achieving managed targets with no real intent in solving any actual crime.'

I smile. 'When did you speak to him?' I ask.

Sam furrows his brow. 'Ben, these are purely inferences I'm able to draw after speaking to a number of his colleagues and close friends. Nothing is directly attributable to DS Moore. You'll be able to read the full story in Wednesday's paper.' Sam turns and looks behind us, back towards the river. 'Isn't that his wife?' he asks, pointing in Dani's direction. 'He said a lot of nice things about her.'

I stop listening. I look beyond Dani, towards the riverside bars that line the water's edge. It's not yet five and most of the bars are yet to come to life. In a dimly lit doorway, a figure conceals itself in the late afternoon shadows.

It's Archie Grace.

CHAPTER 59

Dani turned and looked at the woman's kindly eyes.

'Do you remember me?' asked Pamela.

'You lived in the house next door?'

Pamela nodded. 'I still do.'

'You had a little patch of grass in your back garden where I'd come and play.'

'I'd see you sneaking down the alley and then you'd peek through my back gate. You loved to chase around the garden before coming inside and drinking hot chocolate.'

Dani shook her head. 'I don't remember any more.'

Pamela smiled. 'I've always tried to keep an eye out for you; seen what you've done in life. I did try to get in touch, last year, after the . . . at the supermarket.'

'I went on leave for a few months.'

'Maybe I should have tried harder, found out where you lived.'

'At the top of Haddley Hill on the new housing estate.'

'Not far away – close enough for me to walk.'

'You'll have heard about my mum's body?' said Dani.

'Mr Nowak in the mini market said something, but I didn't want to believe him.'

'It's true. Do you remember her?'

'I didn't know her well,' replied Pamela.

'Anything at all?'

'I met her briefly when she and your father first moved in. Not long after she fell pregnant with you.' Pamela dropped her head. 'I'm sure you brought her a lot of joy.'

Dani took a sudden sharp breath and sat upright in her seat. 'You had a daughter,' she said, quickly. 'She slept in the little bedroom at the front of the house and every inch of her walls was covered with posters.' Pamela looked out at the water and closed her eyes. 'She died, didn't she?' continued Dani, softly. 'I remember my dad telling me. I hate to say it, but I can't even remember her name.'

'Jeannie,' whispered Pamela.

'I'm so sorry.'

A breeze blew off the river and for a moment the two women were silent, until Pamela said, 'I came to your father's funeral.'

'You did?' replied Dani, letting the surprise show in her voice.

'He did a lot for Haddley, went after the right people.'

'The Baxter family,' said Dani, under her breath.

'I wanted to show my respects,' continued Pamela. 'I sat at the back, kept out of the way. I left St Stephen's as soon as the service was over. I'd said my prayer and didn't want to intrude.'

'You should have come to say hello.'

'I felt certain you'd already been through enough,' replied Pamela.

'I still miss him,' said Dani, turning to reach for Pamela's hand, 'almost every day.'

'He was a good man,' she replied.

'I wish he was here now.' Dani felt Pamela begin to trace her fingers around her hand. 'My mum used to do that,' said Dani, 'to help me sleep. Ever so gently, around and around.'

Pamela gave her a sad smile.

And suddenly, Dani understood. 'That was you?' she said. Standing quickly, she hurried away.

CHAPTER 60

The crowd in front of the supermarket has grown. I can move quickly between people with little danger of being seen. I climb the first three steps of the flight that leads back up to the bridge and look across the courtyard. His black hood pulled up over his head, Archie Grace remains hidden in the unlit doorway.

I realise if I cross the courtyard directly towards him, he will see me instantly. Instead, I follow the steps up to the road, sidestepping the last stragglers drifting down to view the reconstruction. At the top of the steps, I dart in and out of the meandering throng and, at the end of the bridge, I turn down onto the footpath that runs behind the glass tower block. From there, I sprint past the back of each of the riverside bars before turning down a narrow alley which loops out onto the riverside walk.

Approaching the waterfront, I slow and catch my breath. I am now just a few feet behind Archie. I know he will be easily spooked but feel certain he won't try to escape me by running towards the supermarket and the police. He is alone, crouched inside the doorway. He is bending forward, his attention caught by the police activity outside the supermarket. I silently approach him until I am only steps away.

Suddenly, from behind, three figures charge forward, running past me along the riverside walk. Hallowe'en masks cover their faces and they yell to each other as they go. I press myself against the side of the building and, while remaining hidden, I see Archie turn to watch the start of the reconstruction.

The three figures sprint towards the gourmet supermarket. The young officer portraying Dani, dressed in police uniform, briefly looks in their direction as they race past. All Dani thought she saw was a group of kids wearing ghoul masks. Watching now, it's easy to understand why. When they reach the front of the shop, the three masked figures stop. They stand for the assembled press photographers before CI Bridget Freeman takes to the podium to begin her appeal.

'Two days before Hallowe'en, did somebody return home with a mask similar to one of these? For no explicable reason, were their clothes torn or damaged? Or were they suddenly flush with cash? During the raid, over four thousand pounds was stolen.'

I look across the courtyard towards Dani. She is standing beside her husband. Freeman tells us PC Cash, unaware of their intention, had followed the three raiders into the store. Inside, one of the raiders had pulled a knife. With the knife pressed against her back, PC Cash was forced to the floor, along with the store owner and a customer.

'With hostages under threat,' continues DCI Freeman, 'police officers with operational command took the decision to enter the rear of the building. After forcing open the back entrance, DS Mat Moore led the team that freed the three hostages. While effecting the rescue, DS Moore suffered a direct knife attack. Due to the injuries he sustained to his spinal cord, he remains paralysed from the waist down.'

I watch as DS Barnsdale joins Freeman on the podium. She holds a knife, believed to be similar to the one used to attack DS Moore.

'Did someone you know return home that evening with blood on their clothes? Did someone appear in a different outfit to the one they had worn earlier in the day? And where is the knife used in the attack? Somebody must know.'

I step forward and grip Archie's shoulder. Startled, he turns and tries to run. I grab hold of his arm, twisting it up behind his back. He cries out in pain. I force him forward and press his face against the bar's glass doorway.

'My guess is that somebody is you.'

CHAPTER 61

Adrian Withers knew exactly the kind of people the reconstruction would attract — rubberneckers seeking titillation. The very worst of humanity. He was desperate to avoid all of the gawping crowds. They repulsed him. Yet, he too had found himself making his way along the river path in the direction of the vulgar glass tower. He needed to hear what the police were saying.

From Haddley Bridge, he descended on the opposite side to the overpriced supermarket, taking instead the steps that led down into the riverside park. At the foot of the steps, he looked towards the playground. Small children were running without a care in the world. How he envied them. He walked back beneath the bridge, following a narrow tunnel under the road, which led towards the open courtyard. In the damp, confined space, water dripping down the brick walls, the smell of urine turned his stomach. Repeatedly he felt the need to bring his hand to his mouth to stop himself gagging. At the end of the tunnel, he concealed himself in a small alcove, and was barely able to see the police officer standing on the small podium.

Ensuring he remained hidden in the gloom, he watched the men charge forward towards the supermarket. When the detective stood on the podium, holding up the knife, a shiver ran through him. He could still hear the officer standing on the podium taking questions from the assembled journalists. She repeated her assertion that somebody must know what happened on that day; somebody was sheltering the truth. She avowed her determination to find the knife and to arrest those responsible for the life-changing injuries suffered by Detective Sergeant Moore.

He whispered a quiet prayer.

'*Make me a clean heart, O God; and renew a right spirit within me.*'

'I think that moment passed many, many years ago,' a low voice breathed into his ear.

He quickly turned his head.

'Hello, Adrian,' said Betty Baxter. 'Still skulking around in dark corners?'

Open mouthed, all he could do was lurch backwards. He pressed himself against the tunnel wall and felt the damp stone beneath his hands.

'Cat got your tongue?' she said, moving a step closer. His mouth quivered beneath his moustache. He tried to smile but his lips froze. 'Strange way to greet an old friend,' she continued.

He could feel her breath on his face. 'I just wasn't expecting you,' he said, wishing he could hide the tremor in his voice. 'I didn't think we'd see you again in Haddley.'

'I don't like it when people arrive uninvited at my front

door, especially nosy journalists asking questions. It makes me think things are getting out of control.'

Nervously shaking his head, Withers stared over her shoulder. In the dark recess of the tunnel, he could see another figure standing in the shadows.

Baxter gripped his face. 'I'm over here,' she said, her fingers squeezing his fleshy cheeks.

'Of course,' he replied, his eyes darting back.

She released her hold and reached into her pocket. The vicar held his breath until he saw her pull a small bottle of hand sanitiser from inside her coat.

'Can't be too careful these days,' she said, 'never know what you might pick up. Shall we walk and talk?'

He knew very well it wasn't a request. Briefly, he looked towards the courtyard and the police but realised there was nobody who could help him now. He felt Betty take hold of his arm and together they crossed back beneath the bridge, away from the reconstruction.

'Smells like you've pissed yourself, Adrian,' she said, as they walked under the road. He hated the sound of his own pitiful laugh.

It took his eyes a moment to adjust to the bright glare of the daylight. As they walked in the direction of the children's playground, he risked a glance at Betty Baxter. Even in her early seventies she somehow still maintained the same menace from thirty years before. When he looked over his shoulder and saw the giant forearms of the man walking only three paces behind, he felt even more feeble.

'Eyes forward,' said Baxter. 'Everything behind you you've seen before.'

Withers locked his eyes on the path ahead. 'Sorry, Betty.'

'I don't like it when dead bodies turn up unannounced,' she said.

'I'm sure everything will blow over soon.' Even he thought his answer sounded pathetic.

'Blow over!' she replied. 'Have you been shoving too much of that stuff up your nose?'

He forced himself to look in her direction. 'The dead body has nothing to do with you, Betty,' he said, hesitantly. 'Has it?'

He regretted it as soon as the words left his mouth. She gripped hold of his arm as her minder moved two steps closer. 'Where's Luke?' she said.

'I don't know, I really don't. Honestly, I've been trying to contact him. I knew you'd want to speak to him – we all do – but we don't have a number for him or any way of reaching him. I haven't seen him for over two decades. I'm sure if anybody knows the truth, he does.'

Baxter took a step back. 'Calm down, Adrian. We don't want you pissing yourself again.'

His laugh was little more than a titter. 'But then again, I really don't think he knows anything.'

'He built the bloody place!' Betty again grabbed hold of his face. He felt her nails dig into his cheeks. 'Find him,' she said. 'Or I will.'

CHAPTER 62

As the woman on the podium held up a knife that was four times the size of anything Pamela had in her kitchen drawer, Pamela winced. She was standing at the back of the crowd, near the steps, and even from there, she could see it was a vicious weapon. When the police officer placed the knife at the front of the podium, Pamela saw its jagged edge. To her, it looked more like a saw than a knife. She flinched at the thought of it piercing her skin. She couldn't stop herself looking towards Dani and her husband, together outside the supermarket. Sitting upright in his chair, he looked like a very proud man.

The officer on the podium continued talking but Pamela kept her eyes on Dani. She watched as Mat Moore opened his hand and reached up in search of his wife's. Dani let her fingers briefly touch his before taking her hand away and resting it upon his shoulder. Slowly, he dropped his arm back down onto his chair.

Dani's expression was blank, her eyes dull and sad. Pamela remembered the noisy toddler she'd chased around Haddley

Hill Park, who grew up wanting to be just like her daddy. On the days when Jack worked long into the evening, she would take Dani up to bed, only for her to creep down, minutes later, to ask when her daddy would be home. She would carry her back up to bed, often sitting with her throughout the evening, making up stories about each of the toys that covered Dani's bed. How she'd loved to make Dani laugh, to see her bright blue eyes sparkle. How she wished it was as easy to make her eyes shine in the same way now.

The police officer stepped down from the podium. She kept talking as a television cameraman and a small group of journalists followed her inside the supermarket. Pamela felt there was little more for her to see and decided she was ready for home. Jeannie would be long gone from the playground, but she still thought it was probably wise to keep her distance. She would walk on the opposite side of the bridge.

The stench of urine hit her as soon as she entered the tunnel. She dropped her head and quickly made her way through the underpass. Not looking where she was going, she walked straight into a figure moving in the opposite direction.

'I'm so sorry, all my fault,' she said, her eyes still fixed on the floor. 'I wasn't looking where I was going.'

'I'm sure I'm equally culpable,' replied the man.

At the sound of his voice, Pamela froze. She knew it was him, she didn't need to look, and yet she found herself lifting her gaze to his. She shuddered, fear coursing through her.

'Pamela,' said Adrian Withers. 'After you, I insist.'

Her coat brushed against the wall as she stepped around

him. Hurrying up the stairs, she felt her legs begin to cramp but she was determined not to slow down. Instead, she forced herself to quicken her pace, pushing herself forward until she reached the middle of the bridge. Only then did she begin to slow and steady herself. She looked back over her shoulder and breathed a sigh of relief when there was no sign of him. Resting her hand on the side of the bridge, she took a deep breath. Again, she checked behind her before, at a slower pace, she walked on, the hate within her burning brighter than ever.

CHAPTER 63

'If you try and run, I will break your arm,' I say to Archie, before I release him.

In the doorway of the bar, he turns and looks at me. His face is dirty, his hair a mess. He smells just as you would expect a teenage boy to smell after three days without a shower. The fight has gone from his eyes. He knows he's cornered. Now all I can see is fear.

'I want to try and help you,' I say, 'if it's not too late.'

He says nothing, his breathing heavy. We can both hear Freeman fielding questions from journalists. She tells them whoever fled the supermarket that evening was covered in blood. Somebody saw them. Somebody helped them.

'Somebody helped them,' I repeat.

Archie's breathing quickens. I think he is going to cry.

'Pull your hood up,' I say, 'and keep your head down. Walk alongside me. If you run, the only place you'll end up is in a police cell.'

He nods.

'Come on,' I say. 'Let's go.'

We push past the bar's outside tables and chairs and continue along the river before turning onto the path that leads us away from Haddley. The paved path becomes more of a gravel track as we reach the derelict industrial railway arches. When I kick open the door to an old London taxicab repair shop, pigeons fly in all directions.

Inside, the floor is stained with oil. Metal tools, coated in rust, cover an abandoned workbench. Rotting tyres are stacked along the wall. Before I flick on my phone, I push the door closed behind us. In the far corner of the garage is an abandoned office. Little remains other than two desks, facing each other across the room. Plastic letter trays and a Rolodex filled with faded business cards still sit on one of the wooden desks. I shove them aside.

'Sit down,' I say. The room is barely illuminated. Its only window, a narrow gap at head height, is obscured by a thick layer of cobwebs. 'Tell me everything.'

Archie lifts himself up and sits on one of the desks. From beneath his unkempt hair, his dark eyes hang heavy, his gaunt cheeks sagging like a man's more than thirty years his age. He stares at the floor. I lean against the opposite desk and wait.

Eventually he speaks. 'I wasn't there. It was nothing to do with me. I didn't even know it was them. I would never have got involved with them if . . .'

He stops.

'Take a breath,' I say, 'and start at the beginning.'

Archie sighs. 'They came to me,' he replies, his hair hanging over his face. 'But I suppose I didn't take much persuading. I wanted the money.'

'To help your mum and dad?'

He laughs. 'I'm not a stupid kid. The money I could get would never be enough to help them, but it would help me. I wanted stuff. I wasn't going to be the poor kid at school. And I didn't want that for Ted, either.' I think of his Nike trainers, his Maverick clothes, the latest iPhones for him and Ted. 'I earned enough to buy things.'

'Expensive things.'

He looks up at me. 'I was stupid, but I just wanted a bit of cash.'

'How did it start?'

Archie pushes his hair out of his eyes. He pulls his legs up onto the desk and then wraps his arms around them. 'They needed somebody to sell stuff at school.'

'Drugs?'

He nods. 'I'd never been interested in any kind of pills or even weed, so hadn't had much to do with them. That probably made me more appealing, no danger of me feeding my own habit.' His smile is a fatalistic one. 'At first all I did was drop-offs.'

'How old were you?'

'Fourteen. Not long after, a couple of kids dealing for them in school were caught sampling the goods. That meant they were out, and I was in.'

'And over time you were expected to do more and more?'

'Pretty quickly, I had a couple of other kids working for me in school. I started dealing out of the boathouse. They gave me a list of regulars. I was their contact point. Higher-priced deals meant a bit more commission for me.'

'Didn't your mum and dad ever ask where all the clothes and the phones came from?'

'I told them they were second hand. They think I've got a job cleaning up at the boathouse. In a way, I do.' Archie smiles nervously. 'My dad was always working, and my mum thought praying was somehow the answer. If she knew the truth about Reverend Withers. He gave the dealers my name.' I raise my eyebrows. 'And he's by far my biggest customer.'

'Tell me what happened on the night of the fire.'

Archie rubs his hand across his face. 'You saved my life,' he says, quietly.

'Why were you there?'

'They paid me two hundred quid to get rid of the knife.'

'You decided to hide it in the community centre?'

'No,' replies Archie. 'It's been hidden there for the last year, under that old weights machine.' I suddenly realise why Archie was so slow to leave the burning building. 'My job was to get hold of the knife and get rid of it, but the machine was bolted to the floor. I tried everything to free the knife but couldn't. When you screamed at me to get out, I had no choice but to leave it.'

'Who has the knife now?'

'I don't know. I was glad to be out. They could have killed me.'

'You think they set the fire?'

'Who else would?' I don't answer but I can't help but wonder why anybody would want to kill Archie after paying him to retrieve the knife. 'Why are you still working for them?'

'You don't decide when to stop. If I tried to quit, that would make things worse.'

'They're desperate to get hold of the knife,' I say, 'because it was the knife used to stab Mat Moore?'

Archie nods.

In the dim light, I look directly at him. 'Tell me you had nothing to do with that.'

'Nothing,' he replies. I hear an urgency in his voice. I think of the way Ted idolises his older brother. I want to believe Archie is a good kid who's made some stupid decisions.

'If you want me to help you, you're going to have to tell me who *they* are.'

Archie drops his head and covers his ears with his hands. He raises his eyes to me.

'You work for Bertie Baxter?' I say.

CHAPTER 64

Pamela stopped when she reached the bottom of the high street. Still catching her breath, she looked back over the bridge to where people were now moving away from the reconstruction.

Her body tensed.

On the opposite side of the road, there he was, scurrying past. He didn't see her. She waited and watched him hurry away towards St Stephen's. For a moment, she felt paralysed. She forced herself to breathe before taking slow, hesitant steps forward.

She looked at her watch and saw it was just after five. At the bottom of the high street was her favourite Haddley pie shop. She could see the shop was still open and decided to treat herself to a beef and stilton. With some mash and gravy, she would sit in front of the television and eat her dinner. And she would open one of her miniatures. Perhaps two.

Traffic was heavy, so she began to walk a short distance down the Lower Haddley Road to cross at the pedestrian crossing. As she did, her attention was briefly caught by a couple standing on the riverside towpath. It was the sight of the man grabbing hold of the woman's arm, as if he was restraining her, that made her stop.

Still on the pavement, Pamela moved towards the river wall. From there she could look directly down onto the embankment and the couple below. Her arm outstretched, the woman was attempting to walk away. The man grasped hold of her hand and refused to let go. From behind, Pamela could see the woman was straining to move away.

The noise of the traffic meant Pamela was unable to hear any conversation, but squinting she could see the man was now forcibly restraining the woman. Quickly, she opened her shopping bag to rummage for her glasses. Of course, they were right at the bottom. By the time she had her glasses on, the woman had broken free. Pamela could see her walking away, but the man was going after her.

Suddenly, the woman stopped and turned to confront him. Pamela held her breath. Was the man going to hit the woman? Pamela was ready to scream but instead of hitting the woman, the man wrapped his arms around her. Seeing the couple embrace, Pamela wondered if they were simply quarrelling lovers. She narrowed her eyes and could now see the woman was much older than the man. Surely they couldn't be lovers, although these days you did see some of the oddest pairings.

When the couple split apart, Pamela looked again.

To her surprise, she recognised the woman. It had been a number of years since she had seen Emily Withers close up, but it was definitely her.

Briefly, the man turned his face in her direction. Pamela looked again. At first, she wasn't sure but when she leaned forward and he turned again, she felt certain.

She held her breath.

CHAPTER 65

A train rattles overhead when I step outside the derelict railway arches. I pull the door of the garage closed before forcing the gatefold lock back into its original screw holes. With the padlock hanging in place, only a close examination would reveal the door has been recently opened.

I hurry back down the alley, leaving Archie hidden inside the garage. He is ready to talk to the police, but first I need to speak with Dani. I want Archie treated more as a witness than a criminal. Jack Cash tried for two decades to convict Betty Baxter. Now, Archie can testify to the illegal activity of the latest successor in her crime lineage.

For a Monday evening, the riverside bars are conducting a brisk trade. Journalists from the reconstruction drift down the river walk to fill the tables beneath the outdoor patio heaters. At the front of the supermarket, two young officers begin to dismantle the podium. Dani sits beside her husband as he conducts a final interview. I walk directly towards them.

'I need to speak with you,' I say quietly to Dani.

'We'll be done here in ten minutes. Fifteen at the most.'

'I really need to talk to you now.'

Mat Moore looks towards his wife. She catches his eye before turning back to me. 'You're going to have to give me ten minutes.'

PC Karen Cooke crosses towards me. 'Mr Harper, any news on Archie?' she asks, as she approaches.

I smile. 'Shouldn't I be asking you that?'

'The boy will have been away from home for forty-eight hours this evening. At that point, we will be reviewing the situation and a decision will be made as to whether we increase the search area.' I nod before Cooke asks directly, 'Is there something you need assistance with?'

Mat Moore is concluding his interview with a local London journalist. 'Thanks for your time,' he says. 'We're wrapping things up here now.' I recognise the woman from the free London evening paper and smile as she steps away. Moore turns his chair towards me. 'You must be the famous Ben Harper.'

'I hope today proves to be a success,' I reply, offering my hand. 'We'll be running the story on our site.'

Moore takes a moment to respond before reaching for my hand. 'Thank you,' he replies. 'Any coverage you can give us would be much appreciated.'

'I should probably get going,' I say, looking towards Dani. 'I only came over to say hi.'

'You know my wife?'

I take a step back, unsure how to respond. 'We worked together in finding the truth of how my mum died.'

Moore nods. 'I think I read something about that,' he replies. 'We should let you go,' he continues. 'I'm sure there's always another story to cover.'

'Good to meet you,' I say, half holding up my hand. At the bottom of the steps, I turn and look back towards Dani. She is facing away from me. Slowly, I make my way up the stairs, hoping she will find an excuse to follow, but she doesn't.

As I walk onto the bridge, the church bells of St Stephen's begin to ring out across Haddley. Early-evening traffic is still heavy, and I have to wait before dodging between cars to cross to the other side. By the time I reach the embankment path on the south side of the river, the clang of church bells has become more rapid and irregular. Early on a Monday evening, I know the sound coming from St Stephen's cannot be a call to prayer. I quicken my pace.

The church bells continue unabated, their sound becoming faster and faster. I approach St Stephen's and the noise becomes increasingly erratic. I stop outside Haddley Grammar School boathouse and look towards the church.

Smoke is pouring from the bell tower.

CHAPTER 66

I sprint along the towpath, the fitful ringing of the church bells reverberating in my ears. I race up from the river, past the Neptune Boathouse and the back of the burnt-out community centre, and up to the front of the church where, once again, I can taste dry smoke filling the air.

People swarm outside the churchyard gates. When I reach the imposing wooden door, Sam is at my side.

'Ben, thank God you're here,' he says, pointing up at the bell tower. 'Somebody must be trapped inside.' The ringing of the bell continues, its tempo seemingly more and more desperate. 'The front door is locked,' continues Sam, 'bolted from the inside.'

'There's another door round the back, one that leads from the vestry.'

I look around at the crowd and see Jason Grace standing with his wife and youngest son.

'Jason,' I yell. 'I need your help.'

Black smoke continues to pour from the bell tower. Jason follows me down the gravel path at the side of the church. The sound of approaching sirens now blends with the clanging bells.

I stop, suddenly. On the wooden bench, where I had sat with PC Cooke on the night of the last fire, sits a solitary figure.

When she sees me, Betty Baxter barely lifts her head in acknowledgement.

'Ben, come on,' shouts Jason, running ahead of me.

I stare at Betty and am able only to walk past her in disbelief.

'Ben,' shouts Jason, and again I run forward. 'We'll need bolt cutters to get through that,' he says, looking at the chain holding the gate at the back of the vestry. 'All we can do is start smashing windows.'

Together, we run back to the front of the church. The numbers in the crowd have grown larger, and I notice Pamela Cuthbert is among them. Standing alone on the path leading into the graveyard is the vicar's wife. I turn to see Dani running through the gates, but as I do the ringing of the bells abruptly ends.

I look up and see a figure clambering out from inside the bell tower. All the crowd can do is stand and watch as the Reverend Withers ascends the narrow wall that stands beneath the bronze church bells.

Dani shouts at him to stop.

The reverend stands on the edge of the wall and opens his arm wide.

He cries out. 'My own shame is so great, I choose to destroy this life belonging to God. For all of my sins, take me now to my eternal damnation.'

Dani shouts again but the vicar steps forward.

And then falls silently to the ground.

Nine

'I learned from Madeline how dangerous it is to ever make assumptions about anyone.'

CHAPTER 67

Evening creeps across the churchyard and, in the fading light, the last shadow falls across the bell tower. Smoke is still rising through its roof. Four firefighters wrench open the church door and within seconds they are inside. The fire is soon extinguished.

The body of the Reverend Adrian Withers lies on the gravel path in front of St Stephen's. Alone, his widow walks towards the church. Onlookers take a step back while PC Karen Cooke moves forward, offering support. With her hand resting on the police officer's arm, Mrs Withers stands beside her husband's body, then, with heads bowed, they turn and walk back past what remains of the crowd.

Sam is at my shoulder. He has his phone in his hand. Using me as cover, he edges forward and captures an image of the widow.

'Sam!' I whisper.

He stands close at my side. 'It's news.'

'How much will you run?'

'I have to go with the suicide.'

'If it was suicide,' I reply.

'We just saw him jump,' says Sam. 'If I'm feeling charitable, I might hold off on the picture of the late vicar in the vestry. Good taste and all that.'

'Do you think that tipped him over the edge?' I ask, quietly.

'What, his years of substance abuse? I'd say probably so.'

'No, I mean us bursting in.'

'We weren't the ones with a twenty-pound note dangling from our nose. I can't believe that alone was enough for him to decide to kill himself. He must have known the risk he was taking. If you ask me, it's more likely the discovery of Angela Cash's body a few feet away from his front door had something to do with it.'

I turn to Sam. 'There's an old friend of yours sitting by the side of the church.' He raises a quizzical eyebrow. 'Betty Baxter,' I say.

'Betty spends one afternoon in Haddley and there's a dead vicar in the middle of his flock. There's no such thing as coincidence, Ben.'

Sam moves from my side and begins to drift across the churchyard. Over so many years, he has perfected the impression of aimlessly wandering while actively observing every angle of a story. I watch him disappear, and then Dani walks out of the front of the church.

'It was Withers ringing the church bells?' I ask.

Dani nods. 'We have to assume his aim was to draw a crowd to witness his final act. Whatever we might think of him, it's horrible he was driven to end his life in such a desperate way.'

'Horrendous,' I reply, 'for him and his wife. He set the fire as well?'

'Looks that way. After bolting the main door, he locked himself in the belfry. The key must be somewhere on his body.'

Dani and I turn away from the front of the church. 'Why now?' I ask.

'The shame of being exposed?'

I shake my head. 'I think there's something more.'

We walk past the front of the church and stop where the path begins to turn. I look towards the wooden bench, but it stands empty.

'What makes you say that?'

I take hold of Dani's arm and we walk down the side of the church. 'Archie Grace.'

'You've found him?'

'He's hiding in an abandoned garage, under the railway arches.' I stand with Dani beside the wooden bench. 'Your dad was right,' I say. 'Bertie Baxter did expand the family business. Withers supplied the kids to ferry drugs across county lines. I need you to hear what Archie has to say.'

'Give me ten minutes,' replies Dani. 'I'll speak to Cooke and ask her to cover for me.'

CHAPTER 68

The first thing Pamela thought when the Reverend Withers hit the ground was she'd never make it back to the pie shop before closing now. Even if she did, they were sure to have sold out of beef and stilton. She did have a chicken Kiev at the back of her fridge, although she felt certain the use by date was sometime last week. She'd have to find something in her freezer.

After that, she thought how glad she was the vicar was dead.

Pamela watched Emily Withers move slowly back from her husband's body and stand by the small, wooden gate that led through to the vicarage garden. Seeing the police officer step away, Pamela walked forward. Finding herself standing directly in front of Emily, suddenly she was at a loss for words. She simply held out her hand and was surprised by the warmth with which it was received, Emily clasping it firmly between her own.

That was how the two women stood until Pamela said, 'Nobody deserves to die in such a way.'

'I'm not sure I agree,' replied Emily.

Pamela didn't feel the need to answer. She stood beside the vicar's wife and together they watched as his body was carefully lifted onto a stretcher and a white sheet placed over him.

'The church teaches us suicide is a sin,' said Emily. 'In this case, I would call it a rare act of charity.'

Pamela wasn't quite sure how to respond. 'He's with his maker now,' she replied, which she thought sounded suitably religious.

Emily tutted. 'He will answer for all of his sins.'

'I hope so,' said Pamela, quietly. She felt Emily reach again for her hand.

'Since the night of the fire,' said Emily, 'I've been hoping I might speak with you.' Pamela waited for her to continue. 'That evening, I had supper with an elderly parishioner before I came home on the bus. It was so crowded, I had to sit upstairs. From there, I noticed a woman hurriedly crossing the common. For a moment, I thought it was you, but so late in the evening, I'm sure it wasn't?'

Pamela smiled as she felt Emily squeeze her hand. 'No, it wasn't me.'

'I thought not.'

Looking past Emily, Pamela saw a figure standing at the back of the vicarage garden. His hair was longer, softening his face, and she decided it quite suited him. He'd never been the most handsome man in the world but, if she was being kind, she'd say his nose was distinguished.

'I always knew he wasn't a bad boy,' said Emily, bringing her eyes to Pamela's.

Pamela nodded before turning and walking away.

CHAPTER 69

I see Pamela Cuthbert leave through the front gates of St Stephen's. Before she can hurry down the Lower Haddley Road, I call after her.

'Mrs Cuthbert!' I say, following her out onto the roadside.

Her mind is elsewhere, and I call again. She turns sharply. Only when she recognises me do I see her face brighten.

'Pamela, please,' she says, stopping and smiling as I approach. 'We must stop meeting like this, although it's lovely to see you again,' before quickly adding, 'even though it's in such terrible circumstances. Are you working?'

It takes me a moment to understand what she's asking. 'For the website, you mean?'

'You are a reporter, aren't you?'

'Not really that kind of reporter. I write longer stories, almost like you might see on television.'

'You mean investigative,' she replies. 'I might be old, Ben, but I'm not stupid.' We laugh but I feel suitably reprimanded. I learned from Madeline how dangerous it is to ever make assumptions about anyone. 'Any sign of the missing boy?' she asks.

'You heard about that?'

'I read it on the neighbourhood app.'

'Of course,' I reply.

'He lives just across the common from you?'

'I'm hoping he might be home by tonight.'

'That would be some good news, at least. It has been quite a day,' she says.

'Did I see you at the reconstruction earlier? I think I saw you with Dani Cash.'

'You *think* you did?' she replies.

'I did see you.'

'It's a long time since she and I have spoken. It was nice to talk.'

'You still remember Dani?'

'As I said to you, I used to see her running up and down the alley behind my house.'

'Perhaps she owes you her life?' A frown creases Pamela's brow, but I press on. 'Weren't you the neighbour who helped Dani and her father escape from the house fire? If it was you, you saved their lives.'

'We all did what we could. Jack Cash did a lot for Haddley, went after the right people – people like the Baxter family.'

I wait for her to say more but she doesn't. Pamela is proving harder to pin down than the few politicians I've interviewed during my career. I change tack.

'Was that Emily Withers I saw you with just now? Do you know her well?'

'Only as the wife of the vicar,' she replies, as she glances up at the smoke still swirling above the trees of the graveyard.

'Another fire at St Stephen's. Terrible, isn't it?'

'Awful,' she agrees.

'You saw the vicar fall?'

'Like everyone, I was drawn by the ringing of the bells. He must have been deeply troubled.'

'Did you know him, too?'

She shrugs. 'He came to see me after Thomas's death. That was a long time ago.' Pamela looks at her watch. 'I really must get going, but you should call in for coffee again sometime soon. It's always nice for me to have company.'

'That would be lovely,' I reply, admitting defeat. 'No more sign of those boys, I hope?'

'Happily, not.'

'You still need to be careful.'

Pamela, who has already started moving up the Lower Haddley Road, looks back over her shoulder. 'I always am, Ben. I always am.'

CHAPTER 70

'Is that your new girlfriend?' says Sam, when I walk back towards the church. We stand together at the entrance gates.

'She lived next door to Jack Cash for over five years.'

Sam's interest perks. 'Has she got a connection?'

'She knows more about what happened on the night of the original fire than she's saying.'

Sam and I watch in silence as the ambulance carrying Reverend Withers pulls out of the churchyard.

'Written your headline yet?' I ask Sam, as it disappears down the Lower Haddley Road.

'Drug-addled vicar leaps from burning bell tower,' he replies. 'Too much?'

'A touch.'

I see Dani exit the front of the church. 'I've got to go,' I say, before taking a step closer to Sam. 'I've found Archie Grace.'

'Is he okay?'

'He's fine.'

'Where is he?'

'Hiding in a disused garage under the railway arches.'

'What did he tell you?'

'On the night of the community-centre fire, he'd been paid to find the knife and get rid of it. The heat of the fire forced him to leave without it.'

'So, somebody else did take it.'

'Definitely.'

'That leaves us with PC Cooke, or perhaps the only other person lurking around the church that night – the late Reverend Adrian Withers.'

'We know he liked to keep his most precious things hidden in the vestry,' I say.

'Leave it with me,' replies Sam, before hurrying off in the direction of the church.

CHAPTER 71

A heavy dance rhythm echoes between the buildings as Dani and I cut behind the riverside bars. Outside a deserted bar entrance, a group of teenage girls stand in a ring, giggling and passing a joint back and forth.

'Archie will tell the police all he knows,' I say to Dani, 'but I want you to hear him first – in your unofficial capacity.' Dani nods as we hurriedly make our way towards the railway arches. 'He's done some stupid things,' I continue, 'the main one being getting mixed up with Bertie Baxter. But he knows a fair bit, possibly including who stabbed Mat.'

Dani stops. We are standing behind the last of the riverside bars. The sound of breaking glass fills the air as a barman steps outside and pours a bucket of empty beer bottles into a giant green recycling bin. Although he is some distance from us, Dani waits for him to return inside.

'Ben,' she says, once she sees the barman disappear through a rear fire door, 'what's any of this got to do with Mat's stabbing?' I can hear the disbelief in her voice.

'The knife,' I reply. 'On the night of the fire, Archie was

paid to retrieve the knife. It had been hidden in the community centre since the stabbing.'

'Was Archie involved last Hallowe'en?'

'He says not and I believe him. He was paid a couple of hundred quid by Bertie Baxter, or more likely somebody who works for him, to get rid of the knife. Archie's only job was to get the knife out of the community centre and toss it in the river or bury it in the weeds.'

'Why?'

'Because if Withers got his planning permission the land would have been sold and the knife discovered. Plus, with all the noise around the reconstruction, they wanted to get rid. It wasn't worth taking the risk.'

A train rattles over the railway bridge. Dani looks at me. 'But then the fire started and Archie had to leave the knife in the community centre?'

'Until somebody else came along to collect it.'

'Could he be lying to try and save is own neck?' asks Dani. 'He is a dealer, after all.'

'He's a kid who helps funnel drugs down the pipeline, no more than that. I believe him when he says he wasn't involved in Mat's stabbing.'

We walk on. Away from the riverside bars, the path becomes dark. Streetlights work only sporadically, and we approach the garage in the gloom. On my phone, I flick on the torch. Immediately I see the garage door swinging open.

'Fuck,' I say, and run forward.

'Ben?' replies Dani, quickly following me.

'Archie's done a runner,' I say, reaching the derelict garage.

Inside, it's dark. 'I should never have left him.' I point my phone towards the deserted office.

'I'm sure we can find him,' says Dani. 'Let me call it in.'

I hesitate. I still hate the thought of the police pursuing Archie as a criminal. I want him to have a second chance. 'If you have to,' I reply, reluctantly. I turn away from the office and scan my torch around the rest of the garage.

The light falls upon the abandoned mechanic's pit.

'No!' I shout, running across the garage and standing at the edge of the pit. I jump down.

Archie is lying face down on the oil-covered floor. I turn him over and blood bubbles from his mouth. He is barely breathing.

'Call an ambulance,' I scream. When I cradle his head, my hands are covered in blood.

Ten

'The hardest thing for any parent is to see their child unhappy or unloved. That's all Jack wanted to avoid.'

TUESDAY

CHAPTER 72

It's still dark when I cross the gravel path at the front of St Stephen's. In the hope of keeping intruders out, a panel of wood has been jammed across the church door. I take three quick steps up and push the plank aside. Inside, I light my phone and in the eerie silence walk down the aisle towards the altar, before following the same path Sam and I took to the vestry on Sunday night.

The vestry door stands ajar. The top drawer of Withers's filing cabinet is open but empty. I step back out of the room and walk towards a small wooden door hidden at the back of the church, behind the altar. When I twist the heavy iron handle, the door slides silently open. I feel the cold as I follow the narrow flight of stone stairs down into the concealed crypt. Hunched beneath the main body of the church, I point my torch along the narrow passageway that leads off in the direction of the vicarage garden. There is nothing more I need to see.

I leave through the front of the church and cross into the cemetery. Autumn leaves, crisp with another early-morning frost, rustle beneath my feet. I walk towards a police cordon where PC Karen Cooke stands alone. Behind her, a small group of officers are gathered beside the gravestones of Jack and Angela Cash.

'I must ask you not to cross this line,' says Cooke, as I approach.

'Good morning, constable,' I reply, adopting a suitably hushed tone. 'I take it you're here to hold back the media hordes?'

She doesn't respond. I'm the only onlooker present.

I look past Cooke to where a lone gardener is cutting back the holly bush that surrounds the two graves. A white tarpaulin is unravelled and laid on the ground. Once it's lifted into place, the exhumation of the body hidden in Angela Cash's grave for over twenty years will begin.

When the curtain is raised, I think immediately of the white curtain swept around Archie's bed last night. The ambulance crew lifted him from the garage pit before racing him to Accident and Emergency. Dani and I rode with him, and his parents arrived at the hospital minutes later. Together, we waited. Jason and Amy clung to each other throughout the interminable hours. With the news Archie was out of danger, his mother sobbed. Her palpable relief was matched only by my own.

For much of the night, I lay awake, questioning my motives. I'd thought I was protecting Archie, convincing myself over the last few days I was helping him, trying to give him a second chance. In the depth of the night, I saw in reality I'd chosen to keep him away from the police until

I'd secured all of the information I could. I'd gambled with Archie's life.

A cool breeze blows up from the Thames and I zip up my jacket. A movement between the back of the cemetery and the embankment path catches my eye. Scrambling up from the water's edge, pushing his way through a clump of overgrown bushes, is Sam. Hidden among the trees, he finds himself the very best uninterrupted view of the exhumation. I leave PC Cooke at her cordon, cross the graveyard and climb over the rear stone wall to join Sam.

'Wouldn't be my first career choice, digging up dead bodies,' he says, slipping his phone out of his pocket to take a quick snap of the approaching gravediggers. 'Of course, you've already made a bit of a career of it.' He chuckles at his own joke.

I stand beside him and keep my voice low. 'Any joy in the vestry last night?'

'The reverend had a nice little stash ready for a couple more toots, but the top drawer of the filing cabinet had already been cleared out.'

'Somebody beat us to it?'

Sam nods as he captures another image of the gravediggers pulling on their white coveralls. 'If the knife was there, they got to it pretty quick.'

'Just as Withers did on the night of the fire,' I reply.

We watch as heavy shovels are handed to the men digging the grave. 'Whoever's hidden in there, it was a big risk for Jack Cash to bury her as his wife,' says Sam.

'Perhaps he was left with no other choice. I get the

impression Angela Cash was the kind of person people remembered. She was the wife of a senior officer. Good or bad, people were used to seeing her around. Suddenly, at some point in the run up to Christmas, she was gone.'

'Buried under the community centre.'

'That we know for definite,' I reply. 'There was only so long her disappearance could go unnoticed.'

'People would begin to ask questions.'

'And you'd think the first person to be asking questions would be Jack. Unless . . .' I raise an eyebrow at Sam.

'Unless he knew, and it was other people's questions he was trying to avoid,' he replies, finishing my thought.

For Dani's sake I'm trying to keep an open mind about Jack's involvement, but I'm finding it increasingly difficult. 'For a couple of weeks, Jack could get away with it – Angela's visiting family or friends – but, at some point, she has to come home.'

'So, he burns another woman's body at the bottom of the stairs and buries her as his wife. Job's a good 'un.' Two of the gravediggers lift a wider tarpaulin at the side of the grave, obstructing Sam's view. 'Spoil sports,' he says, and we step back towards the river. 'How's the boy doing?' he asks.

'He's going to be okay.' I messaged Sam last night while I waited at the hospital. We pass through the trees and stand together looking out across the river.

'If Withers did take the knife,' begins Sam, 'how did he get it?'

'On the night of the fire, after he'd spoken with Dani, he goes back inside the church. Watching from the back of the vestry, he sees Cooke and me leave, giving him all night to collect the knife.'

'Except, until then, anyone connected to Archie thought he had the knife,' says Sam.

'Archie messages Bertie's thugs telling them he doesn't have it, and the instruction is given to the good reverend to step in and save Bertie's neck.'

'But who has the knife now?'

'I still like Cooke for it,' I say.

'Why?' asks Sam, turning to face me.

'Yesterday evening, somebody tipped off Baxter's heavies and they went after Archie. Only you, me, Dani and Cooke knew where he was hiding.'

Sam clicks his tongue. 'You can't prove anything.'

'No,' I reply, 'not yet.'

Sam moves deeper into the woods, looking for a spot beyond the grave that might still give him a clear shot. I follow him.

'I understand the need to move the knife from the community centre, but why burn down the building?' he asks.

'That takes us back to Jack Cash,' I reply. 'If he hid Angela's body in the foundations, it seems unlikely he did it alone. Whoever set the fire wanted to destroy the evidence of what lay beneath the floor once and for all.'

CHAPTER 73

I leave Sam lurking among the trees, hoping to capture a distant image of the coffin rising from the ground. As I walk back through the graveyard, where Karen Cooke still stands sentry at her deserted cordon, I catch sight of a figure seated at the side of the church.

Dressed in a full-length, black fur coat, with her face nestled in its thick collar, is Betty Baxter. I follow the path towards her and when she hears the crunch beneath my feet, she lifts her eyes to mine.

'Ben,' she says, softly.

'Ms Baxter,' I reply. 'I'm surprised to see you back in Haddley.'

'Really? I'd be disappointed if you weren't expecting me.'

'May I?' I say, now standing beside the bench.

'Please do,' she replies, and I take a seat next to her.

'Why are you here?' I ask.

She turns to me, resting her face in her collar. 'I find this a reassuring spot for quiet contemplation.'

'A long way to come for quiet contemplation?' When I

lean back, my shoulder rests against hers. I can sense her slow and controlled breathing.

Betty turns and looks over her shoulder, towards the graveyard. 'Yesterday showed us the stupid ones always come to a sticky end.' I realise she is sitting in the same spot from where she would have witnessed Reverend Withers fall. She turns back to me. 'My sister, Charlie, was more stupid than most. You don't compete with family, ever,' she tells me, repeating a phrase she used at her home in Southwold. 'I have to admit there were times when she could be great company, amusing, even entertaining, but she was always exceptionally stupid.' She raises her face above her collar. 'My sister's been dead to me for more than two decades, but despite everything I thought it was only right I came to pay my respects.'

'You think your sister's in Angela Cash's grave?'

'I'd imagine, just like you, Ben, of that, I'm certain.'

We are silent for a moment. I wonder how much Betty suspected about her sister when we went to visit her. 'I'm sorry,' I say.

'No reason you should be but thank you.'

'Are you here alone?'

'Geoff will be sneaking around somewhere in the shadows, but I don't think I've anything to fear from you, do I? At least not in the physical sense.'

I smile. 'Did you have a chance to speak with the Reverend Withers, before his . . .'

'Demise,' she continues, elongating the word. 'What makes you think I came back to Haddley to see Withers?'

'Old friends, perhaps?'

'Never.'

'Business acquaintances?'

'The vicar shared some of the very same qualities as my sister, except he was never amusing, nor entertaining but always very, very, stupid.'

'He sent you children from church groups, or perhaps care homes, mostly boys, to ferry drugs.'

'That's a big accusation, Ben. I hope you can back it up if you ever plan on putting it in print. All I ever tried to do was give local people some small opportunities.'

'You told me every generation likes to put their stamp on a business. That's what Bertie did when he used the boys to ferry drugs across county lines. Jack Cash got close. My guess is somebody tipped you off and, much to Bertie's displeasure, you stepped in and closed the operation.'

'Like so many journalists these days, you have an enormously fertile imagination. All I ever wanted to do is run a successful business. The youngsters I employed were purely for warehouse work and the occasional building project.'

'Did that include the vicar's son?'

Betty pulls her coat close, nestling her hands inside the sleeves. 'I told you when we first met, Luke built the community centre. That's at his door.' She pauses. 'Have you spoken to him?'

'I don't know him.'

'I didn't ask if you knew him, I asked if you'd spoken to him.'

'No,' I reply. 'Have you?'

'It would appear he's not easy to find. In the past, Ben, Haddley police have drawn me and my family into crimes we didn't commit.' I raise my eyebrows and beneath her collar I think I see Betty smile. 'Or ones they couldn't prove.'

'I'm not sure that's quite the same thing.'

'Isn't it?' she replies. 'I can assure you in this case my family was not involved, unless of course you count the fact that it was my sister Jack Cash buried in his wife's grave. Luke built the community centre. I think he owes us all an explanation.' She holds my eye. 'I won't allow Angela Cash's death to be put at my family's door. I will always protect them.'

'A fifteen-year-old boy was badly beaten last night. I wonder who's protecting *him*?'

'I understand he's going to make a full recovery.'

'You have an uncanny ability to keep yourself well informed.'

'Haddley will always hold a special place in my heart,' she replies. 'I feel for his parents. I can appreciate how incredibly worried they must have been. We all want the best for our children – even me.'

'I don't doubt that,' I say. 'When Sam and I came to your home, we saw Bertie storm out of the house.'

'He still has so much to learn. Nobody likes having that pointed out to them.'

'Is he still learning?'

'Sometimes a parent needs to set stricter boundaries. From now onwards, I'll make sure to do that.'

When I get to my feet, Betty slips her hands out of her sleeves. I wonder if she's signalling for Horsfield.

'Somebody tipped you off that Jack Cash was getting close,' I say, dropping my voice. 'Now, Bertie's thugs beat up Archie Grace. Did the same person tell him where Archie was hiding?'

Betty runs her hands down the length of her coat. 'Ben, I'd hate it if you and I didn't part as friends. Jack Cash asked a lot of questions, and look where it got him – a career ended in disgrace before he drank himself to death. Turns out, in the end, he had more to hide than anyone.'

I lean forward, closer to Betty. 'A man was left paralysed in the raid on the supermarket. Archie Grace would have died last night if Dani and I hadn't found him when we did.'

'I told you, Bertie will learn.'

'But he'll be dealt with by you, not by the police.'

'As a parent you'll do anything to protect your child. What makes you think I would be any different?' Betty looks back towards the graveyard. 'I'm sure even Jack Cash convinced himself, in all he did, he was protecting his daughter.'

CHAPTER 74

When I exit Isleworth railway station, it is already mid-morning. I stop at the Ballucci coffee bar. A smooth flat white gives me a much-needed caffeine shot. I check the time on my phone and walk quickly into the nearby Primrose Park. Except for an elderly couple and their black Labrador, the park is deserted. I find a bench and am halfway through a cheese toastie when Dani arrives and sits beside me.

'Breakfast or lunch?' she asks.

'Bit of both,' I reply, my mouth still half full. 'Thought you might need a coffee.' I pass Dani a takeaway drink before reaching for my own second cup. She holds the cup between her hands, and I watch her take her first sip. 'How's Archie doing?'

'He's stable,' she says, exhaling. 'He hasn't said anything yet about what happened. His mum and dad are with him. I shouldn't be away long.' The park where I asked Dani to meet me is a five-minute walk from the hospital.

'Did you stay all night?'

She nods. 'I dozed on and off, but I couldn't really

sleep. We should have got to him sooner. If I'd come when you'd asked.'

'Dani, none of this is your fault,' I say. 'I could've taken Archie straight to the police station. If I had, he wouldn't be where he is now.'

'You were trying to help him.'

'Or did I think he'd help me be first to a good story?'

'Maybe in part, but that is your job. In everything you did, you wanted to help Archie,' she replies, before hesitating. 'You were trying to give him the second chance Nick never had.'

I drop my head and for a moment I'm silent. 'Does that make me stupid?'

'It makes you who you are,' she says, bending her head towards mine.

I lean towards her. My lips brush hers.

'No, we can't,' she whispers in my ear.

I'm quick to my feet, pacing in front of the bench. 'How did the Baxters discover where Archie was hiding?'

'You're certain it was them?' she replies, looking directly across the park. I tell Dani of my conversation with Betty. 'Then we should bring Bertie in,' she says.

'Betty would deny our conversation, Bertie would have the best lawyer and we have zero evidence.' I force down the last bite of my sandwich before tossing the empty bag into a neighbouring bin. 'You, me and Sam knew where Archie was hiding.' I say before I pause. 'And Karen Cooke.'

'Karen wanted to help.'

'Of course she did. If you want someone to share

information with you, first you need to build trust. That's how she works.'

Dani shakes her head and gets to her feet. 'I should head back inside,' she says. We begin a slow walk across the park. We watch the elderly woman throw a ball for her dog, which exhibits as little enthusiasm for the game as its owner. 'Anybody could have seen you take Archie to that garage. Or seen you leave. It's a big leap to assume someone in the force gave Bertie Baxter that information.'

I say nothing more. I feel certain the disappearance of the knife on the night of the fire and yesterday's attack on Archie are directly linked, and that Cooke is the most likely candidate, but I can see there's no point pressing it. We walk through the entrance of the West Middlesex Hospital.

'I remember my dad bringing me here when I was eleven,' says Dani. 'I had to stay in for three nights to have my appendix removed. I missed my first two weeks of secondary school. I thought I'd never get over it, never make any new friends, but a couple of weeks later it was all forgotten. Years earlier, my mum had had her appendix out on the same ward.'

I can't stop myself wondering if Angela Cash ever did have her appendix out, in the same way I still can't help wondering if anything Jack Cash told Dani is true. I press for the lift and, in silence, we wait.

When we walk onto the small ward we find Archie's parents sitting beside his bed. I wince at the sight of him. Blood still seeps from his lips; his mum, standing beside him, gently dabs his mouth. On the right side of his body his arm is broken, his shoulder dislocated and his leg in plaster, all a result of the impact from when he was tossed into the garage pit. He's been lucky. Archie is telling his parents what he told me yesterday. His voice is raspy and weak. His father listens intently, his face frozen. His mother continues to tend gently to her son. I doubt she hears all he is saying.

Pulling chairs from the opposite side of the room, Dani and I sit across the bed from Jason. Dani starts to ask Archie a series of questions. Did he know where the drugs were distributed from? Did he ever see them being packaged? Did he ever meet Bertie? After each question he shakes his head.

'What about the money you received from buyers?' asks Dani, pressing Archie for any information.

'I left it locked in a drawer in the boathouse. It was always gone by the time I returned.'

'Phone messages?'

Again, Archie shakes his head. 'Very rarely and always from an unidentifiable number.'

'And the man who did this to you. Did you recognise him?'

'It was dark, I never saw him. He came at me from behind and tossed me around as if I was a little kid. I thought I was going to die.'

'You're safe now,' says Amy, stroking her son's forehead.

I lean forward against the bed. 'What made you believe the knife was the one used in the raid on the supermarket?'

We wait for Archie to reply.

'People talk. Suddenly there was an urgency. They wanted the knife gone before the reconstruction. An instruction had been given.'

354

'Why hide it there in the first place?'

'I wasn't involved, I knew nothing about it,' replies Archie, talking now to Dani, not to me.

'We know,' I say. 'But why do you think?'

'The community centre had been abandoned for years. In the past we'd done some dealing out of there.' Archie drops his head. 'I guess they knew Reverend Withers would never question us.'

'Did he buy from you there?'

Archie nods. I look at his mother. Her eyes are closed.

Dani stands and moves to the end of the bed. She looks directly down at Archie.

'Were you part of the raid on the supermarket?'

'No, I never did anything like that, ever.' Archie looks at his dad. He's still a child.

'Was Bertie Baxter?' asks Dani.

'Nobody ever dare say for definite but yes, I think so.'

'Why?' asks Dani, raising her voice. Two nurses tending another patient on the opposite side of the ward look across in our direction. Dani drops her voice. 'Why would he get involved with a raid on a supermarket?'

'For the thrill,' replies Archie.

Dani steadies herself, resting her hand on the bed. 'Was it Bertie that stabbed the officer involved?'

There is a moment's silence and then Jason says, 'You need to answer, Archie.'

Archie looks at his father. 'All I know is they were desperate to get rid of the knife. There had to be a reason why.'

Dani moves away from the bed and walks out of the ward. I follow her.

'All so futile,' says Dani, as we stand together by the deserted nurse's station. 'He got a kick out of a badly planned raid. And in that moment he stole away so much of Mat's life.' Dani looks at me. 'And so much of mine.'

'Can you arrest Bertie?'

'We could bring him in for questioning,' replies Dani, 'but just like whoever beat up Archie, we've nothing to hold him on. His fancy solicitor would have him home within the hour.'

'We've got Archie, though. Can't he give evidence?'

'A fifteen-year-old drug-dealing kid who has never met Bertie but heard a rumour from his other drug-dealing pals that Bertie was involved in the raid,' replies Dani, painting a stark picture. 'Archie was involved in the small-scale supply of pills to school kids and cocaine for middle-class dinner parties. He never saw the scale of the operation, just his tiny piece of it. That's how they work. Is what he's telling us about the raid true? I'm sure it is but the only evidence is a knife which doesn't exist.'

'I'm beginning to understand why your dad was so obsessed with the Baxters.'

'I should have listened to him when I had the chance.'

'It's not your fault.'

Dani sighs. 'I need to go and talk to Mat.'

I watch her exit through the double doors at the end of the corridor. When I turn, I find Amy standing behind me.

'I'm sorry,' I say. 'If I'd brought him straight home . . .'

She shakes her head. 'You didn't do this, Ben. I'm just glad he's alive and we get the chance to try and start again.'

'Promise me you'll take that chance.'

'We will,' she replies.

'I'm going to head off,' I say. 'Get him home as soon as you can.'

'Ben,' says Amy, as I'm about to leave. 'You saw me at St Stephen's on Sunday evening?' I nod as Amy continues. 'I needed to pray for Archie but stepping back inside that church left me feeling physically sick.' I wait for her to tell me more. 'I stopped attending more than a year ago. Reverend Withers didn't just buy drugs from teenage boys. He was vile towards women. So many under his supposed *pastoral care* were left to physically fight off his unwanted attentions.' Amy pauses and I can see her whole body tense. 'More than a year ago, he invited me to meet with him in the vestry. He pushed me against his filing cabinet and forced his tongue down my throat. I should have said something then. He was the devil himself.'

CHAPTER 75

My train back to Haddley is quiet. I sit alone and stare out of the window at the passing rows of terraced houses. We think of our homes as a shelter from the outside world. Jason and Amy believed their home provided safety to their family until a deadly menace reached their door. My own mum thought our home would protect us. But it didn't. In everything Jack Cash did, was he really seeking to protect Dani? Perhaps he was. Even Betty Baxter has shown me how potent the love of a child can be.

Reaching Haddley railway station, my train slows and then stops. I exit quickly and take the stairs up from the platform into the main body of the station. At the touch of my phone, the ticket gates open and absent-mindedly I glance across into the station coffee shop. Occupying a small table by the window is Pamela Cuthbert. With her is a man I saw standing at the back of the vicarage garden yesterday evening. My attention caught, I stop and look directly at them. Sitting close across a small table, there is a warmth between them.

From behind me, an older man comes through the ticket gates. He makes a show of having to walk around me, grumbling under his breath as he does. I step aside and call a dutiful apology then cross to the small station newsagents, stand in the doorway and look back over the concourse towards Pamela. Her hands are wrapped tightly around her cup and she is absorbed by whatever the man is saying to her.

I meander around the small shop, casting my eyes over an assortment of newspaper headlines covering the latest government crisis. I pick up one paper and pause to read the first two paragraphs before placing it back down. Then I pick up a packet of chewing gum and scan it through the self-scan. As I tap my phone to pay, I turn towards the coffee shop again. Pamela is getting to her feet. The man does the same before stepping forward and briefly wrapping his arms around her. I decline the machine's offer of a receipt and move back to stand in the shop doorway. Pamela leaves the coffee shop alone. Her eyes are red and puffy. She doesn't see me as she hurries down the steps at the front of the station.

I look back at the man she was with. He has resumed his seat and is typing into his phone. Crossing the concourse, I enter the coffee shop and order a cappuccino. As the barista froths my milk, I look more closely at the man. His hair is long but pulled neatly back. He is clean-shaven and, viewing him close-up, I would guess he is somewhere close to forty.

I thank the barista for my coffee and walk across to the man's table.

Pulling out a chair I ask, 'May I?'

Other tables are empty, and he looks pointedly around the café. I take the seat opposite him.

'I'm about to leave, anyway,' he says, turning to reach for a rucksack hanging off the back of his chair.

'I saw you in the vicarage garden yesterday evening,' I say. He turns back to face me.

'Do I know you?' he asks, narrowing his eyes.

'My name is Ben Harper.'

He shows a flicker of recognition. 'I'm sorry,' he says. 'I've read about your family.'

It's a response I've grown accustomed to, especially in Haddley. I simply nod in acknowledgement.

'Can I ask how you're connected to St Stephen's?' I ask directly.

'Emily Withers is my mother,' is his equally direct reply.

'And Reverend Withers your father?'

'Indeed.'

It's my turn to express sympathies. His response is muted. I move on. 'Luke, can I ask why you came back to Haddley now?'

There is a scrape of his chair as he gets up to leave. 'Sorry but I have to go.' He gets to his feet and swings his rucksack over his shoulder.

'Was it anything to do with the fact that Angela Cash's body was discovered beneath the community centre, the one you built?' I ask, pressing him. 'Or with the fire that nearly killed a boy?'

'I didn't know anything about the fire,' he replies. 'The first I heard of it was from my mother.'

'But you felt it was necessary to come back?'

'Ultimately, it was easier for her and me to speak face to face.'

'Because she was afraid you might have been involved?'

'I was able to reassure her.'

'Did you speak to your father yesterday?'

'No, I didn't.' He walks away from the table and towards the exit of the café.

I call after him. 'How do you know Pamela Cuthbert?' He stops, shaking his head, and is about to deny it, before I add, 'I saw you together just now.'

He turns and walks slowly back towards me. 'Mr Harper,' he says, quietly. 'In your life, you've been through more than it's possible for most people to imagine. Because of that, I'd ask you to please let this go.'

CHAPTER 76

I walk slowly up the high street and wait at the junction with the Upper Haddley Road. I sip my coffee. When the traffic stops I cross, and my pace slows even further as I begin the climb up Haddley Hill. The noise of the heavy traffic does nothing to stop Luke Withers's parting words filling my head.

Archie is safe. The Reverend Withers's death has come as a relief to many. His son is returning to wherever he came from. I could do as Luke asks and stop now, turn around and head for home.

But I don't.

I have promised Dani I will help her find the truth behind the death of her mother. It's impossible for her to move on with her life until she does.

And I need to be able to tell the whole story of Angela Cash.

The air is cold, and I pull up the hood on my sweater. I turn into Haddley Hill Park, follow the path around the edge of the playing fields and begin to arrange the thoughts in my mind. Exactly what is it Luke Withers wants me to let go? When he told me he'd first learned of the community centre fire from his mother, I believed him. Whoever started the fire at St Stephen's ensured it had the fuel to burn, in the same way the fire at Dani's childhood home burnt so many years before. Could the same person be involved with both fires? I'm beginning to believe they could. Did Luke know of the concealment of Angela Cash's body from the very beginning? Why else would he have returned to Haddley now?

My feet drag as I walk back towards the road. At the crossing I hesitate before hitting the button. I know I must and seconds later the traffic stops. I pass in front of the stationary cars and stand before the small row of terraced houses that look out onto the park.

I knock on the front door of one, and wait. A moment later, I hear a bolt sliding back followed by the turn of a key.

'Ben,' says Pamela, opening her door to greet me. 'I wasn't expecting to see anyone else today. I was all locked up.'

'I was hoping you might be able to spare me a few minutes. Perhaps we could have that coffee?'

She smiles and steps aside. 'Of course. I'm always glad of some company.' She ushers me into her living room where her fire is beginning to burn. 'It'll soon warm up in here,' she says. 'I'm only just back in myself.'

'Been anywhere nice this morning?' I ask. It's a clumsy question and I immediately regret it.

Pamela backs out of the room. 'I need to get these shoes off. I'll be down in a minute.'

I mustn't rush her. Alone in the room, I go to the small

bookshelf and pick up the photograph of Thomas standing proudly in his dress uniform. Again I think of what Pamela said to me the first time we met. *I could have made him who-ever I wanted him to be.* I feel certain that is what Jack Cash did with Angela. I look again at the photograph of Thomas and for the first time I ask myself the question, did Pamela do the same with him?

'That's better,' she calls, coming down the stairs. 'You make yourself comfortable and I'll pop the kettle on.' I hear her run the kitchen tap. She sparks the gas on the hob and then comes back to join me in the living room. 'Can I make you a sandwich? I've some roast beef or honey roast ham and some lovely cheese I picked up at the farmer's market at the weekend. I could make yours toasted if you like?'

'No, no, I'm fine,' I reply. 'Coffee's plenty.' When I take a seat on the sofa, Pamela perches on the arm of her chair. 'I was with Dani this morning,' I say. 'We were with the missing boy, from the neighbourhood app.'

'You've found him. That's a relief.'

'He's the same boy who was trapped on the night of the community centre fire.'

'Really?' Pamela raises her eyebrows. 'But he's home now?'

'He soon will be.'

The kettle starts to whistle, and Pamela is quick to her feet. I follow her and stand in the kitchen doorway. 'He could have been killed in the fire,' I say.

'He's a lot to thank you for,' she replies, picking up the kettle and filling her teapot.

'In the same way Dani and Jack owed their lives to you?'

Pamela returns the kettle to the hob. 'You asked me that question yesterday,' she says.

'I did, but you didn't give me an answer.'

'Yes, it was me who helped them on the night of the fire. Jack always left his back gate open. When I heard him shouting I ran straight around. I'd borrowed his ladder a couple of times and knew he always left it resting along the side of the fence. I was relieved I was able to help but it was purely by being in the right place at the right time. I'm only sorry I was too late to help Angela.'

I look at Pamela. 'But I think we all know now, Angela was already dead.'

She reaches for a spoon and quickly stirs the pot. 'We'll just leave that to stew for a couple of minutes.' She busies herself in the fridge, opening a carton of milk and pouring some into a small jug. 'If you won't have lunch, I know you'll eat a couple of biscuits,' she says, reaching for her tin. 'Now, let's see what we have in here. Chocolate digestives, bourbons and some Jaffa cakes. Will that do you?'

I step forward and pick up the tray she's loaded. 'Let's go and sit down,' I say. 'You lead the way.' I follow Pamela back into the living room and she sits in her chair by the window. For a moment, she closes her eyes. 'Shall I pour?' I say, and before she has time to answer I add milk and tea to our cups. I place Pamela's on the table next to her. 'Take a couple,' I say, offering her the plate of biscuits. When she reaches for them, I see her hand shake. She picks up a chocolate digestive. 'Go on, have another.'

'Dr Jha wouldn't like that,' she says.

'I won't tell her if you don't,' I reply, smiling, as Pamela places a Jaffa cake on her saucer. I sit in the corner of the sofa closest to her. She sips on her tea and bites into a biscuit. When I lean back on the sofa, Pamela relaxes into her chair.

'Dani told me of your conversation by the river. She remembers the inside of your house,' I say.

Pamela nods. 'Surprising what remains hidden deep inside our memories. I was touched that it was Jeannie she remembered. She was so good with Dani; they spent hours playing in her bedroom. Jeannie would've been a lovely mother.' She pauses before getting to her feet and kneeling by the cupboard under the window. 'I've got some photographs of the two of them together.' She pulls out an old album and comes to sit beside me on the sofa. She flips the pages. 'Jeannie would be fourteen, perhaps fifteen,' she says, pointing to a photograph of her daughter standing beside a pushchair. 'Dani wouldn't be quite two.'

'Is that taken in your back garden?'

Pamela leans forward. 'I think it is.' She turns the pages and shows me more pictures of Dani and Jeannie together, taken in Haddley Hill Park. Her hand rests on a smiling image of her daughter. 'I still miss her every day,' she says, her voice fading to a whisper.

We sit in silence until I turn the page again.

'Look at my hair!' says Pamela, wiping a tear from her eye. 'Such a long time ago.'

I rest my hand on the page and stare at the image. Pamela has her arm wrapped around Dani, who curls into her as they sit together inside a pedal boat.

'Where was this taken?' I ask.

'Jack needed a break; we all needed to get away. It'd been such a horrible year.'

'But where was it taken?'

'A place on the North Yorkshire coast, a lovely little seaside town called Filey. I'd visited as a girl. It had hardly changed. We did have a lovely week but by then I already knew . . .' Pamela closes the album and gets to her feet. 'I'm sure Dani would remember the place. I think she and her father kept going after we . . .' She pushes the album back into the cupboard and returns to her chair.

I realise now the distant memories of her mother, which Dani clings to so desperately, are in fact memories of Pamela. I wait for her to continue. 'We went to Filey six months after Angela's death. Jack and I were close for a while, but I knew by then it couldn't last.'

'Why did you lie to me?'

'After the fire, when Dani and Jack moved away, I was forced to let them both go. Jack built his life around Dani and the police. In the end there wasn't room for me.'

'You and Jack?' I ask.

'That feels like a long time ago. Thomas I adored,' she says, looking fleetingly towards his photograph. 'And I know he felt the same way about me. I hope you find that person one day, Ben.' I half smile and wait for her to continue. 'Jack, I cared for, but never in the same way. He was a hard man to love. His job defined him, everything else came second. Except for Dani.'

'And Angela?'

'I'm sure at first there was passion between Jack and Angela, but anyone could see they were never really suited. She could never live with coming second to Jack's job. He was a workaholic, she needed constant attention. How was that ever going to work?

'By the time Angela fell pregnant with Dani, it was clear the marriage was struggling. Very quickly she'd become bored. He was out most nights and so, in the end, was she. I think they both thought having a child would make things better. It rarely does.'

'I'm sure you've heard it was Angela's body discovered beneath the community centre,' I say.

'Mr Nowak seems to be the first to know everything. He should be on the neighbourhood app. He'd be sure to get lots of followers.'

'Early this morning, the police exhumed the body buried in Angela Cash's grave. Tests are still to be done but I will be very surprised if it doesn't turn out to be the body of Charlie Baxter.'

Pamela is quiet. She looks out of the window with an expression on her face I can't read. Then she says, gently: 'Are you tightening your net around me, Ben? It feels that way.'

I pause.

'Why don't you tell me about Angela and Charlie? They did know each other, didn't they?' I say, thinking of Charlie's rant at Sam in the pub.

'It's impossible to win against drugs and dealers. However hard you try, in the end, they will destroy you. They don't play by the same rules. Charlie didn't care what drugs she sold and she didn't care who bought them. Or, what happened to people's lives afterwards.'

'She sold drugs to Angela?'

'Supposedly they were friends, but yes. Angela was an addict. Charlie supplied her; perhaps they even dealt drugs together. I don't know, or care. In that last year they were out most nights, and often days. So many times, Angela came home in a terrible state.'

'Jack tried to help her?'

'We both did.'

'But there was no way to stop her?'

'No,' says Pamela. 'Jack hated the Baxters with a passion the like I'd never seen. Because of Angela, it was all so personal to him.'

'So he did the only thing he really knew how to – went after them in court?'

Pamela nods. 'And even that didn't work. He was willing to do anything to destroy them.'

'Including burying Charlie Baxter in his wife's grave?'

'Yes,' Pamela replies, her voice barely audible.

CHAPTER 77

'I'm sure we could both do with some lunch now,' says Pamela, getting to her feet. I watch her walk slowly back into her kitchen. After a moment I follow and find her busying herself with bread from the cupboard, ham and cheese from the fridge.

'The bread's fresh this morning. I bought it while I was...' For a second she hesitates but then quickly continues '...while I was shopping on the high street. Are you sure I can't make yours toasted?'

'A regular sandwich is fine,' I reply, pulling out a chair from the small table tucked in the corner of the room. 'Why don't you tell me more about you and Jack?'

'I don't know if there ever really was a me and Jack. We were both a bit lonely, perhaps a little unhappy. It never was a great romance. We cared for each other.' Pamela stops buttering bread and turns to face me. 'We were both trying to protect that little girl.'

I think of the way Pamela looked in that picture with her arm around Dani, and nod.

'In the three months after the fire, before Jack found the house in Clapham, we lived here together. I thought we were happy but in the end, after everything that had happened, it was all too hard.'

Pamela crosses the kitchen, bringing a plate of sandwiches to the table. 'You start,' she says, 'I've made you two rounds.' She goes back to the sink and runs the tap. 'Glass of Ribena?'

'I haven't had that for years,' I reply.

'I tell Dr Jha I buy the sugar-free variety, but I don't. It doesn't taste the same at all.'

Pamela brings our drinks and sits across from me.

'You said Angela and Jack hoped having a child would save their marriage. What happened after Dani was born?' I ask.

'Angela struggled,' replies Pamela, picking up a sandwich. 'I tried to help where I could. Perhaps I shouldn't have got involved, I don't know. I said to Angela if she wanted the odd night out, I'd take care of Dani. It wasn't long before Angela fell back in with the wrong crowd.'

'Charlie Baxter?'

Pamela nods.

'That's when the drugs started up again?' I ask.

'Started? Who knows? Maybe she'd never stopped, but things got a lot worse. She tried to hide it from Jack, and stupidly I would help her. You always tell yourself you're helping, trying to do the right thing, that things will change. They don't. She soon spiralled downwards. Jack realised and got more angry with her. He thought he could make her stop if he tried hard enough. It doesn't work like that.'

When she looks across at me, Pamela's eyes are dark and tired. She's hidden the truth for too long.

'I found Angela sick in the back alleyway,' she says. 'And then I found Dani wandering alone. It wasn't just once, it was time and time again. By the end it felt like it was almost every single day.'

'Is anything Dani remembers about her mum real?'

Pamela takes a deep breath. 'Ben, the hardest thing for any parent is to see their child unhappy or unloved. That's all Jack wanted to avoid. He didn't want Angela's story to become Dani's. Turning Angela into something she wasn't made Dani happy. Is that so wrong?'

'When Dani doesn't know what's true and what's not, I think it is.'

Pamela picks up her glass. 'After Jack and I drifted apart, I think he relied even more on Angela, or the woman he'd created, to help him parent Dani. He never meant any harm.'

'Will you tell me what happened to Angela?'

'I think it's time I did,' she says softly. 'It was the first week of December. I heard her leave the house around lunchtime and almost immediately Dani wandered into my back garden. No shoes on. You should have seen her, Ben. Those soft blonde curls and bright blue eyes. She was such a lovely little girl. I brought her inside and made her macaroni cheese. That was always her favourite. I phoned Jack, told him I was happy to look after her but we both knew what state Angela would be in by the time she got home. Dani and I spent the afternoon decorating my Christmas tree. We stood it in the window and covered it in lights so everyone who walked past could see. I still do that now.'

Pamela rubs her neck before resting her hands together on the table. 'I had a key for Jack and Angela's, for emergencies. It was early evening and Dani needed a bath and her bed, so I carried her round and let myself in. She loved a bubble bath, covering her face with a Father Christmas beard.

'I heard Angela come in through the front door. That time of year she'd had no problem finding some fool to buy her drinks, drugs and whatever else she wanted. I could hear her struggling to get up the stairs. When she eventually did, she stumbled into the bathroom. She was in a terrible state and could barely stand.

'I told her to go and lie down, and once Dani was in bed I would come and help her. She started shouting, grabbing at Dani. Dani was scared, crying. When Angela grabbed for her again, Dani slipped under the water, hit her head on the side of the bath. I was terrified.'

'What did you do?' I ask.

'I managed to get Dani out of the water somehow, but Angela wouldn't leave her alone. She began clawing at Dani, screaming at me to get away from her child. Dani fell from my arms onto the bathroom floor. I needed to get Angela away from us.' Pamela's eyes are wide; she's willing me to understand.

'I pushed her. But I was angry and scared, and I pushed too hard. She fell straight back, smashing her head on the sink as she fell. As soon as she hit the floor, I knew she was dead.'

Eleven

'I don't think he ever saw it as lying. He loved you.'

WEDNESDAY

CHAPTER 78

Beneath a brilliant blue sky, I sit on a wooden bench in the middle of Haddley Hill Park and wait. Making their way towards the Grammar School are the last of the morning stragglers, their late arrival for mid-week lessons already guaranteed. Yesterday afternoon, I had no desire to push Pamela any further. She ended our conversation by asking me if she could be left alone to spend the night in her own home. It was where she felt closest to Thomas. It would've been heartless not to agree. Late in the evening I met Sam at the Cricketers, and over one too many pints, I told him what I'd learnt. We agreed Pamela posed no threat.

Early this morning, I messaged Dani asking her to meet me and when I look towards Haddley Hill Road I see her entering the park. A bright smile lights her face as she crosses towards me. She has no idea of what I'm about to tell her.

'I can't believe it's still so cold,' she says, her gloved hand touching my arm. 'Archie's had a good night and the doctor's pleased with his progress. He could be discharged by the weekend. Mat's still pushing hard for Bertie Baxter to be questioned.'

'I think he should be,' I reply.

'I'm officially on leave but I spoke to Barnsdale last night. She's going to talk to Archie today before deciding if there is a chance of building a case against Bertie.'

I nod, but I'm not really listening. I'm focused only on what I'm about to tell Dani.

'Ben?'

'Let's walk,' I say, my hands deep in my jacket pockets.

'Sure,' she replies, after a slight hesitation.

As I tell Dani everything I learned from Pamela yesterday, her eyes remain fixed on the path ahead. Listening intently, she says nothing until I reach the end of Pamela's story. When I do, we stop, and she turns to face me.

'I don't believe her, not what she says about my mum. She's lying. She's turning my mum into something she wasn't. I won't let her do that. The picture she's painting of her protecting me, of what happened to my mum being an accident, it's simply not true. That's not how it happened; I know it's not. That's not who my mum was.' She turns away from me and begins to walk quickly across the park in the direction of Pamela's home. I go after her.

'Dani, stop,' I say, reaching for her hand.

'Was she jealous of my mum and dad? Is that what drove her? She'd lost her own husband and her own child, so she killed my mum to get my dad all to herself.'

'Dani, listen to yourself. That's not who Pamela is.'

For a moment, we stand in silence. Then Dani's shoulders

drop and she exhales. Keeping hold of her hand, I lead her towards the nearest bench.

'She killed my mum?' says Dani, her voice breaking as she lowers herself onto the bench. 'Did my dad know?'

'I think you should hear it from her.'

Dani's breathing slows.

'I want us to meet with her,' I say, 'but first I need to show you something.'

Before I left Pamela's home yesterday afternoon, I asked her for the photograph of her, Dani and Jack together on Filey boating lake. 'I believe Pamela genuinely cared for you and for your dad,' I say, as I reach inside my jacket for the image and pass it to Dani. She studies it carefully and, as she does, her hand begins to shake.

'This was my mum,' she says, 'not Pamela.'

'I wish it was,' I reply.

'There must be an explanation. This must have been taken a year later.'

I shake my head. 'Filey was a place Pamela knew, not your mum. Whatever she might have done, Pamela loved you. And I'm sure she still does.'

Gripping the photograph, Dani leans against my arm. 'Everything's different to how I remember?'

'You were four years old; memories become fragmented.'

'But the woman I remember is Pamela, not my mum? My dad replaced whatever memories I had?'

'I'm sure he thought he was doing what was best.'

'Even if that meant lying to me?'

'I don't think he ever saw it as lying. He loved you.' I look

381

at Dani and in her expression I see the vulnerability Pamela must have seen all those years before. 'Are you ready to hear what Pamela has to say?'

It's some moments before her answer comes.

'Yes,' she says, in a hushed tone.

We walk towards the Haddley Hill Road. Waiting for the lights to change, Dani presses her fingers into the corners of her eyes. When we cross, she walks quickly forwards, past the front of Pamela's house before turning down the path at the end of the terrace. I follow her along the alleyway that runs behind the houses. She stops at the wall at the back of her old garden. The gate is unlocked, narrowly ajar, and she edges it further open. The small garden has been modernised with a raised wooden terrace and outdoor gas heaters.

'It means nothing to me,' she says, immediately moving back.

She takes the small number of steps from her old home to Pamela's. With her hand resting on the thumb latch of the battered wooden gate, she pauses. As she hesitates, I wonder if she will go in. Does she want to hear Pamela's truth?

'Dani?' I say.

'I'm ready,' she replies, before pushing the gate open.

Inside, the garden is small. A pathway of cracked paving stones runs across a carefully tended square of grass. A wooden patio chair is folded neatly by the backdoor.

'She'd sit on that chair while I played on the grass,' says Dani.

I look at my watch. I agreed with Pamela we would come to her home at ten o'clock. I step forward and quietly tap on the door.

CHAPTER 79

Through the mottled pane of glass in the middle of her back door, I see Pamela reach up for the bolt before turning the key.

'Right on time,' she says, opening the door. Holding her hands tightly together, she moves to one side.

When Dani walks past her, both drop their heads. Dani keeps moving, walking straight through into the living room. I step inside and smile softly at Pamela.

'I've already got the kettle on,' she says, as she closes the door behind me.

'That'd be nice,' I reply.

'I've cake as well.'

'Maybe not today.' I gently touch her hand before reaching into my jacket pocket for the Filey photograph. I carefully place it on Pamela's kitchen table. 'I'll go and see how Dani's doing.'

I stand in the living-room doorway. Dani has her back to me as she stares out of the front window. I drop my jacket on the sofa before crossing towards her.

'We need to listen to her. She's the one person who can help us understand,' I say. Dani doesn't respond and keeps her eyes locked on the road. 'You will get through this. I promise.' I step back. 'I should go and help with the tea.'

Pamela is busy loading her tray when I enter the kitchen. 'I've been up since five,' she says. 'I couldn't sleep so I came downstairs and got out my best china.' She stops what she's doing and looks towards me. 'I don't know why, it's not even very expensive.' She quickly turns away, touching her eye. 'Stupid, really.'

'Not at all,' I reply, wanting to find some way to reassure her. 'I think it's lovely.'

She looks over her shoulder and smiles. 'Thank you,' she says.

'Shall we go and sit down?' I ask, moving forward and picking up the tray.

I follow Pamela into the living room. After placing the tray on the small coffee table, I sit beside her on the sofa. While she adds milk to our cups and pours the tea, Dani continues to stand and stare out of the window.

'Are you both warm enough?' asks Pamela, breaking the silence. 'I put the heating on early so hopefully it's warmed through by now, but I can turn it up a notch if you're feeling chilly.'

'I'm sure we're fine,' I reply, taking a cup from Pamela. I place it on the small table nearest Dani.

Suddenly, Dani turns and faces Pamela directly. 'So, I'm listening,' she says, 'but I don't want to hear your pack of lies about my mum.'

Pamela responds to Dani's hostile tone by sitting bolt upright. Her eyes wide, she looks to me, but Dani continues.

'Tell me the truth, and after that you'll be dealt with by the police.'

I move towards Dani. 'We should let Pamela tell us what happened in her own words. When we're finished, she knows she will have to be interviewed at the station but right now this is your chance to hear what happened,' I say.

Dani slowly sits. I return to my seat and Pamela hands me my tea. 'Can you tell us what happened after Angela hit her head?'

'Nobody ever meant to hurt Angela, nobody,' says Pamela, speaking first to me. 'It was the last thing any of us ever wanted, of course it was. I wanted to help her. Both Jack and I did.' She turns to Dani, but Dani immediately looks away. 'We'd tried so hard for so long, but your mum found everything so difficult. Somehow, in his mind, your dad had shaped the perfect family, with Angela as a doting mother.'

Dani glances towards Pamela but says nothing.

'He meant no harm. He only ever wanted the very best for you,' Pamela continues. 'Your dad wasn't the easiest person in the world to love. He could be a grumpy sod and his job ate away at him, but he was a good man.' When Dani turns away, back towards the window, Pamela reaches out her hand. 'I would have given anything for it not to have happened the way it did, I would have, Dani. I would have given my life for none of this to have ever happened.'

Pamela's eyes glisten with tears. She takes a sip of her drink followed by a deep breath.

'You were going to tell us what happened after Angela hit her head,' I say.

Pamela sets the cup back on the saucer, the china rattling in her shaking hands. 'I knew she was dead. Dani was screaming,' she says to me, before looking back at Dani. 'You were scared, of course you were. I wrapped you in a towel, scooped you up as quickly as I could and carried you out into your bedroom. I needed to settle you first, so I surrounded you with all of your favourite toys and, once you were calm, I called Jack. He said he was coming straight home. I went back into the bathroom. Your mum wasn't breathing. I promise you there was nothing I could do. I only wish there had been.'

'What happened when my dad came home?' asks Dani, still looking towards Haddley Hill Park.

'He could see it'd all been a terrible accident. I'd been trying to protect you.'

'Why the cover-up? Why not tell the truth?'

Pamela takes a moment to finish her drink. She passes me the empty cup. 'Both your dad and I knew what any post-mortem on Angela would reveal. Beside her head injuries, her system would have been full of who knows what. Jack had been so outspoken against drugs and well, here was his wife . . .' Pamela pauses. 'We were scared his whole career might be at risk.'

'And of course, covering up her death would avoid any awkward questions about you and my dad, or about how hard you'd pushed my mum.'

Pamela leans forward. 'Your dad and I had been close for a few months, perhaps a year. But he wanted to help your mum. Did we panic? Yes, of course we did, but in that moment we agreed it was the right thing to do. Jack knew the community centre was under construction. We needed to get the body out of the house and hiding it in the foundations seemed the perfect solution. We waited until three in the morning and then took the body over in the back of Jack's car.'

'You weren't worried it would be discovered?' I ask. 'If not then, in the weeks following?'

Pamela glances towards me. 'We were careful with exactly where we hid the body.'

'What date was this?' asks Dani.

'December the second. I'll never forget it.'

'What happened in the days that followed?' I say.

'Hiding the body bought us time but we knew at some point people would start asking questions. Angela had disappeared before, sometimes for days at a time, but she always came back. This time she wasn't coming back. We knew Christmas was around the corner and people would want to know where she was, but then we had a piece of luck.'

'Luck?' says Dani.

'We'd never planned it but suddenly we'd been thrown together into a funny little family – you, me and your dad. We still wanted you to enjoy Christmas, so we booked the panto-mime in Richmond – *Peter Pan*. You screamed so loud at the crocodile I thought you were going to burst. We queued for ice creams at the interval and that was when your dad received a callout. There'd been an incident at a bar on Haddley High Street – a fight, a drug-fuelled fight. A young man had been stabbed – a child really, fifteen years old. He survived, but each time Jack saw the effect of drugs, it ate away at him a little bit more.' Pamela stops and wearily rests her face on her hand. 'After talking to witnesses, your dad walked out into the back alley. That's where the deals were done. The alley was deserted but slumped behind an industrial bin was a woman, a needle sticking out of her arm. Her face was blue and when Jack looked closely, he saw it was Charlie Baxter. She was dead.

'That's when he came up with the idea of the fire.'

CHAPTER 80

Pamela pushes herself up from the corner of the sofa. She crosses the room and perches on the arm of Dani's chair. 'I know it sounds cruel to say but Charlie Baxter's body was like a gift from God. It gave us a way out.' Pamela takes hold of Dani's hand. 'Burying her in your mum's grave haunted your dad for the rest of his life, but we knew a funeral would give us a chance to draw a line. We needed your mum's death to become official.'

'What happened on Christmas Day?' asks Dani.

'It almost sounds silly saying it, but we spent Christmas Eve at my house wrapping presents.' Pamela winces, rubbing her leg. 'My knees don't get any younger,' she says, returning to sit beside me on the sofa. 'Your dad and I had both splashed out, wanting to make it a special day. We'd ended up with so many gifts, it was nearly midnight by the time we were done. After that your dad and I had a drink together.' Pamela pauses. 'I'll never forget seeing your face on Christmas morning.'

'My red scooter,' says Dani.

'With a giant pink bow,' replies Pamela. 'You were so excited. We all shared a lovely breakfast and then I got lunch on the go. We knew it was a risk having your presents at mine, but your dad was desperate for you to keep them. He felt if anybody ever asked why they were there he could somehow explain it away, but nobody ever did.' Pamela leans forward and pours herself a half cup of tea. She takes a drink before continuing. 'We had our turkey early in the afternoon. Just the three of us; hats and crackers, a whistle in yours. After lunch we all went out into the park. You did love that scooter. Your dad didn't stay long. I knew what he was doing. He'd left the body hidden inside the bin. I never went back inside your house again.' Pamela pauses, her head in her hands.

'Keep going, please,' says Dani.

'It was almost dark by the time you and I went back inside, back inside my house. Jack came in about an hour later. I could tell he was nervous; we both were but we tried to keep everything as normal as possible. We gave you a bath, your dad read you one of your Christmas storybooks and then we put you to bed in Jeannie's room. Your dad and I watched some television and a little bit after midnight, he went down the alley back to your house. We'd already agreed an exact timeline of events. At five past two I was to call the fire brigade and then head straight into your back garden.'

'Timing was everything?' I say.

Pamela nods. 'We couldn't risk the fire spreading. Even then, when I stepped into the garden, I could feel the intensity of the heat. It was terrifying. I lifted the ladder, and Jack was already at the window. He climbed down carrying your duvet.' Dani furrows her brow and Pamela explains. 'We needed it to look like you'd been in the house and for the duvet to smell of smoke. From the bottom of the ladder, he ran into my house, raced up the stairs and wrapped you in the duvet. You were never at any risk. He carried you out through the back door and together we ran around to the front of the house. Two minutes later the fire engines arrived, the police not long after. Jack dealt with everything. I was simply the friendly neighbour. Three days later the body was released for burial. We knew then it was all over. In the weeks which followed, you and your dad stayed with me. We were happy in each other's company, but I knew it couldn't last. Your dad needed to get away from here. The trip to Filey was our farewell.'

My heart breaks for Dani. All those trips with her Dad to commemorate a family holiday that never happened, not in the way she remembered.

'Did you love him?' asks Dani, eventually.

Pamela smiles. 'You were five years old by the time you left Haddley. The day you moved to Clapham, you sat at my kitchen table and cried. You gave me the biggest hug when you left and waved frantically as you and your dad pulled away. After that, I sat here in the living room and sobbed. I knew it was you I'd miss. Occasionally, I'd pop over to see you, but once your dad and I were living three miles apart it might as well have been three hundred.'

Sitting alongside her, I turn to face Pamela. 'When Jack planned the fire, he knew he had to keep it fuelled to ensure the body burnt?'

'There were so many empty boxes, plus a dried-out Christmas tree, and I doubt the sofa was overly flame resistant. Jack added some turpentine and the fire raced away.'

'And you made sure you did the same at the community centre?'

'He taught me well. Is that how you knew?'

'It caught my attention. Even though the building had been empty for so long, the fire was still well fuelled.'

'If I'd known somebody was inside, I'd never have set the fire. You know that don't you, Ben?'

'I know,' I reply. 'You'd seen the planning application?'

'When I saw Jack, in the days before he died, he said I only had to worry if the community centre was ever pulled down. Then a few weeks ago, I read about it in the local paper. With all the dry weather, I had to take my chance. You'd have laughed at me dragging all the chairs into the middle of the room. I ordered turpentine from an art shop. It came in the post.'

'Quite simple,' I say.

Pamela shrugs her shoulders. 'It would have been if it had worked. The fire was meant to destroy the whole building and the remains of Angela's body with it. I didn't reckon on you, Ben,' she adds with a smile.

Dani turns slowly back to face Pamela. 'I should call for a car now,' she says, softly. 'You might want to think about a solicitor.'

When Dani walks across the room, Pamela holds out her hand. Dani stops. Closing her eyes, she gently squeezes Pamela's fingers before walking into the hall.

'Can I ask you one more question?' I say, as Pamela and I sit together on the sofa.

'Of course.'

'At the railway station yesterday, I saw you with Luke Withers. To me, you looked quite close.'

Pamela rests her hands in her lap. 'He was the boy, Ben, the older boy who Jeannie became involved with. It was all such a long time ago but over these years I've come to understand he did care for her. I should accept that.' I reach across and hug Pamela. She wraps her arms around me. We can both hear Dani on the phone to Haddley police.

'Thank you,' whispers Pamela. She leans back and looks at me. 'You're a good man, Ben.'

Slowly she gets to her feet and crosses to the cupboard under the window. She kneels before pulling out Thomas's flag. When she closes the cupboard door, I go and help her back to her feet.

'I am getting old,' she says.

She drops her head, and inhaling deeply, sinks her face into the flag. Then, she clutches it to her breast before holding it out in front of her. 'I'd like you to take this.'

She hands me the flag, and I take it uneasily, unsure why she is offering it to me.

'Are you sure?' I ask.

'I couldn't be more certain.'

And suddenly, I understand.

CHAPTER 81

I race down Haddley Hill, dodge through the traffic on the Upper Haddley Road and when I enter the railway station, I'm running. The information board tells me my train is pulling into platform one. I tap my phone, sprint through the ticket barriers, and charge down the stairs. The train doors are about to close when I jump on board a deserted rear carriage.

Catching my breath, I sit in a block of four seats and avoid the need to have my knees tucked beneath my chin. Carefully I place Thomas's wrapped flag on the seat beside me. I feel for my earphones and eventually find them tucked away in my inside jacket pocket. I flip them open, and wait for them to connect with my phone before I call Sam. His answer is instant. He listens quietly as I recount the conversation Dani and I shared with Pamela.

'Dani's called Barnsdale,' I conclude, 'and she's taking Pamela in for questioning this afternoon. There's nothing more I can do for Pamela right now.'

'Did she say anything this morning to change your mind?'

'Nothing,' I reply, 'in fact I'm more certain than ever. Pamela Cuthbert did not kill Angela Cash.'

Last night, when Sam and I met at the Cricketers, we replayed all that Pamela had said to me. We both agreed her confession didn't ring true.

I pushed too hard.

She fell straight back.

As soon as she hit the floor, I knew she was dead.

Tucked away in Sam's favourite corner of the pub, we reread the police forensic report.

A series of significant blows to the back of the victim's head; or the victim's head was repeatedly hit against a hard surface.

A single blow against a bathroom basin could not have inflicted such damage.

'What's your plan now?' asks Sam, as my train slows on its approach to Waterloo station.

'There's a train from King's Cross leaving at one. I should be in York by three and then I can get a cab out to the North Yorkshire Moors. Any joy in finding an exact address?' I ask.

'Not an easy one to track down,' replies Sam, 'but Maddy says she'll have it within the hour. Her tentacles reach a lot further than mine.'

'A lot further than most,' I reply, laughing.

I step off the train at Waterloo and promise Sam I'll call him back once I'm on the train to York. I walk quickly along the platform before following the escalator down to the Underground. It's approaching lunchtime and the trains are relatively quiet, so I easily find a seat. My journey beneath the capital city is less than fifteen minutes but as the carriage rattles from side to side, I close my eyes and replay the conversation I had with Pamela this morning. I feel certain she told us the truth about Charlie Baxter and the fire but, given the inconsistencies in her confession, I struggle to believe it was her who hid the body with Jack.

We were careful with exactly where we hid the body, was what she said when I questioned her. To me, her answer felt vague and too practised.

I'm certain somebody else was involved.

My Tube train comes to an abrupt stop at King's Cross Station. I walk up the escalator and at a sandwich shop on the main concourse grab a takeaway. Once on board my train, I again place Thomas's flag carefully beside me. As the train leaves the station and begins its journey north, I flick on my phone. I write an apologetic note to the podcast producers, requesting a couple more days' grace on the delivery of my final script. I promise them this will be the last delay.

The train starts to pick up speed. My phone buzzes with a message from Sam. He tells me he's arranged a last-minute lunch date with Mrs Wasnesky but ends his message with an address in the village of Cropton, on the edge of the North Yorkshire Moors National Park.

It is the home of Luke Withers.

CHAPTER 82

My taxi driver stops directly in front of the New Inn. It is the only pub in Cropton. I hand the driver cash before stepping out into the cold. The map on my phone tells me I'm a ten-minute walk from Luke's home but I want to use the last of the fading daylight to wind my way through the village. Stone cottages with tended gardens line the narrow roads of what I already know, after reading on the train, is a village of little more than three hundred inhabitants. There are no shops, and the village feels like the perfect place to retire.

Or to hide away from the world.

Off the main street is a small road identified as *unsuitable for large vehicles*. I walk up the track, passing homes built more than a century ago. Beyond the cottages, at the end of the track and standing alone, is a neat, modern bungalow. All the lights at the front of the home are lit, while a lantern brightly illuminates the bungalow's dark blue front door. It's as if I'm expected.

I stand in the garden at the front of the house and look out across the vast moorland. The scenery is striking, and I'd forgotten the sense of calm open countryside brings. I follow the path to the front of the house and gently knock on the door. Darkness is descending, with a sharp chill creeping across the hills. I shiver as I wait. When the door is opened, I immediately feel the warmth from within.

'I guess I knew when I asked you to let this go, I was being unrealistic.'

'Hello Luke,' I reply. 'I'm only here to help Pamela, if I can.'

He steps aside. 'You'd better come in.'

I follow Luke into a small living room. An open log fire is burning and, as I sit on the sofa, he pulls the heavy curtains closed across the front window.

'The winter battle with the elements has begun,' he says.

'It must be a beautiful place to live,' I reply, 'but I'm guessing everything comes at a price. It really does feel a long way from anywhere.'

'Suits me on both counts, weather and location,' he replies, sitting on a rug-covered rocking-chair that neighbours the fire. 'I like the isolation.'

In the warmth of the fire, I slip off my jacket and put it on the seat beside me. I rest Thomas's flag on top of it. 'How long have you lived in Cropton?' I ask.

'From the moment I left Haddley,' he replies, 'over twenty years ago. At first all I could afford to do was rent a couple of rooms, but that improved over time, and I built this place about a decade ago. It took me two years to complete.'

'You did a great job. My guess is you could live here for years and pretty much never see a soul.'

He stares at me across the room. 'I'm not going to waste your time,' he says. 'I spoke with Pamela last night.'

'Are you in regular contact with her?'

'Only when it's needed,' he replies. 'Thank you for letting her spend last night at home. That meant a lot to her.'

'You know I met with her again this morning?'

'Yes – along with Jack's daughter?'

I nod. 'I presume you know what Pamela planned to say?'

'I do.'

'I struggle with the fact it was you building the community centre, you on site day after day, and for most of the time you alone. For a body to be successfully hidden, you'd have to have been involved.'

'When I spoke to Pamela last night, she insisted on sticking to the story she'd agreed with Jack. It was the story they'd planned for her to tell if the body was ever discovered.' Luke reaches across to a basket by the fire and throws a small log onto the flames. 'In truth, Jack and I hid the body together.'

'A secret you, Pamela and Jack were all committed to keeping. But where does your mother fit in?'

Luke narrows his eyes as sparks hiss in the fireplace.

'She never knew about the body,' he replies. 'When I originally left Haddley, I left very suddenly.'

'What happened?'

'It was a Sunday morning, I was tidying up on site, finishing the last bit of decorating. Everyone else was in church when one of Betty Baxter's heavies appeared, persuading me to sell pills for her in the pub at the top of Haddley Hill.

There was a few quid in it for me and I needed the money, so I thought why not. I should never have agreed. Like most kids, I'd smoked a bit of dope but dealing pills wasn't me. I was a bloody disaster. The landlord threw me out and threatened to call the police. I did a runner from the pub, but my mum found the pills in the pockets of my jeans. Stupid of me, really. I had a blazing row with the reverend and left Haddley for good.'

'What about Angela's body?'

'By then, it was already done. The community centre was built. Ironically, building it I'd been the happiest I'd ever been. I knew that was what I wanted to do in life but to do it as far away from Haddley as possible.'

'What changed with your mum to make you go back this week?'

'I'd only seen her twice since I left. That was tough, for us both, but if I was going to have my own life it had to be disconnected from Haddley. With the discovery of the body, she became terrified that I'd been involved. I needed to stop her contacting me.'

'You told her the truth?'

'I had to. In the end it was simpler if she knew.' Luke gets to his feet. 'You've come a long way. Can I offer you a drink?'

I hold up my hands. 'I'm fine, thanks.'

'You don't mind if I do?' He crosses the room to a small drinks trolley and pours himself a generous shot of whisky.

'Your mother told your father?'

'I argued with her on the embankment path. She'd made me a promise to tell no one but she was so angry.' Luke returns to his seat by the fire. 'She needed him to know about all of the pain he'd caused.' He sips on his drink.

I ask him another question. 'Did you tell her everything?'

'What's everything?' he replies, answering my question with a question.

'Pamela Cuthbert didn't kill Angela Cash,' I say. Luke rolls his glass between the palms of his hands. When he stares into the fire, I can see the flames dancing in his eyes. 'I saw the state of her shattered skull,' I continue. 'A single blow on a bathroom sink didn't kill Angela. You and I both know that.'

He drinks again from his glass but, as he does, I hear the living-room door slowly creak open behind me.

I turn my head.

For a moment, all I can do is stare. A waif-like figure stands in the doorway.

'Hello, Ben,' the figure says.

'Hello, Jeannie,' I reply.

CHAPTER 83

Luke stands beside Jeannie and offers her his arm. Leaning heavily on him for support, it takes all her effort to move towards the sofa.

'You shouldn't be out of bed,' he says. 'You need to rest.'

'It's time,' she replies, in a quiet but resolute voice.

I reach for my jacket and move the bag containing Thomas's flag. I stand at the side of the sofa.

'Please, sit,' says Jeannie, as she and Luke edge forward. Holding onto his arm, she slowly lowers herself onto the sofa. When asked again, I resume my seat beside her.

From a wicker basket beside the fireplace, Luke pulls a thick rug, which he carefully lays across Jeannie's lap. 'I'll get you a lighter blanket for your shoulders,' he says to her.

'I'm fine, I promise,' she replies, but Luke is already disappearing out of the room. 'Twenty-three years and not on one single day has he ever stopped looking out for me.' Her voice remains strong even when her body appears to be failing her. When Luke returns, he carefully wraps the blanket around her shoulders. He stands beside her, and she reaches up for his hand. 'That's perfect,' she says. Luke quietly steps back and returns to his seat by the fire. 'Twice I've been in remission over the past five years but this time the bloody thing's got me,' she continues, turning to me. 'I try and tell myself I've been lucky to enjoy these last few years, but I don't really believe that. Cancer's a fucker.' She smiles and it's impossible not to respond in the same way.

I look at Luke. 'Yesterday, when you met Pamela at the station?'

'He told her I was dying,' replies Jeannie.

Luke sips from his drink. 'At any age, that's an impossible thing for a parent to hear,' he says. 'We'd all have done anything for it to be different, for Pamela and Jeannie to be together, but it's never been possible.'

'You haven't seen her since you were a teenager?' I ask Jeannie.

'We had to break all of our ties, every last one of them,' she replies. 'I hated it but it was the only thing we could do.'

'That was the plan you and Jack Cash came up with?'

She glances fleetingly towards Luke before replying. 'It was what the four of us agreed and Jack put into place. We're forever grateful to him.'

'The first time I met your mum,' I say, 'she spoke with what I thought was such a painful honesty. She told me how you spiralled downwards into a world of addiction.' Jeannie listens to me intently. 'And then when I spoke to her yesterday, she used that same phrase about Angela – how she'd spiralled downwards. When she first spoke to me about you, was that simply part of her prepared script?'

'Mum was worried about me. I'd put off going to university,' she replies. 'She thought drugs and boys were to blame but Luke and I were kids messing about, nothing worse than that. Angela went to a very dark place.'

'Tell me about Angela,' I say to Jeannie. Her breathing is laboured, her skin pallid. I can see she doesn't have very long to live. 'I know your mum didn't kill her.'

Luke moves to stand but Jeannie lifts only her fingers on one hand and he lowers himself back in his seat.

'Everything my mum told you is true, except it was me giving Dani her bath on the night Angela died. Dani was a sweet little girl. I enjoyed spending time with her.' Jeannie stops and looks across at Luke. For the first time, his eyes turn away from her and he gazes back into the open fire. 'I'd spent the afternoon with her, and Jack had asked me to babysit until he got home. Mum and I had argued, she'd tried to forbid me seeing Luke so, of course, I took the chance to invite him over.

'It was just us and Dani in the house. We needed milk for her bedtime but there was nothing in the fridge.' Jeannie brings her eyes slowly back to mine. 'Luke said he'd pop down to the mini market while I ran Dani's bath. It was her favourite time of day, splashing about in her bubbles. I remember there was a plastic frog, stuck on the wall at the side of the bath. When you poured water into the top of its head, its mouth opened and closed. It made Dani laugh every time.'

Jeannie pauses, searching through her fading memory. 'I was kneeling by the side of the bath, about to shampoo Dani's hair. I heard the door open downstairs and of course,

I thought it was Luke back with the milk. I think I even called out how quick he'd been.

'There was banging on the stairs and the next thing I knew, Angela fell through the bathroom door. She was wasted. I don't think I'd ever seen her so bad; shouting, screaming, I don't remember what. Dani started crying so I scooped her out of the bath and wrapped her in her towel. I can still feel her clinging to me now.' Jeannie stops.

'Are you okay to go on?' I ask.

She nods. 'I dashed out of the bathroom and quickly carried Dani through into her bedroom. Angela was still screaming, so I closed Dani in her room and went back into the bathroom. As soon as I walked in, Angela was in my face, shouting that I was trying to steal her child. She yelled over and over that I would never take her baby, that I would never take Dani away from her.

'I tried to calm her. I told her I didn't want to take Dani away, that I was there to help. She didn't hear anything I said. She kept bawling at me until finally she lunged forward. I turned away but she grabbed hold of my hair and pulled me back.

'We both fell to the floor. I can remember a blinding pain in the back of my head. I tried to get up but Angela was on top of me, pinning me down. I could taste the alcohol on her breath. I was terrified. She hit me again, but then dropped down, pressing her face against mine.

'*Are you stealing my child because you'll never have one of your own?* She spat on my face and then said with real venom, *You disgust me. You're sleeping with your own brother.*'

CHAPTER 84

The crackle of burning wood is the only sound in the room. Jeannie looks towards Luke, but his gaze is trapped in the flames of the fire. She slowly pulls the blanket around her shoulders and I wait for her to continue. She turns back towards me.

'Angela began laughing hysterically, like a woman possessed. She screamed at me: *Didn't I know Luke and I had the same father? Didn't I know Reverend Withers was my father? Didn't I know I was sleeping with my brother?*

'I snapped. I flipped her over and pinned her to the floor. All I could hear was her callous laugh, taunting me. An unrelenting noise, until I grabbed hold of her head. And hit it against the floor. Over and over and over. And then there was silence.'

Luke moves away from the fire and comes to sit on the arm of the sofa, beside Jeannie. 'Less than five minutes later, I was back in the house,' he says. 'We called Pamela and she spoke to Jack. That night she told us the truth – Adrian Withers is Jeannie's biological father, not Thomas.

'Jack and I hatched the plan to hide Angela's body at the community centre. We moved it that night. Jeannie left Haddley early the following morning. I stayed on a couple of weeks to finish the building, before leaving under the guise of a blazing row with my father – although that wasn't difficult to create.'

'You never told him?' I ask.

'I hated going back to live with him, even if it was only for a couple of weeks, but we knew the only safe way out was for us to completely disappear. Confronting him directly – however much I despised him – would have put us at greater risk.'

'How did you convince Jack to go along with the plan?'

'He cared for Pamela and hated what had happened to her family, and his. I think he rationalised it by blaming it on the drugs and the dealers he'd spent a lifetime pursuing.'

'The Baxter family?'

'We never spoke of them that night, but yes.'

Both Luke and Jeannie look towards me. I see the years of sorrow in their eyes. I realise what they are asking me. They want me to keep their secret.

'In all of the years since, I've never been back to Haddley, not once. Luke and I stayed close, and I moved in here five years ago when my cancer struck,' says Jeannie. 'I haven't seen my mother in more than twenty years.'

'I'm sure you've both suffered,' I reply.

'We have.'

'But however you justify it, and whatever you might have thought of Angela, you killed a woman.'

'I did and if there is a heaven, then I'll be judged. But I have paid.' I look at Jeannie. She is dying. I doubt she will live longer than two or three weeks. I can't help but think of what Pamela would want me to do. 'I've been lucky to spend so many years with Luke,' says Jeannie, 'but I lost my home and lost all connection with my mother. I don't want her to suffer any more.' She looks up at Luke and then turns back to me. 'When I'm gone, the truth must be told.'

I don't say anything. Pamela confessed to the killing with the sole aim of protecting her daughter. Who am I to undo that desire? I doubt she would have acted any differently if Jeannie's condition gave her two months, two years or even longer to live. If I were to act now, I know it would be against Pamela's wishes.

I open the bag resting on my knees and reach inside. I put the empty bag on the floor and hold the neatly folded flag in my hands. Jeannie's breath quickens and when I stand before her she touches a tear from her eye.

I place the flag in her hands, and she clutches it to her face.

Unable to say anything more, I leave the room. As I do, I hear Jeannie quietly whisper, 'Thank you.'

Alone, I stand in the small hallway at the front of Luke and Jeannie's home. Jeannie killed a woman. Luke, Pamela and Jack helped her cover it up.

As journalists, we all make choices.

The words Sam spoke to me in Southwold rattle around my mind.

I can wait to tell the truth. As I've learned in life, evil comes in many forms. Good people do bad things.

The door to the living room opens behind me. Luke crosses to the front door of his home and, together, we step outside.

'I'm sorry for all you've suffered,' I say, 'you and both of your families. You'll be relieved to know the police have concluded your father's death was suicide.'

He meets my gaze. 'That will provide my mother with at least some comfort.'

'I'm sure it will,' I reply. 'I can't begin to imagine how distraught she was when you told her the truth. Separated from you for so many years, the loss and humiliation caused by your father, the intolerable pain he inflicted on so many others.'

A howling wind blows across the moors. Luke walks slowly across his garden. 'After we'd argued on the embankment path—' he begins.

'I don't need you to tell me any more. Your father was in the bell tower. Perhaps his decision was already made. Maybe his conscience finally drove him to it, or equally, his fear of being caught, but it was your mother who set the fire?'

Luke closes his eyes. 'She locked the doors ...' He swallows hard.

'And then left the church through the crypt,' I say.

I hold Luke's shoulder before turning and walking away across his carefully maintained garden.

It's a secret I will never share.

Good people do bad things.

TUESDAY

CHAPTER 85

Six days later, I walk through airport-style security at the entrance to Silvermeadow Prison. I raise my arms and a security officer pats me down. I'm allowed to move forward but must wait for the inner door to be unlocked before stepping into the vast visitor centre. Row upon row of tables and chairs fill the room, while a low hum of hushed chatter hangs in the air.

Pamela is already seated at a table neighbouring the tea bar. I've been told I'm allowed to briefly hug the prisoner I'm visiting, both on arrival and departure. She stands and I wrap my arms tightly around her. I say nothing but as I hold her close she whispers, 'I'm doing just fine.'

The day after I saw her daughter, I made the appointment to visit Pamela. After confessing to killing Angela Cash and concealing her body, Pamela is now held on remand awaiting her court appearance. My aim is to help secure her release long before that day arrives.

We sit. Immediately, she says, 'Tell me about Jeannie.'

I look at Pamela. Her eyes are wide, still somehow full

of hope. She is desperate to hear whatever news I bring. 'She's loved,' I say. 'And cared for, and as comfortable as she can be.'

She briefly closes her eyes. Almost imperceptibly, she slowly rocks her body backwards and forwards. 'That's all I can ask for. You gave her her father's flag?'

I fleetingly touch her hand. 'I did.'

She smiles. 'They can be together now.'

A woman walks past our table collecting empty teacups, her trolley rattling as she pushes it forward. 'Luke will speak to the police as soon as Jeannie . . .'

'I don't want you to worry about me, Ben,' Pamela replies. 'I'd stay in here for ever if it meant I could give Jeannie just one more day. I'd give anything to keep her alive, to hold her for a single fleeting moment.' Pamela pauses. 'You noticed I could never say she was dead?'

'I did,' I reply, thinking back to our first meeting. 'In the plan you agreed with Jack, you were meant to say she was?'

Pamela nods. 'It was the only thing I couldn't do. I was terrified if I said it, it would become true. After she left, I really did leave a downstairs light on each night for over two years. Stupid really. She wasn't dead but I knew she was never coming back.'

'Even Dani remembered her as dying.'

'Just as Jack had told her, like he did with so many things. He didn't want her mother's life to cast a shadow over hers, so he made Angela into something she wasn't. He was only trying to protect Dani, to keep her safe from the past.'

'Something you'd already done with Jeannie,' I say.

412

Pamela lowers her head in response before I continue. 'The very first afternoon we met, it struck me when you said you could have made Thomas into anything you wanted him to be. You told me you didn't need to because he was a genuine hero but, in reality, that's exactly what you did. You made him Jeannie's father.'

'One day you'll learn you'll do anything to keep your own child safe.' Pamela rests her hands on the table and lifts her head. 'In over twenty years, not a single day has passed without me thinking of Jeannie, imagining what she was doing. Can you believe that? Every day, for over twenty years. I loved watching the children walk past my window. I never believed that little girl was Jeannie, and I probably sound a bit like a stupid old woman, but I really loved her. After I'd set the fire at the community centre, all I could think about was Jeannie, and little Jeannie. I couldn't bear the thought of something being wrong at home. I wanted to take care of her.' Pamela's eyes fill with tears. 'I'd love a cup of tea,' she says, a smile again lifting her face.

The volunteer at the tea bar pours our drinks and I add a splash of milk to Pamela's tea. I pick up two bars of chocolate and tap my phone to pay.

'Lovely,' says Pamela, as I return to our table. 'I do miss something sweet in the afternoon. Dr Jha will be back next month. I wonder if she'll come and visit me here.'

'Let's hope we've got you home by then.'

Pamela gently shakes her head. 'That's not something I can wish for,' she says, before sipping her tea. 'Jeannie had no idea Thomas wasn't her father. In my mind, I think I somehow convinced myself he was and that made it so much easier for me to convince Jeannie. For years, I never told a living soul.'

'What changed?' I ask.

'I saw him, Withers, talking to Jeannie and I panicked,' she replies. 'It was Jeannie's first Christmas at secondary school, and he hosted the carol concert. For so long, I'd done all I could to avoid him; never attended his church, politely declined any wedding invitations where he was presiding. And suddenly there he was, talking to Jeannie. I was petrified. Of course, he had no idea. I doubt he even knew she was my daughter, but I needed to talk to somebody.' Pamela looks at me, over the top of her teacup. 'You're thinking why Angela? I hadn't known her long. She and Jack had only recently moved in next door and at first we seemed to hit it off. Naive of me, I know, but she was different then, or I thought she was. We sat together in my living room and for the first time I said the words out loud. Adrian Withers raped me.'

CHAPTER 86

Pamela sips again from her cup of tea.

'The week Thomas was killed, Withers came to visit me three times. I was a mess. Thomas was one of the first to die in the war. The Royal Navy was trying to contact me, but I couldn't face all the formalities. I didn't want to speak to anyone but for some reason, I trusted him.

'The third time he came, he brought a bottle of wine. He said it would settle my nerves, help me relax. I'm sure he referenced Jesus. He sat beside me on the sofa and when he handed me the glass, the acid stuck in my throat. He asked if he could hold me; said it would make me feel better. When he pushed me down, he was still telling me it would make me feel better.

'It sounds a stupid thing to say now but it took me a long time to realise it was rape. I'd drunk with him, sat with him. Hadn't I let him?'

I slowly shake my head. 'No,' I say, quietly.

'Whenever I could, I started listening to other women's stories – on the radio or on television or read about them in the newspaper. I realised their stories were my story; that what had happened to them had happened to me. But by then my only concern was Jeannie and I'd long since decided to make Thomas her father.'

'Jeannie had no idea until the night Angela was killed?'

'None,' replies Pamela. 'Like most eighteen-year-olds, she was incredibly headstrong. I wanted her to go to university and she'd got a good place, but then out of nowhere she told me she'd let the place go. She'd started seeing a boy who was a couple of years older than her. It wasn't until the middle of November that I found out it was Luke and I realised who he was. Simply telling Jeannie not to see him was never going to work and I couldn't bear the thought of her knowing the truth. My plan was to try and get her to start university in the January and separate them that way, but of course that never happened.'

'That night you were left with no other option.'

'I sat with Jeannie at the kitchen table. I told her it was true; Adrian Withers was her father. We cried together but as dawn broke we knew we had to make a decision. We agreed the only thing to do was for her and Luke to leave and never come back. I gave her all the money I had, just to try and give her a second chance. Saying goodbye was the hardest thing I will ever do.'

'You've never seen her since?'

Pamela shakes her head. 'We all agreed it was the safest thing, for Jeannie and for Jack. I'd be lying if I didn't say I hadn't been tempted; the thought of spending just one day with her. But deep down, I had to accept Jeannie had killed a woman and somehow we all had to pay.'

'And Jack?' I ask, quietly.

'He wanted to kill Withers and at first I feared he might. In the weeks that followed, after the fire, I told him the violence had to end. And Jack knew if Jeannie was ever to be safe, we had to keep the secret of who her father was.

'I went to see Jack the week before he died. I could see he was fading. His hatred of the Baxters had destroyed him. That and the drink.' Pamela gives a weak smile. 'We talked about our children. He was so proud of Dani. Both of us had only ever tried to do our best.'

CHAPTER 87

In the early evening, Haddley CID office was almost deserted.

'Only if you're sure?' said DS Barnsdale, before stepping away from Dani's desk. 'I'm happy to speak with him if you'd prefer.'

'No, I'm quite certain,' replied Dani. 'It's best that he hears it from me.' Dani leaned forward, resting her elbows on her desk. Behind her, she heard her superior press the exit button to leave the station. Before the doors had even begun to close, Mat was moving towards her.

'What did she say?' he asked, positioning himself at Dani's side.

'Bertie Baxter's been released. We couldn't hold him any longer.'

Despite only limited evidence, Mat had persuaded his superiors to question Baxter on events surrounding the raid on the supermarket one year earlier. Arriving with an £800-an-hour lawyer had ensured Bertie left relatively soon afterwards.

'For fuck's sake,' said Mat, lashing out across Dani's

desk. She sat motionless as her computer mouse flew through the air, hitting the wall behind her. 'I told you Barnsdale would get nowhere. I should have been in the room with him.'

'We both know that was never going to happen,' replied Dani, waiting for her husband's anger to subside. 'There was no evidence to connect him to your stabbing other than what Archie gave us. If Archie'd been a witness to any kind of criminal activity it might have been different, but he'd never even met Bertie Baxter, not once.'

'So, Baxter walks free?'

'Barnsdale had no other choice.'

'He'll be laughing at us right now, laughing at me.' Mat slammed his hands against the arms of his chair. 'Is there nothing else we can get from the boy? If I had him in a room, I'm sure—'

'Mat, listen to yourself. He's a fifteen-year-old boy. We're not going to charge him.'

'Doesn't this station even put dealers away any more? Your dad will be turning in his grave.'

'Archie's a kid, working at the bottom of the dealers' food chain. He tried to help us, gave us all he had and right now he deserves a second chance.'

'Fuck off, Dani,' said Mat. 'Don't tell me about second chances.'

Dani stared at her husband as he frantically rubbed his hands across his unshaven face.

'I need a drink.'

'Not now,' she replied.

He leaned forward. 'Come with me,' he said. 'Let's go and get absolutely wasted.'

'I can't.'

'Why not?' he said, anger still in his voice.

'I don't want to go out and get drunk.'

'You don't want to get drunk with me.'

'Don't be stupid. It's a Tuesday night. We've both got work tomorrow.'

'A few drinks, that's all I'm saying. And then we'll order a Deliveroo.'

'I've told Barnsdale I will speak to Archie and his parents.'

'Send Karen.'

'I was with them at the hospital. It should be me. Why don't we go out for a meal at the weekend, just the two of us? We can book somewhere nice.'

'I'm going to the Watchman tonight and I'm going to pour a bottle of the finest Polish vodka down my throat.'

Dani held her head in her hands and spread her fingers across her face. She knew if Mat left now he would do exactly as he said. In the early hours, he'd arrive home barely conscious. She wouldn't see him until he appeared at the station late tomorrow morning.

'I've told Barnsdale I will speak to Archie's family and that's what I'm going to do.'

Mat said nothing in reply. He manoeuvred himself back across the room, reached for his jacket and grabbed his phone off his desk. He turned and without looking at his wife, exited through the rear of the station.

Alone in the room, Dani sat back in her chair and blew

out her cheeks. She reached down and picked up her mouse before plugging it into her computer. She read one last message on her screen and then clicked twice on the mouse to log off. She reached for her jacket, walked across the room before standing in the corridor outside Freeman's office.

Again, she found herself thinking of her father, blameless in the death of her mother and justified in his pursuit of the Baxter family. She would continue his search for justice, although she feared the necessary evidence to convict Bertie had travelled with Adrian Withers to his grave.

She took a deep breath and knocked on the chief inspector's door.

'Come in,' called Freeman, from behind her desk. Dani entered the room and took a seat opposite her. 'I haven't had the opportunity to say,' continued Freeman, 'but I'm very happy to see matters have been satisfactorily resolved in your mother's case.'

'Thank you, ma'am,' replied Dani, thinking herself naive for expecting anything more from the chief inspector.

'You must be pleased?'

'For my father, I am.'

'He was an honest officer. I'm sorry we haven't achieved a better result for DS Moore. It wasn't for want of trying.'

'No, ma'am,' said Dani. 'It was on a related matter that I wanted to speak with you.'

'Go ahead.'

'I was the first officer to enter the church following Reverend Withers's death. I entered immediately after the fire service.' Freeman nodded and Dani continued.

'Withers was locked inside the bell tower, but we never found the key.'

Freeman glanced at the MacBook on her desk. 'You have to remember he fell from a great height. In the chaos that followed evidence may easily have been displaced. From his words at the time and what we now know about his criminal activities, I think we can call this case closed.' Freeman reaches for her bag. 'It's late and I'm heading for home. I think you should do the same.'

'Yes, ma'am,' replied Dani, getting to her feet.

'Don't look so worried,' said Freeman. 'You've done good work in clearing up this matter so quickly. Withers was an addict who kept his stash shut away in the bottom drawer of his filing cabinet. Don't waste your energy worrying about him.'

Dani nodded and swiftly exited the room. Following the dimly lit corridor towards the kitchen, she stopped briefly. Did her report detail Withers keeping cocaine in the bottom drawer of his filing cabinet? Perhaps it did.

She wandered into the kitchen where she found Karen Cooke filling the kettle.

'Tea?' asked Cooke.

'Thanks, no,' replied Dani. 'I'm heading out. You on a late?'

'Here until midnight. Too much to hope it'll be a quiet night?'

Dani smiled. 'Karen,' she said, standing beside her fellow officer as she brewed her drink, 'last week, immediately after Reverend Withers's death, when I left the churchyard . . .'

'Yes?' replied Cooke, crossing to the small fridge and reaching for a carton of milk.

'Who did you speak to when you called in the incident?'

'Whoever was on the desk. I wasn't really paying much attention. I told them you'd been called to another incident at the railway arches, I was on my own and could they send me some support.'

'Your request would have been logged?'

'I guess so. They sent me Fidler and Higgins from the reconstruction. Why?'

'No reason,' replied Dani. 'Just making sure my final report tallies with yours.'

Cooke smiled. 'Thanks.'

'Hope you have a quiet evening,' Dani called, as she left the building.

CHAPTER 88

Freeman waited until the constable had closed the office door behind her. Dani Cash had the potential to be a successful officer and an asset to her team. But Freeman worried that, just like her father, she had a nasty habit of asking too many questions.

She glanced over the daily call log before shutting down her screen. Closing her MacBook and slipping it into her bag, she paused. She felt inside her bag and pulled out the key for her desk drawer.

Inside the drawer was a stack of papers detailing Haddley's latest crime statistics, which she was still to review. Right now they would have to wait. Lifting the papers, she looked at the knife hidden beneath.

Taking the knife herself had been a risk, but following Withers's death she was left with no other choice. She'd always said he was a weak link and she'd been proved right. However he'd died, he was better off dead.

She pushed the papers back into the drawer and turned the key.

She would deal with the knife in the days ahead.

CHAPTER 89

The rusting gate at the side of St Stephen's cemetery squeaked open when Dani stepped into the graveyard. She looked across at the sixteenth-century church, once more tranquil in its surroundings. Then she followed the gravel path until she stood in front of the brightly coloured holly bush.

'The berries are turning red,' she said aloud, as she knelt beside her father's headstone, gently placing a fresh bouquet of blue irises there. 'Your favourite time of year. And Mum's – or at least that's what you always said.'

She twisted to sit on the edge of the grave. 'You could have told me the truth,' she said, 'about Mum. I wouldn't have loved you any less. Or her.' As she said the words, she wondered if what she was saying was really true. Would she have loved her mum any less? The more she thought, the more she began to understand what Jack had done – the life he'd built for her, the mother he'd given her. And she forgave him.

'I'm sorry I didn't listen to you more,' she told her father, as she thought about his pursuit of the Baxters in the last year of his life. 'We all make mistakes, we just need to make sure we learn from them. I promise I'll keep trying to learn from mine.'

She closed her eyes, and images of her father flashed before her: Jack spinning her round in the desk chair; Jack, his eyes bright with exhilaration as his voice boomed across the office at a briefing; Jack as he looked in that last meeting in his office, when he told her he was leaving.

She brought her fingers to her father's headstone. 'I worry it isn't only the Baxters you were right about. I'm afraid – afraid somebody inside the force was working against you. If that is true, I promise I'll find them.'

Dani slipped out of the churchyard through the side gate. She thought of Mat's silence as he left the station earlier, the coldness in his voice when he'd spoken to her. Standing in the lane, the cold snap replaced by heavy clouds and the first drops of rain, she was aware of how alone she felt.

She walked to the end of the lane and looked across the Lower Haddley Road. Leaving her car, she hurried across the road and onto the common, walking quickly towards Ben's house.

CHAPTER 90

I'm woken by the sound of rain lashing against my bedroom window. Autumn gales blow through the woods and across the rain-sodden common. In the darkness, I reach for my phone and flick on the screen. It's three o'clock. The brightness from my phone briefly lights the room. I look at Dani sleeping beside me.

I push my phone back onto the table beside my bed but, as I do, Dani stirs.

'I'm sorry,' I whisper. She closes her eyes and curls closer to me.

I'm yet to reveal anything further about Angela Cash's death, even to Dani. I don't want to compromise her position with the police and I've sworn to Pamela I will say nothing until Jeannie passes. Having spoken briefly with Luke last night, I expect that to be any day.

I sink back down and Dani wraps her arm around me. I wish this moment could last for ever.

ACKNOWLEDGEMENTS

This book is dedicated to the memory of my brother, James. He passed away in late 2019 at the relatively young age of fifty-one, having suffered with motor neurone disease. I know his wife and children miss him every single day, as does our mum. His two children play a key role in this book, which I'm sure will amuse them and I know it would have entertained him.

Thanks go to all my family for their support of me in writing this book and their constant understanding when I have to hurry away, time and again, to get back to 'my book.' Love to my mum, especially for always being my number one fan and for hand-selling copies of Robert Gold to any new readers she can find. And, as always, thanks to O, H and W for the loan of the name.

Thanks also go to young Max for being the inspiration for so many of the lines spoken by younger characters both in this book and in *Twelve Secrets*. Max, you are the real character.

This is my second published, full-length novel. Starting

a second novel can feel quite daunting so a big thank you goes to all the team at Little, Brown for their unflinching encouragement and support. Special thanks go to Rosanna Forte for being a marvel in terms of feedback, direction and most importantly patience. And in Gemma Shelley I am lucky to have someone who champions my books with both an incredible passion and an enthusiasm that is unrivalled across the publishing industry. Publishing a book is a true team effort and many thanks go to all of the editorial, sales, publicity and marketing teams at Sphere that helped this book find its readers.

Juliet Mushens is a one-of-a-kind agent, and without her the residents of Haddley and St Marnham would never have reached readers. She and all her team are simply brilliant to work with.

And, finally, my thanks go to you the reader. Finding and choosing a book, before taking the time to read it, is an investment from you for which all authors are incredibly grateful. I hope *Eleven Liars* kept you entertained until the last page.

Thanks for reading.

Revisit the first Ben Harper mystery . . .

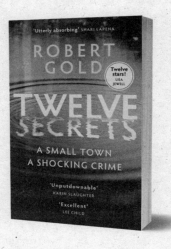

A SMALL TOWN. A SHOCKING CRIME.
YOU'LL SUSPECT EVERY CHARACTER.
BUT YOU'LL NEVER GUESS THE ENDING.

Ben Harper's life changed for ever the day his older brother
Nick was murdered by two classmates. It was a crime
that shocked the nation and catapulted Ben's family and
their idyllic hometown, Haddley, into the spotlight.

Twenty years on, Ben is one of the best investigative
journalists in the country and settled back in Haddley,
thanks to the support of its close-knit community. But
then a fresh murder case shines new light on his brother's
death and throws suspicion on those closest to him.

Ben is about to discover that in Haddley no one is
as they seem. Everyone has something to hide.

And *someone* will do anything to keep the truth buried . . .